Blake's Pursuit is a work of fiction. Names, characters, places, and incidents are the products of the author's imagination and are used fictitiously. Any resemblance to actual events, locales, or persons, living or dead, is entirely coincidental.

Cover design: Leah Kaye Suttle
Cover photo: Curaphotography
Author Photo: © Marti Corn Photography

Printed in the United States of America

Books by Tina Folsom

Samson's Lovely Mortal (Scanguards Vampires, Book 1)
Amaury's Hellion (Scanguards Vampires, Book 2)
Gabriel's Mate (Scanguards Vampires, Book 3)
Yvette's Haven (Scanguards Vampires, Book 4)
Zane's Redemption (Scanguards Vampires, Book 5)
Quinn's Undying Rose (Scanguards Vampires, Book 6)
Oliver's Hunger (Scanguards Vampires, Book 7)
Thomas's Choice (Scanguards Vampires, Book 8)
Silent Bite (Scanguards Vampires, Book 8 1/2)
Cain's Identity (Scanguards Vampires, Book 9)
Luther's Return (Scanguards Vampires, Book 10)
Blake's Pursuit (Scanguards Vampires, Book 11)
Fateful Reunion (Scanguards Vampires, Book 11 1/2)
John's Yearning (Scanguards Vampires, Book 12)
Ryder's Storm (Scanguards Vampires, Book 13)

Lover Uncloaked (Stealth Guardians, Book 1)
Master Unchained (Stealth Guardians, Book 2)
Warrior Unraveled (Stealth Guardians, Book 3)
Guardian Undone (Stealth Guardians, Book 4)
Immortal Unveiled (Stealth Guardians, Book 5)
Protector Unmatched (Stealth Guardians, Book 6)
Demon Unleashed (Stealth Guardians, Book 7)

Ace on the Run (Code Name Stargate, Book 1)
Fox in plain Sight (Code Name Stargate, Book 2)
Yankee in the Wind (Code Name Stargate, Book 3)
Tiger on the Prowl (Code Name Stargate, Book 4)

A Touch of Greek (Out of Olympus, Book 1)
A Scent of Greek (Out of Olympus, Book 2)
A Taste of Greek (Out of Olympus, Book 3)
A Hush of Greek (Out of Olympus, Book 4)

Venice Vampyr (Novellas 1 – 4)

Teasing (The Hamptons Bachelor Club, Book 1)
Enticing (The Hamptons Bachelor Club, Book 2)
Beguiling (The Hamptons Bachelor Club, Book 3)
Scorching (The Hamptons Bachelor Club, Book 4)
Alluring (The Hamptons Bachelor Club, Book 5)
Sizzling (The Hamptons Bachelor Club, Book 6)

BLAKE'S PURSUIT

SCANGUARDS VAMPIRES #11

TINA FOLSOM

1

She shouldn't have ignored the phone call.

Lilo stared out the window of the taxi as it made its way through rush hour traffic. Her flight from Omaha had been delayed due to heavy snow in Nebraska, and the plane had touched down in San Francisco well after sunset. Anxious, she tapped her fingers on the smooth leather of her handbag and replayed Hannah's pleading message in her mind.

"Lilo, you have to call me back. I have nobody to talk to about this. I need your help. You always know what to do."

A faint smile stole over her lips, and involuntarily she shook her head. Her best friend since high school had such confidence in her. As if she could fix anything. But what if she couldn't fix this? What if it was already too late?

Hell, she didn't even know what there was to fix. Hannah was gone. Vanished from the face of the earth.

Mrs. Bergdorf's call the previous evening had confirmed it. *"Hannah never called me for my birthday. Lilo, you know she always calls. She's not answering her phone. I'm worried about her."*

And so was Lilo. Because despite all her faults, Hannah had always been a considerate daughter. If she hadn't called her mother with birthday wishes, it meant she hadn't been able to get to a phone. Had Hannah fallen ill and wasn't aware of the important date she'd missed? It was unlikely that a flu or cold would make her so delirious that she'd forget her mother's birthday. Perhaps Hannah had had an accident and was unable to communicate. But even if she'd been taken to a hospital, the hospital staff would have notified her mother and Lilo, too, because both were listed as Hannah's emergency contacts. No, something was wrong. She could sense it: something terrible had happened to Hannah.

Guilt surged through Lilo. She'd been under deadline stress, having had difficulty finishing her latest mystery novel. Her editor had been breathing down her neck, so she'd hunkered down and shut out the outside world to finish the damn book. But at what cost? She'd broken her promise to Hannah, a promise they'd made in ninth grade: that they would always be there for each other. But instead of calling her friend to find out what was wrong, she'd finished her book so she wouldn't miss her deadline.

Lilo sighed. What kind of friend did that? She'd heard the pleading tone in Hannah's voice message when she'd called only a few days before her mother's birthday. Hannah had sounded tense, worried. Lilo wished she hadn't let the phone call go to voicemail and instead picked up and talked to her friend. What if Ronny, that no-good loser she was dating, had hurt her? Why else would Hannah say she couldn't talk to anybody but Lilo? If only she knew more about Hannah and Ronny's relationship, but her friend had been very tight-lipped about it, never revealing much about what Ronny did. As if she was ashamed of him in some way.

The only thing she knew was that Ronny was very possessive, and that was a trait Lilo had never liked in men. It was one reason why her relationships never lasted long. She needed to be independent, and trusting somebody didn't come easily. Maybe her mystery writer brain had something to do with it. She simply knew the darkness of the human psyche, and was more aware than others what could lurk beneath the surface.

After Mrs. Bergdorf's call, Lilo had booked the first flight out to San Francisco, determined to find Hannah and figure out what had happened. And she wouldn't go home until she'd accomplished that task. She only hoped that she wouldn't have bad news for Hannah's mother when she did.

"This is it," the cab driver said, as he came to a stop in front of a three-story apartment building. "Number 426."

Hannah had raved about the neighborhood when she'd first moved in, but now, at night and with few streetlights to illuminate the area, Lilo couldn't understand the attraction of this steep street in North Beach. She was glad that the cab driver had stopped directly in front of the garage, so she wouldn't have to haul her suitcase up the hill.

After paying for her ride, Lilo walked up to the front door. There were six door bells, one for each apartment. *Bergdorf* was written on one of the bells. She rang it. As she expected, there was no reply. But she wouldn't let such a small obstacle stop her. She wasn't a mystery writer for nothing. And she knew Hannah better than her own sister. After locking herself out of her new apartment and paying an exorbitant amount for a locksmith—a story that her friend had recounted in minute detail—Hannah had been determined never to get caught without a key again, and together they'd figured out the best hiding place for a spare.

Lilo let her eyes wander around the entrance. A bougainvillea snaked up one side of the wall along a trellis. It wasn't in bloom. Even in San Francisco, where it was a balmy fifty degrees outside in early January, it wasn't warm enough for the plant to flower. The leaves hid most of the wooden trellis, but Lilo knew what she was looking for: a brown string with a key tied to the end of it, blending perfectly into the wall. She pulled on it. The key emerged from its hiding place, a deep crack in the foundation, probably caused by an earthquake.

Key in hand, Lilo let herself into the building and found Hannah's apartment on the first floor. She listened for sounds coming from inside the unit, but it was quiet. As she pushed the door open and stepped in, she crinkled her nose. It smelled of rotten food.

She flipped the light switch and closed the door behind her.

The place was nothing special, a one-bedroom apartment with a large living room, a separate kitchen and a small bathroom. Despite its size, Hannah's touch was everywhere. The funky furniture and decorations from around the world were quintessential Hannah. This was her home.

Lilo shrugged off her coat and placed it over a chair, then walked to the open doorway from which the strong odor emanated. It was the kitchen. The under-the-counter light was on, and the cause of the smell was immediately evident: a half-eaten can of dog food sat on the kitchen counter. She glanced around. There was another door, leading back into the small hallway that connected to the bathroom and bedroom on one end and the living room and front door on the other.

On the floor near the refrigerator stood two bowls, one filled with water, the other empty, but not clean. A dog had eaten from it recently. Frankenfurter.

"Frankenfurter?" she called out to Hannah's terrier, but got no reply.

Lilo grabbed the spoiled can and tossed it in the trash, then opened the kitchen window to let in some fresh air, before returning to the living room.

Had Hannah fed the dog, then taken him for a walk and never come back? Or had she left in a hurry to get away from Ronny, taking

Frankenfurter with her? What if Ronny had shown up at her apartment and fought with her? Hurt her or kidnapped her? What if he'd killed her, and removed her body…

She shuddered at the thought, looking around for signs of a struggle. But the place was tidy. A few magazines on the coffee table, a blanket on the couch, a chew-toy for the dog next to a chair. Nothing out of the ordinary. Certainly no blood stains on the carpet. She lifted one edge of the old rug. No blood stains underneath it either. She breathed a sigh of relief.

On the dining table, Hannah's computer sat open. She touched the mouse to wake up the system, and a login screen appeared within seconds. But without knowing Hannah's password, she couldn't unlock the screen. She tried a few different combinations: Frankenfurter, Bergdorf, IloveMom, even her own name, but none of them worked. Clearly, her friend was too sophisticated to use a password that could easily be guessed by anybody with a passing knowledge of her.

If she wanted to find out what Hannah had been doing before she disappeared, she needed to get into her computer. She wanted to check her recent search history and her inbox to see if she'd received any worrisome emails. Either might provide a clue as to where she was. But first of all, she needed to go to the police to report her missing. And she would do that right after she'd taken a quick shower and gotten changed out of her thick clothes, which made her feel like she was in a sauna. Her skin was sticky, and she felt tired from the trip. A shower would revive her again and lend her the strength she needed to look for her friend.

2

Blake shoved his cell phone back into the pocket of his cargo pants as his long legs ate up the distance between his office and the conference room at the other end of the long corridor in Scanguards' Mission headquarters. Despite the stress and the long hours that came with his job, he loved it. He loved being in charge of security for the hybrid children of some of the most powerful vampires on the West Coast—even if it meant putting his own needs before theirs. When he'd been human, and much younger, he'd been a selfish and entitled trust fund baby. Now he was making up for it.

He nodded to Oliver, his de-facto brother, who was coming out of the elevator.

"You're only now just rolling in?" Blake asked, grinning. "Trying for another baby?"

Oliver shook his unruly mane. His hair wasn't long, but thick and stood out in every direction. "One is enough, thank you very much. And if you could play uncle and take care of Sebastian for a few hours this week, so Ursula can get the house in order for her parents' visit, I'd appreciate it."

"Hey, your son practically lives at my place!" Or rather in Blake's refrigerator, which he had trouble keeping stocked, given the amount of food the twelve-year-old could devour.

Oliver chuckled. "Shouldn't have bought that big house. Now you'll never get rid of the youngsters. Let's face it, they'd all much rather hang out with you than with their parents."

Blake smiled. "Only because I let them run wild." He motioned to the conference room. "Zane and the rest of them are way too strict with their offspring. Too much discipline isn't good. They need an outlet."

Oliver smirked. "As I said, you'll never get rid of them now." He turned and sauntered in the other direction.

For a moment, Blake just stood there. He and Oliver hadn't started off on the right foot, when they'd first met over twenty years earlier. But they'd been thrown together because they were kin: Quinn Ralston, Blake's 4th great-grandfather, was Oliver's sire, and they'd lived together under Quinn and Rose's roof for several years. Rose, who wasn't related to Oliver by blood, had borne Blake's 3rd great-grandmother shortly before her turning, and thus ensured the survival of the Ralston clan.

Smiling to himself, he opened the door to the conference room and let himself in. Several members of the Scanguards management team were assembled around a large conference table. A speakerphone stood dead-center on the table.

"Sorry, running late," he apologized to nobody in particular and sat down next to Amaury.

The linebacker-sized vampire with the shoulder-length dark hair and the piercing blue eyes acknowledged him with a sideways glance, pointing to the phone as he murmured, "Donnelly is giving us the weekly crime report. You haven't missed anything."

"What worries me, Samson," Detective Donnelly was saying through the speakerphone, "is that there are way more robberies and home invasions than usual. Something is up."

Samson, Scanguards' founder, a tall vampire with sleek black hair and a chiseled face and physique, rested his elbows on the table and leaned a little closer to the speakerphone. "What do you want me to do, Mike? You know as well as I that Scanguards only gets involved in city business when it concerns infractions committed by vampires. That's our deal. And from what you're telling us, most of these crimes are committed during daylight."

The implication was clear: the crimes couldn't have been committed by vampires, who needed the cover of darkness to operate safely.

Zane grunted in agreement. Blake tossed him a quick glance. As usual, the bald vampire looked like he was ready to rip somebody's head off. Zane glanced down to his watch and then he pushed his chair back, nodding to Samson. "Flight's in a few hours. Gotta get ready."

Samson nodded back, and then exchanged a look with his second-in-command, Gabriel.

Gabriel shrugged indifferently, but the scar that marred one side of his face ticked, a sure sign that he was affected by the matter. The scar stretched from his ear to his chin, a gruesome reminder of the emotional and physical pain he'd endured as a human.

"Come on, guys, the city compensates you handsomely for your consulting services," Donnelly added now. "Just this once. Just have one of your guys look into it."

Gabriel sighed and met Samson's eyes directly. "How about John? Maybe he can check it out, determine whether there's anything odd about these robberies? Won't take him longer than a day or two, I reckon."

Quinn, who'd been silent until now, ran a hand through his blond hair. He looked no older than mid-twenties, though he was close to two hundred years older than Blake. "I can pull John off patrol duty for a couple of nights, but I'll need a replacement for him."

"Take Grayson," Samson agreed. "I'm sure he'll be chomping at the bit."

Gabriel chuckled. "You're gonna let him go out there on his own?"

"You know my son as well as I do. He's been badgering me for months to give him his own patrol. Maybe this is a good opportunity to see if he's ready."

"He's twenty-one, it's about time he pulled his weight!" Quinn interjected, laughing.

Amaury shook his head. "Wait until the twins find out. They'll want their own patrol, too. You're opening a big can of worms here." Amaury's twins Benjamin and Damian were twenty, only one year younger than Grayson, and absolute hellions.

"Don't you trust your boys to do a good job?" Gabriel asked.

"It's not Benjamin or Damian I'm worried about. Nina isn't ready to let them go."

Blake had to smile. Amaury's blood-bonded mate was a force to be reckoned with. Though she was human, Amaury was putty in her hands. "You've gotta put your foot down, Amaury."

Quinn's eyes sparkled with mischief. "Too late for that. That comes from letting your mate wear the pants."

Amaury grunted and shot Quinn a look. "Like you have any more control over your woman than I have over mine!"

Samson raised his hands in a conciliatory gesture. "Hey, guys, let's get back to business."

Blake glanced at his boss. Yeah, Samson was in exactly the same boat as the rest of the blood-bonded vampires: they were all dependent on their women, and they wouldn't have it any other way.

"So we got a deal?" Donnelly asked through the speakerphone.

"Yeah, we got a deal. I'll have John call and coordinate with you. You get forty-eight hours. Then I'm pulling him off."

"Okay. Thanks." There was a soft rustling of papers, then Donnelly continued, "Can we go over the vampire case files now? I've got a few updates."

"Go ahead," Samson agreed.

There was a faint knock at the door, followed by a creak as it opened a sliver. Finn, a young employee of *Vüber*, one of Scanguards' subsidiaries, popped his head in. Several heads turned to him.

"Sorry," Finn apologized quickly, "but it's important. Blake, a word."

Blake rose. "Excuse me for a sec." He walked outside, and eased the door shut behind him. "What's going on?"

Finn shifted from one foot to the other, appearing nervous. "Well, I'm not sure. But you told me if there's ever a problem with Hannah Bergdorf, I should let you know personally."

Blake's heartbeat instantly went into overdrive. Hannah, one of the many human drivers who worked for *Vüber*, a company that transported vampires around the city during daytime, stood under his personal protection. "Hannah? What's going on?"

"I'm not sure, but she hasn't accepted any fares lately. And she didn't call in sick or anything." Finn shrugged.

"How long has she not worked?"

"Maybe two or three days."

Blake felt heat rise to his head. "And you didn't tell me earlier?"

"I didn't even notice at first. I mean, the *Vüber* drivers don't have fixed hours. They accept the fares as they come in. I figured she was taking a few days off, since she worked over Christmas."

"Did you call her?"

"She's not picking up her phone. Goes straight to voicemail."

"Has anybody checked her house?"

Finn shook his head. "Can't spare anybody right now. It's really busy. And maybe she just forgot to set her app to the *Away* mode. I don't wanna intrude if she's just taking time off."

Blake nodded, worried and anxious. Nevertheless, he didn't want to shoot the messenger. "I'll take care of it. In the meantime, send the details of her last fare to my phone."

"Will do." Finn turned on his heel and rushed away, clearly relieved at being allowed to leave.

Blake didn't waste time either. He marched to the elevator and pressed the call button. As he waited, he tried to calm himself. Maybe Hannah had just forgotten to tell Finn's team that she wasn't working for a few days. But as much as he wanted to believe in that scenario, he knew better.

Hannah was too generous and charitable for her own good. She'd probably helped somebody and gotten in trouble as a result. Just like she'd helped him on that wet March day four years ago. The day he would have died, had it not been for Hannah's fearless action.

3

Lilo towel-dried her blond hair, before reaching for her hairbrush to comb the damp strands into submission. Normally she'd let it air-dry, but since she was planning to go to the nearest police station and didn't want to freeze, she bent down to the cabinet below the sink and pulled Hannah's hairdryer from it. She was about to plug it in and switch it on, when she heard a sound coming from the other room.

She froze in mid-movement, her heart skipping a beat.

Had Hannah come home? She listened, instinctively, hoping against hope it was her friend. If it was Hannah, she would see the suitcase and know she had a visitor. Judging by the stickers on Lilo's luggage—stickers Hannah had sent her from her numerous trips—she would also know immediately who it was.

Lilo waited another two seconds, but whoever was in the other room didn't call out her name. It couldn't be Hannah.

It was an intruder, probably a burglar. It had to be. She'd written enough mystery novels to know how this would go down: he'd steal everything valuable in sight, including her handbag and computer, which would leave her stranded. And she already had enough problems to deal with. Getting her valuables stolen wasn't on the agenda tonight.

She stretched her hand toward the glass shelf above the sink, reaching for her phone, but stopped.

Crap, she cursed silently.

Her cell phone was still in her handbag in the living room, out of reach—which meant she couldn't call the police for help. She had no choice. She'd have to take the initiative and surprise the guy. Most burglars, she knew from her research, turned tail and ran the moment they realized they weren't alone. She'd just have to make enough noise to wake the neighbors should the guy not flee instantly.

Gripping the hairdryer more tightly, she looked down at herself. It would help if she weren't dressed in Hannah's short pink bathrobe. Oh well. She'd have to confront the intruder dressed as she was. She'd left her clothes in the living room because there was no space for them in the tiny bathroom without risking getting them wet.

Just pretend you're Morgan West. The protagonist of her popular bounty hunter mystery series would definitely not be quaking in his boots the way she was right now. Then again, in her defense, she wasn't wearing any boots. She was barefoot. Great, she was about to become the main character in a horror movie: a scantily dressed blonde, without shoes, running for her life. Could this situation get any more pathetic?

Stop it, she admonished herself silently. If only her imagination wasn't so active; she could come up with all kinds of possible scenarios for this moment, all of them turning out badly. Sometimes it was a curse to be a mystery writer: she knew too much about the dangerous and evil elements of society. Elements like the burglar she could now hear clearly rummaging through the living room. In a few minutes, he'd be gone and with him, her handbag and computer.

It's now or never.

Taking a deep breath, she turned the doorknob with her left hand while gripping the hairdryer tightly in her right. At least she could hit the guy with it if he approached her.

Lilo eased the door open just enough so she could peer out into the short hallway. But she couldn't see anybody from that angle. Cautiously, she opened the door wider and took one step forward. Beneath her bare foot, the old wooden floorboard creaked. The sound seemed to echo loudly, though that could just be the result of her nervous, overactive imagination.

Another step and she was in the hallway. The part of the living room she could see was empty. Her suitcase was still where she'd left it, though somebody had rifled through the contents, and tossed them onto the armchair.

That proved it. It was definitely not Hannah who'd entered the apartment. Slowly and silently, she stalked into the living room, staying as close to the wall as she could, before peeking around the corner so she could see the entire room. It was empty. The small reading light she'd turned on earlier was still burning, but otherwise it was dark, probably giving the intruder the impression the apartment was empty.

Another sound reached her ears. The burglar had moved on to the kitchen. Was that how he'd gotten in? Through the kitchen window she'd opened to get rid of the foul smell?

As she approached the open doorway to the kitchen, she hesitated. If she surprised him in that small, confined space, he might panic and lunge at her. No, it wasn't smart to corner him like that. What if he fought back?

Her eyes fell on the contents of her handbag on the armchair. If she could get to her cell phone, she could then sneak out the front door and call the police without the burglar hearing her, and everything would work out fine.

She placed the hairdryer on the couch, then bent over the armchair, rifling through her possessions. She shifted involuntarily. Her foot landed on something soft. A squeaking noise ripped through the silence.

Shit! She'd just stepped on one of Frankenfurter's squeaky toys.

Frantically she tried to find her cell phone, but it wasn't on the chair. The intruder must have taken it.

Damn it!

Heavy footsteps behind her made her whirl around. It was too late. A strange man charged into the living room, glaring at her as if *she* were the intruder. Light reflected from somewhere, making his eyes appear red, as if he were the devil incarnate.

Fuck! This guy wasn't the type to just turn tail and run.

Lilo lunged toward the front door, desperate to escape. She could always buy a new computer and get her credit card company to issue her a new card. Better run now and deal with the consequences later.

Her hand was on the doorknob when she was jerked back by two strong hands gripping her shoulders. The guy flipped her around and tossed her in the other direction. She landed with her back on the old couch, legs in the air.

She pulled herself up quickly, trying to get away, but he was already charging at her again.

"Help! Somebody help!" she screamed from the top of her lungs, but in the next instant all the air was pushed from her lungs as the intruder pressed her back into the cushions as easily as if she were a toddler and not a grown woman.

She knew instantly that despite the self-defense classes she'd taken in college, she had no chance against an assailant this strong.

Her next scream for help was smothered beneath his broad palm and only came out as a muffled cry. Nobody would hear her.

Shit! What would Morgan West do now? How would he get out of this predicament? Kick his attacker in the nuts? Yeah, if she could lift her knee, which she couldn't, because he'd disabled her with his weight. Besides, Morgan wouldn't be in this situation in the first place.

"Where is it?" he grunted.

She ignored his question, not understanding what he was talking about, and instead tried to burn his face into her memory. No matter what happened now, she would do everything she could to be able to identify him in a lineup later.

His eyes were still glaring red, though this was probably an illusion caused by her fear, since there was no way the light in the room could reflect off his irises at this angle. Deep lines ran across his forehead, and his mouth was set in a grim line. His dark hair was shaggy, his face clean-shaven. He had prominent high cheekbones, but no other marks that would make him easy to identify.

The sound of a door opening made her shift her gaze from her attacker's face and peer past his shoulders.

Another man, one just as tall as her attacker, charged toward them.

Oh fuck! Could her luck get any worse? The burglar hadn't come alone. He'd brought an accomplice. Now there were two of them.

4

Blake lunged at the attacker. He'd heard a woman's scream coming from inside Hannah's flat just as he was picking the lock on her door.

There was no doubt that the man was a vampire. Just as it was evident that the woman being attacked wasn't Hannah, but a blonde in a skimpy outfit, her long bare legs sticking out from under her aggressor.

Blake gripped the attacker by the shoulders and jerked him off his victim. The hostile vampire wheeled around, growling viciously, but Blake didn't waste time and delivered a blow to the guy's face. It whipped to the side for an instant, before snapping back. Now even more pissed off at having his fun interrupted, the asshole fought back.

Fending off the guy's punches, Blake didn't get a chance to verify that the woman was unhurt. He only heard her frightened screams and saw a flash of something pink move in his peripheral vision. He had to keep all his wits about him to keep his attacker at bay. The stranger had an advantage over Blake, because he was heavier, though his fighting technique was less refined. That's where Blake had the upper hand. Even so, the guy still managed to land a few minor kicks and blows.

When the jerk's fist came at him again, Blake ducked away and rammed him against the bookcase. Books and trinkets crashed to the floor, but the vampire didn't give up. He grabbed the standing lamp to his left and flung it at Blake, who dove away, letting it slam harmlessly against the wall.

But the attacker didn't slow down. He pushed away from the bookshelf and reached for a chair that was covered with a stack of magazines. Blake knew exactly what the guy planned to do with the chair—the wooden chair. But he didn't intend to give him the chance.

"Nice try, buddy!" Blake grunted and jumped, knocking the chair out of the assailant's hand before he could slam it against the wall and make himself a stake. As Blake wheeled back to deliver a punch to the attacker's head, a balled-up fist hit him in the gut, making him fold over for a split second.

But he'd had worse than that. Scanguards had trained him well in hand-to-hand combat. Nobody would defeat him that easily, not even a vampire who weighed a good thirty pounds more than him.

He continued to trade blows with the assailant, avoiding as many direct hits as he could, though the attacker landed a few well-placed fists, just as Blake managed to deliver some decent blows to the guy's increasingly agitated face. It wouldn't be long before both he and the attacker would bare their fangs, despite the human in the room. Not knowing whether the woman knew what they were, he wanted to avoid that complication.

It spurred him on to go even harder at the hostile vampire, and he now used his legs to deliver powerful kicks, moves he'd learned from various martial arts disciplines. But the assailant didn't go down. He kept coming, kept punching and kicking more ferociously by the minute, as if the fight was replenishing his energy. There was no stopping him with ordinary means. Only a stake or a silver bullet would bring this determined jerk down. But that wasn't an option right now, particularly since he wanted him alive.

Blake gritted his teeth and drew on all of his reserves, pummeling the assailant with vampire force and speed. In return, the vampire turned even wilder. His eyes glared red now.

A high-pitched shriek from the woman in the room distracted Blake for a split second. Had she seen the attacker's glowing eyes?

A fist connecting with his temple made him tumble back a step. Blake swung his arm back and aimed for the hostile vampire's chin, but when he stepped forward again to use all his weight against his opponent, his foot got caught in something and he slipped. He caught himself in mid-fall and jumped back, but the other vampire was already heading toward the open doorway.

Frantic, Blake disentangled his foot from the lamp's electrical cord, in which he'd gotten caught, and raced after him. The kitchen was small, and from it a second door led back into the hallway. The assailant was heading for it, but Blake ripped him back and spun him around.

But before Blake could deliver a punch, the attacker braced himself on the kitchen counter and kicked both his legs into Blake's stomach, knocking him on his ass. It gave the hostile vampire enough time to hoist himself over the kitchen sink and lunge for the open window.

Blake was already up again and charging toward the window, when something hard hit him from the side. Momentarily disoriented, he spun his head toward the open doorway, where the scantily-dressed woman stood with a hairdryer in her hand.

"Shit!" he cursed and jumped onto the counter, lunging toward the window. But when he looked outside, the vampire was already fifty yards away from the building and mounting a motorcycle.

He sped away. Despite his vampire night vision, Blake couldn't make out the numbers: they'd been obscured with dirt.

"Fuck," he cursed, slamming his hand against the wall, before jumping down and turning back to the woman. "Why the fuck did you hit me with that thing? I had him!"

She lifted her chin. "You didn't have him! He was beating the shit out of you. I was fucking helping you!"

"Yeah, you were a big help!" he growled. "You should have stayed out of it."

"Oh yeah? And play the damsel in distress?" she griped.

He stepped toward her, furious now. "You *were* the damsel in distress."

He took a deep breath, and for the first time really looked at her. Yeah, and what an utterly beautiful damsel she was. Fuck, he hadn't even noticed. But he sure noticed now.

She was a natural blonde, her hair the color of wheat. It cascaded down her shoulders and touched the exposed skin of her neckline, where her pink bathrobe gaped open. Beneath the fabric, her breasts heaved from the force of her heavy breathing, possibly from the effort of hitting him, certainly from the outrage over his admonishment. Well, he didn't mind the view. Not at all, in fact. She was quite something to look at. Not petite, not fragile, but tall and athletic.

His eyes wandered lower. The robe only reached to mid-thigh, and the legs that he now admired were trim and a little pale from lack of sun. But he could imagine that in the summer her skin would turn the color of bronze, accentuating her golden hair. Involuntarily he shifted, the sudden tightness in his pants forcing him to find a more comfortable position, before the beauty before him noticed that he was sporting the beginnings of a hard-on—and that it was her fault.

A huff made him lift his eyes to her face. Her cornflower-blue eyes scrutinized him with barely-veiled suspicion now. He could get lost in their depths, were they not narrowed at him now.

"Who are you and what are you doing here?"

He tilted his head to the side. "You mean apart from saving your pretty ass from that jerk?" He pointed to the window.

A little bit of color rose to her cheeks. "Yeah, apart from that."

"I could ask you the same thing. 'Cause for sure you're not Hannah. And this is her flat. So what are you doing here?"

"That's rich!" she snapped. "You're breaking in here, and you're asking *me* what I'm doing?"

Involuntarily, he pointed in the direction of the front door. "If I hadn't knocked down that door, God knows what that guy would've done to you. You were screaming for help, so excuse me if I didn't ring the fucking door bell!" Damn it, the woman could rile him up!

She sucked in a breath, but instead of lashing out with another insult, she appeared to calm herself down. "I'm sorry, but so much has happened, and I guess I'm just a little agitated. I mean that burglar… it's not as if I didn't have enough on my mind already."

A burglar? That's what she thought that vampire was? For now he'd let her believe that, but he was almost sure that the attacker had something to do with Hannah not showing up for work. Had the stranger been human, then, sure, he could have been an ordinary burglar, but a vampire, when Hannah worked with vampires? That was too much of a coincidence.

Slowly, he nodded. At least the woman wasn't acting combative anymore. He could work with that. "You're a friend of Hannah's?"

"Lilo. Her best friend from back home. You live in the building?"

"No. I'm a friend. Hannah and I work for the same company. Different divisions." He offered his hand. "I'm Blake."

Lilo hesitated, then transferred the hairdryer to her other hand, before shaking his. "She never mentioned you."

"She never mentioned you either." Though he had no reason to believe that Lilo was lying. "Have you seen her?"

Lilo blinked before answering. "No. The apartment was empty when I arrived earlier tonight."

Blake glanced around. "She hasn't shown up for work. Didn't call in sick, which isn't like her. We're concerned."

"So am I. That's why I flew out here. I think something happened to her." Suddenly she sagged against the doorframe, all the air leaving her lungs.

Instinctively, Blake reached for her, but she eased to the side, stepping into the living room.

"Sorry, didn't mean to…" he started. He shoved a hand through his hair. "It wasn't my intention to frighten you. Guess that burglar did his fair share of it already. Are you okay?"

She forced a faint smile, but shook her head. "No. I'm not okay. My friend is missing. Her dog's gone, too. And she's not answering her cell. Her mother is worried sick." She pulled the robe tighter around her torso. "And I need to file a missing person's report."

"I can take care of that," he offered, though he had no intention of going to the police. This was vampire business. It was paramount that he deal with Hannah's disappearance himself; he didn't want to involve the police.

She shook her head, vehemently. "No. *I* have to go to the police. I owe her. It's my fault she's gone."

Blake instinctively stepped closer. "What? Why is it your fault?"

Lilo's beautiful face took on a pained expression. "She left me a message that she needed to talk. Something was bothering her, and I didn't respond. I was too busy."

"And that somehow makes it your fault?" He shook his head. "That's ludicrous."

Lilo suddenly shivered, and he realized that the cold air coming from the kitchen window was bothering her. He turned around and closed it, then ushered her toward the couch in the living room.

She lifted her eyes, and her gaze collided with his. "I should have called her back when she needed me. It's my fault."

5

"Please sit down. You're more shook up than I thought."

Her rescuer's voice was deep and melodic and made her shiver once more. Lilo realized that she hadn't even thanked him yet. Instead she'd railed at him and treated him with suspicion. Yet here he was, taking the hairdryer from her hand, putting it aside, and guiding her gently to the couch as if she were fragile and would break at any moment. And maybe she would. She wasn't one of the brave characters from her books, who dealt with crime daily and wasn't afraid of anything.

"I'm—"

"What's going on here?" The male voice came from the front door.

Lilo whipped her head in his direction. In the open doorframe stood a middle-aged man, wearing pajamas and a long dark-green bathrobe. He glanced into the apartment.

Blake was already walking toward him. "Nothing to worry about. It's all taken care of." He reached the door and blocked her view, continuing his conversation with the concerned neighbor, lowering his voice so much that she couldn't hear what he was saying.

A moment later, Blake turned around and closed the door behind him. They were alone again.

As he walked toward her with his confident gait, she took the opportunity and eyed him up. He was a little over six feet tall and athletic. His hair was dark, his eyes azure-blue. He had a strong, square chin and a long, straight nose. Underneath his Polo shirt she could see his chest muscles flex.

He was handsome; very much so. Maybe in his early thirties. Rugged, in a romantic kind of way. And he looked exactly like she'd always imagined Morgan West, the bounty hunter from her mystery series, would look in real life.

She shook her head to try to return to reality. She wasn't living in one of her books for a change. This was real life. Real danger. And this man had saved her from a true threat.

"I haven't even thanked you," she started.

He stopped in front of her and sat down on the edge of the old wooden coffee table. He grinned. "No need. I'm just glad you've stopped hitting me."

She cringed. "I only hit you once. And it was an accident. I was after the other guy. I'm sorry."

"Forget about it." He leaned in a little. "Tell me what happened."

Lilo tugged at the bathrobe she'd borrowed from Hannah. "I was taking a quick shower after my flight, getting ready to go to the police, when I heard something. I thought it must be a burglar. So I figured I'd chase him away before he stole something."

"Chase him away? Why didn't you call 9-1-1?"

"I tried." She pointed to the armchair where the contents of her handbag were still strewn about. She still couldn't see her cell phone among her things. "But I couldn't find my cell phone. I think he took it before he went into the kitchen. And then he heard me, and it was too late." She shivered. "I don't know what he would have done."

Blake pressed his lips together and nodded, frowning. "Good thing I got here in time. Well, you'd better get dressed and pack up your things. You can't stay here now." He rose.

She shot up from the couch. "I can't just leave. I need to stay here. What if Hannah comes back? With my phone gone she has no way of contacting me."

"It's not safe here." The sharp edge in his voice brooked no refusal.

And riled her up instantly. "Because of a burglar? It happens all the time in large cities. I'm not some country bumpkin who—"

"It's got nothing to do with that," he interrupted and glared at her. "This was no random burglary. That guy is gonna come back. And I don't want you to be here when he does."

Her heart started to thunder and in the back of her mind something tried to push to the surface. "Why do you think that?"

"I work in security. I have a gut feeling for this kind of stuff. Trust me on that. This guy was looking for something specific." He motioned to the contents of her handbag. "Why take your phone, but not your wallet? What burglar leaves behind cash and credit cards?"

Lilo followed his gesture. He was right; her wallet lay on the armchair, open. She could see that the money was still in it. And then she remembered what the burglar had said to her while he had her on the couch.

"He asked me where it is," she said out loud.

"Where what is?"

She shook her head. "I don't know what he was talking about. He pressed me down on the couch and said: *Where is it?* That's all. Then you came in."

"Do you have anything valuable on you?"

"No. Just my computer, my cell phone, which I can't find, and my wallet. I have no jewelry on me. Nothing of value to anybody but myself. I travel light."

Blake nodded and glanced around, his eyes falling on the computer on the table. "Is that yours?"

"No. That's Hannah's. I tried to get in to check her emails, but it's password-protected."

"That's fine. We'll take it with us. I'll check whether she left her cell phone or anything else that could give us a clue to where she is. In the meantime, get dressed and pack your things. You're coming with me." His voice was commanding, as if he was used to his orders being followed without question.

"But I have to go to the police and report her missing."

For a moment, he just looked at her, studying her face. Then he sighed. "Fine. We'll stop by the police on the way."

She hesitated, instinctively pulling her bathrobe more tightly around her. "I don't know you…"

"I understand that. But if I really wanted to hurt you, I could have done so a million times."

She looked into his blue eyes and saw the sincerity there. Slowly, she nodded. He was right. "Okay, give me a few minutes to get my stuff together."

And to calm down and recover from the shock of being attacked—and then rescued by a man who could make the heart of any woman flutter. Even hers.

6

While Lilo got dressed in the bedroom, Blake used the time wisely and searched the place for anything that could help pinpoint Hannah's whereabouts. He also sent a text message.

Now he hoisted Lilo's suitcase into the trunk of his Aston Martin, a gift from his 4th great-grandparents, Rose and Quinn, after he'd totaled his BMW four years earlier—and a way for them to tease him. After all, in his twenties he'd seen himself as his British namesake, Bond, and tried to pick up girls with 007's signature greeting. How pathetic he'd been back then. Now he was so much more—more than he'd ever dreamed he could be. A member of a group of vampires who had made it their mission to protect the innocent.

Blake placed Hannah's computer and tablet in a bag next to Lilo's luggage. He hadn't found Hannah's cell phone, which could turn out to be good news. If she had it on her, and it was switched on, it would be easy to track: the Vüber app had a built-in GPS. He wouldn't even have to contact his IT crew to triangulate the phone.

Blake walked around the car and got in on the driver's side. Lilo was already sitting in the passenger seat. He unlocked his cell phone and opened the Vüber app. As a Scanguards manager, he had the administrative version of the app on his phone, which allowed him to locate various Vüber drivers and identify them by name, something a regular user couldn't do, in order to protect the drivers' anonymity.

"What are you doing?"

He glanced at Lilo, before tapping the app and entering Hannah's name.

"Hannah's phone has an app on it that shows where she is, so that people who are interested in hiring her know how close she is."

"She told me she was working as a driver. So this is a competitor of Uber?"

"Not really. Vüber only operates during daytime."

Lilo furrowed her forehead. "Why? That doesn't seem like a very good business model."

He smiled involuntarily. Vüber didn't exist primarily to make money. It had been created as a convenience for the vampire population of San Francisco and the Bay Area. "We commissioned a study and found that most attacks on professional drivers are committed at night, but that the majority of rides are needed during daytime. So we decided to create a division which maximizes fares, yet minimizes attacks on drivers." It wasn't exactly the truth, but it was a reasonable explanation, one he hoped Lilo would buy.

"I'd never thought of that. That's actually very... uh, considerate of the company." Now she pointed to the cell phone in his hand. "Is she showing up?"

Blake looked back at the app and saw that the wheel had stopped spinning. *Not found*, the screen told him. He lifted his eyes and met Lilo's hopeful gaze. Wordlessly, he shook his head.

She sighed, and he could sense her disappointment. "I guess that would have been too easy."

He logged out and opened up his messenger app. He pulled up a contact, before handing the phone to Lilo.

"Type in your cell phone number," he said, starting the car.

"What for?"

He pulled into the street and merged into the light evening traffic. "If the intruder still has it, I might be able to find him by triangulating your phone."

She sighed. "I know how it works. But why would *you* do that? The police will take care of that."

"By the time we get to the station and get somebody on the case, he may have already ditched your phone. It'd be too late."

Accepting his explanation, she typed something into the app and handed him the phone. He took it and kept one eye on the traffic, while he forwarded the number, before dialing Thomas's number.

Scanguards' Chief of IT answered immediately. "What's up?"

"I just texted you a cell number. Can you try and track it right now?"

"I suppose it's urgent and can't wait," Thomas replied, a smirk in his voice.

"You guessed right. Call me when you have something."

"Sure thing."

The call disconnected. Blake placed his phone in the cup holder and gave Lilo a sideways glance. "We'll know very soon if it's switched on and he's still got it."

She nodded. "Do you do this a lot? I mean…" She pointed to the phone. "…find missing phones and track down burglars?"

"I do whatever is necessary."

"You said you worked in security. What kind?"

From the corner of his eye, he noticed her studying him. Fair enough. Now that the initial shock of being attacked had subsided, she was bound to have questions. "Personal security."

"You mean like a bodyguard?"

He nodded.

"You mentioned you work for the same company as Hannah. She never said anything about working for a bodyguard company."

He could feel the suspicion rolling off her. At least it meant she had her wits about her, though he didn't relish the fact that he had to give her more explanations. The less she knew about Scanguards the better.

"Different divisions, remember?"

"Yeah, you said. Still doesn't tell me much."

"There isn't much to tell."

"Funny, I had a feeling you'd say that."

He tossed her another sideways look. Her don't-bullshit-me expression was easy to read. It was time to pacify her.

"Listen, Lilo, the company I work for deals with highly sensitive issues. Our clients demand confidentiality. That's probably why Hannah never told you much about her work. But let me assure you, we take care of our employees. And when somebody goes missing, like Hannah, we don't just rely on the police to find that person. We use all our resources."

He stopped at a red light and let go of the steering wheel, reaching for Lilo's hand. Only when he felt her warm skin against his and heard her suck in a breath, did he realize what he was doing. But it was too late to withdraw now. He squeezed her hand, enjoying the tender touch for a brief moment.

"We'll find Hannah. Alive and well. I promise you that." Though he had no right to make such a promise. For all he knew, Hannah could already be dead. But he couldn't share his worries with Lilo or she would fall apart. He needed her to remain strong.

"I hope you're right."

For a moment, their gazes locked. He saw concern in her eyes. He'd do anything to wipe that expression from her face and see her smile instead. There were so many things he wanted to see on her face: laughter, joy... he inhaled... arousal. He eased his torso across the divide between the two seats. She looked so vulnerable... so tempting.

The vampire in him was drawn to her blood. And the man was drawn to her beauty and the strength he'd sensed during their initial argument. She was no pushover—no damsel in distress. Far from it. She was the most fascinating woman he'd ever met. A woman with the most tempting lips...

Honking from behind him made him jerk back and let go of her hand. *Fuck!*

What had he been about to do? He'd only met her less than an hour ago. And he wasn't the kind of guy to paw at a woman just because she was hot. And, damn it, Lilo was hot! But that was besides the point. He wasn't into one-night stands, hadn't been in years. He liked to get to know a woman first, before becoming physical—though in his twenties he'd been the opposite. He'd been the wham-bam-thank-you-Ma'am type. But that had changed with age and his mounting responsibilities as Chief of Hybrid Security. Now he liked to take things slowly. So why the fuck had he leaned in as if to kiss her?

Get a grip, man!

He cleared his throat and turned right at the intersection, then pulled into a parking spot in front of the station. At this time of night, it was only moderately busy.

"Is this the police station?" Lilo asked, her voice a touch hoarse.

Blake pointed to the entry, over which the words *Police Station* were illuminated.

~ ~ ~

As Blake got out of the car, Lilo fumbled with her seatbelt, trembling. She'd mumbled some idiotic question just to escape the silence that had descended between them after that car had honked at them to move.

Embarrassment burned in her cheeks even now. She'd held onto Blake's hand, loving the feel of his gentle touch, when all he'd wanted was to comfort her. Instead, she'd leaned in as if drawn to him by some inexplicable force. She'd never believed in such a thing, never thought that she, of all people, could be drawn to somebody as if hypnotized. She, who didn't trust men, because she'd been disappointed one too many times. But her body didn't seem to remember those times when her trust had been shattered. Instead, her body yearned for the stranger who'd rescued her from the intruder. Maybe that was the reason for her inexplicable attraction: she felt grateful. Of course, the fact that Blake was the personification of her fictional hero, Morgan West, might have something to do with her momentary lapse in judgment. She would just have to ignore this tiny detail and try not to confuse him with her dashing bounty hunter anymore.

Lilo finally undid the seatbelt and took a deep breath. She could do this.

Before she could reach for the door handle, the door opened. She got out and nodded at Blake, who was holding the car door open for her. Clutching her handbag to her side she said, "Let's do this."

She avoided looking at him and walked up the steps leading to the double doors. She heard the car door close, followed by a beeping sound, indicating that Blake had locked the car. His footsteps were close behind her, and by the time she'd reached the entrance, he'd caught up to her and was holding the door open like a perfect gentleman. Not even Morgan West did that. She made a mental note to give her fictional hero better manners.

The station was busy. A few prostitutes sat on a bench, while several officers shuffled papers behind a high counter. In one corridor, a drunken man was being led away, while a well-dressed man argued with a police officer in a cubicle. From down the hall, somebody yelled for somebody else to be quiet. A female police officer stood at the counter with a receiver pressed between her ear and shoulder, scribbling onto a clipboard and simultaneously leafing through a stack of papers.

"Uh-huh," she said into the phone while she waved at one of the prostitutes, motioning to a door on the left. The door opened a second later and a transvestite stalked out, grinning from one ear to the other. She turned toward the open plan area and blew air kisses to the working officers.

"Get out of here, Veronica," one of them called out to her. "Or I'll book you myself."

With a laugh, the transvestite sauntered to the door and left.

"Be right there, ma'am."

Lilo's head snapped to the female police officer behind the counter, who'd spoken, and nodded gratefully.

A police officer in plain clothes came around the corner and approached the counter. "No worries, Mandy, I'll take that."

Lilo took a step closer to the counter, Blake by her side, and gave a faint smile.

"I'm Detective Donnelly. How can I help you?"

Encouraged by the man's friendly demeanor, Lilo sighed with relief. "I'm here to report my friend missing. And also a break-in at her apartment."

He reached for a clipboard and a pen. "Alright then. Your name, please."

"Lieselotte Schroeder."

"I'll need to see ID."

She rummaged for it in her bag, while the police detective addressed Blake. "And you, sir, are you with the lady?"

"Yes."

"I'll need to see your ID, too."

Lilo handed her drivers license to Detective Donnelly.

He looked up. "You're far from home, Miss Schroeder."

"I flew out here, because I'm worried about my friend. Hannah Bergdorf. She's missing."

"Okay." He reached for Blake's ID and looked at it. "Thanks, Mr. Bond."

Lilo whirled her head to Blake. His name was Bond? And he drove an Aston Martin? Really? She managed a glance at his ID. Indeed, it said Blake Bond. Not only did he look like Morgan West, he shared a last name with a fictional secret agent? If she wrote something like this in one of her books, nobody would believe her.

Too far-fetched, her editor would say.

Not believable, her critics would write.

"When did you last see your friend Miss Bergdorf?" the detective now asked.

"Over a year ago."

He raised his eyebrows. "And you're only now filing a missing person's report?"

"She's only been missing for three days. I flew out here as soon as I could to try to look for her. But she's not in her apartment. Her dog is gone. And then this guy broke in and attacked me. He stole my phone, too. And then—"

"You were assaulted? And there's a dog missing? And your phone was stolen?"

She nodded.

"So let me get this straight. We have a missing person, a missing dog, a burglary, an assault, and a stolen phone. Were there any witnesses to any of these alleged crimes?"

"Alleged?" She huffed. Did this man not believe her? But before she could say anything else, she felt Blake's reassuring hand on her forearm.

"I witnessed the assault," Blake said calmly. "I can give a description of the burglar who broke into Miss Bergdorf's flat and attacked Miss Schroeder."

She nodded, thankful for Blake's presence. Lilo added, "And I also think I know who might be behind Hannah's disappearance."

Both Officer Donnelly and Blake stared at her.

"You know?" Blake asked.

"Ronny, her loser boyfriend. I think she wanted to leave him."

"Why didn't you tell me about him earlier?"

She looked at Blake. "There wasn't exactly time for that. I mean, between the break-in, the assault…"

"Miss Schroeder, can you elaborate on this Ronny? What's his full name?" the police officer asked.

"I don't know. Hannah never talked much about him. But from the few things she did tell me, I can tell what kind of person he is." And that he wasn't the kind of man who was good for a sweet and generous woman like Hannah, a woman who believed that everybody deserved help.

The police officer raised an eyebrow, but Lilo continued undeterred.

"He didn't seem to have a regular job. And he was very possessive and jealous." Something she abhorred in a man. It was a character trait that only led to trouble.

"Jealousy is not a crime, Miss Schroeder."

"But it can lead to one. I'm telling you, you have to find Ronny. If anybody knows where Hannah is, it's him."

The police officer sighed. "Fine, Miss Schroeder. But let's start with details about your friend, Miss Bergdorf."

For the next few minutes, Lilo answered questions about Hannah's appearance and habits, which the officer took down diligently.

"You wouldn't have a photo of Miss Bergdorf, would you?"

"Not on me. I have some on my cell phone. But it's gone."

"Not to worry," Blake interrupted. "Hannah works for the same company as I. I can get HR to send over a photo from her personnel file."

Lilo gave Blake a grateful smile. It was lucky that he'd shown up—in more ways than one. Not only had he physically saved her, he was also here to support her in her search for Hannah. And right now she could use all the help she could get.

"Good," Officer Donnelly said. "Now about the break-in and assault. Did you get a good look at the intruder?"

"I did. He was tall."

"How tall?"

Lilo pointed to Blake. "About as tall as him."

"Six foot two," Blake offered.

"But heavier."

Blake nodded. "About two-hundred-ten pounds."

"Any identifying marks? Tattoos? Scars?"

Lilo shook her head. "None. He looked pretty average. Brown hair."

"Brown eyes," Blake continued. "Pretty ordinary."

Ordinary? Lilo clamped her hand over Blake's forearm. "Brown eyes? You didn't see?"

Blake's forehead furrowed. "See what?"

"His eyes were red. As if he had an infection like—"

"You mean like conjunctivitis?" the officer interrupted.

She looked straight at him. "No. It wasn't the white part of the eye that was red; his irises were."

"I've never heard of an illness like that," Blake interjected, making her turn to him. "Maybe it was just a reflection."

"That's what I thought at first, too, but there wasn't a lot of light in the living room that could have reflected off his eyes."

The officer cleared his throat, making her look back at him. "So it was pretty dark then, Miss? I'm surprised you were able to describe the man as well as you did." He made a note on his form. "Well, let's talk about anything that's missing. Your phone, right?"

She wanted to protest, but what if she'd seen wrong? She couldn't swear to it. Maybe it had been a reflection after all, or fear had made her see things that weren't there. After all, he'd been attacking her, and her only thought had been to save herself.

Her mind had played a trick on her.

7

Half an hour later, Blake guided Lilo back to the car.

Donnelly had done his job well. He'd taken down the report and pretended to give the case his utmost attention, when Blake knew all too well that Donnelly would shred the report the minute they left the police station.

Crimes involving vampires were dealt with by Scanguards. That was the deal they'd with the city. Only a few people in the city government knew about this arrangement: the police chief and several police officers, who were spread around the various precincts, so they could alert Scanguards when a vampire-related crime crossed their desks.

While Lilo had gotten dressed, Blake had quickly alerted Donnelly by text message that they were coming and told him to pretend that they didn't know each other. All had gone as planned.

When Blake opened the car door, Lilo turned to him. "Can you recommend a hotel? Nothing too expensive, but in a safe area."

"You won't need a hotel. You're staying with me. I thought I made that clear earlier." He was sure he'd told her that she was coming with him. Why else would he have made her pack her suitcase?

"I can just as easily stay in a hotel. I really don't want to be a burden. And you don't know me."

"You're a friend of Hannah's. That's all I need to know. Besides, if we want to find Hannah, we need to work together."

She gave a hesitant nod, then eased into the passenger seat. He got into the driver's seat and started the engine. He was pulling out of the parking lot and into traffic, when Lilo shifted in her seat.

"You've gotta turn around. We didn't give the police Hannah's computer and tablet," she suddenly said. She pushed a lock of her blond hair behind her ear. "I don't know how I could have forgotten that."

He glanced at her for a brief moment. "The police will sit on her computer for days before they get an IT expert on it and get into Hannah's email. We don't have that kind of time."

"But what are you gonna do with it? I told you it's password-protected. And I already tried a few passwords without success."

"I'll get the company's IT department on it. They'll be able to crack it." He pulled his cell phone from his pocket, but before he could dial Thomas's number, the phone rang. "Speak of the devil." He pressed *accept*, then hit the speaker button. "Hey Thomas, you're on speaker. I'm in the car with Lilo, the owner of the cell phone I had you trace. Anything new?"

"It pinged off a tower at the airport earlier in the evening," Thomas replied. "But nothing since."

"That must have been when I got off the plane and checked my messages," Lilo said.

Blake nodded. "Makes sense. Thomas, keep monitoring it."

"I sent a text message to it and called the number, too, but it's going straight to voicemail. Sorry, it's a dead end for now."

Before Thomas could disconnect the call, Blake stopped him. "Another thing: can you come over to my house and look at a laptop and tablet? They're password-protected. I need to know what's on them."

"Now?"

"The sooner the better."

"Sorry, I'm going into a meeting in a minute." There was some mumbling, as if Thomas was holding his hand over the mouthpiece. "Okay, Eddie just volunteered. He'll be there shortly."

"Thanks, Thomas."

"You bet."

A click on the line, and Thomas was gone.

"Your colleague has a meeting at midnight? Who works those kind of hours?"

Hearing a hint of suspicion in Lilo's voice, Blake met her look and smiled warmly, hoping to dispel all her doubts with his charm. "Security is a twenty-four-seven business."

Slowly, she nodded. "I guess I knew that already." She took a breath. "Your colleague didn't even ask what all this was about. You didn't tell him that we're trying to find Hannah."

"I don't have to. He knows when I ask him for help, it's because it's important. That's how the company works. We don't question our colleagues' requests. It goes both ways."

"That requires a lot of trust," she mused.

"In our business, trust is everything. Sometimes our lives depend on it."

"You mean when you're protecting somebody as a bodyguard?"

"Some assignments can be dangerous, but we're trained well." It also helped that as a vampire he had a few secret weapons up his sleeve. Better than any fictional British spy.

But it was time to stop Lilo from asking any more questions. "So what do you do in Nebraska, Lilo?"

"I'm a writer." She turned to look out the window. "What neighborhood is this?"

Blake suppressed a chuckle. It appeared he wasn't the only one who didn't want to answer questions about his work. "We're driving through Pacific Heights."

"Oh, I've heard of it. Pretty."

"What do you write?"

She shrugged, as if it didn't matter. "Mysteries."

"You mean murder mysteries?"

"Not necessarily. Not every book is about a murder. I write about all kinds of crimes. Or rather solving crimes."

He made a mental note of that. If Lilo wrote crime fiction she had to be smart, and he'd have to be on his toes to make sure she didn't discover his secrets. It would only complicate things.

"So who's your protagonist? A female detective?"

"A bounty hunter."

That response made him toss her a quick look. "Seriously?"

"Why?"

"Well, you've got stiff competition in that genre. Few are as good as Maxim Holt. He's got that market cornered."

"You've read the Morgan West bounty hunter series?"

Blake nodded. "Just finished *Anatomy of a Bounty*." And he would have finished it earlier, if he didn't have to look after thirteen hybrids, who couldn't shut up for even one minute.

"So *he's* the best, you say?"

Crap! He should have just kept his mouth shut. No writer liked to hear somebody rave about another author's books. "Maybe if I read one of yours for comparison…"

"No, no. That's fine. Honestly." She yawned.

Great, now he was boring her to sleep! Way to treat a woman he was attracted to. Yeah, exactly: he was attracted to Lilo. Despite the fact that his mind was working overtime to come up with ideas on how to find Hannah, his body was occupied with other things. Things he had no business imagining.

"We're almost there," he said quickly and turned into the next street.

He pulled into the fourth driveway on his right and drove up to the garage of the two-story Edwardian house that stood on an extra-wide city lot. As he came to a stop, he lowered the window, then reached through it to the electronic reader that was built into the wall that ran along the property line. This part of the driveway was covered so that during daytime it was safe to open the window of the car without being exposed to direct sunlight. In addition, the scanner could be moved closer to the car window by a remote control which was built into his car's steering wheel. And since there was a tall concrete wall on the driver's side, no sunlight could enter the car from that direction.

Blake placed his thumb on the scanner. A moment later, the garage door started to lift.

"You have a high-security, government-style entry system for your home?" Lilo asked incredulously.

He met her wary gaze. "It's very practical. At least I can't lose my keys."

"Unless you lose your thumb," she answered in a deadpan manner.

"If that happens I've got bigger problems than not being able to get into my house."

He put the car back in gear and drove into the garage, parking next to his black-out SUV. Behind him, the garage door lowered again, shutting out the outside world.

"Come, we'll get you settled."

He got out of the car and opened the trunk. Lilo was already next to him and reaching for her suitcase. But he'd reached for it at the same time. Their hands touched, and he felt a charge go through him. He could explain it away as static electricity, but he would be lying to himself. This wasn't electricity; it was chemistry. The kind that could instantaneously combust if he wasn't careful.

With a gasp, Lilo withdrew her hand, and he tightened his grip around the handle. He didn't look at her when he said, "Why don't you take Hannah's computer and tablet?"

"Yeah, sure." Her voice trembled as much as her hands as she grabbed the small bag with the electronics and moved away from the car.

"Listen, Lilo…"

She stopped walking, but didn't turn around.

Maybe it had been a bad idea to bring her here. Perhaps he should have brought her to a hotel. "You don't need to be afraid of me."

Silence greeted him. Then a sigh. She turned slowly and lifted her eyes to look at him. "You saved me from that intruder. You took me to the police like I asked you to. The policeman knows who you are."

Shock coursed through him. Had she somehow guessed that he and Donnelly knew each other?

"I mean, he took down the details of your drivers' license. And there were cameras in the police station. If something happened to me, they would come looking for you." She shook her head. "No, I'm not afraid of you."

"Then why are you shaking?"

"I'm shaking because I've never been in a situation like this. I'm scared."

Slowly he walked toward her, set the suitcase on the floor, and gently drew her into his arms. She didn't protest, and for a long while he simply held her, feeling her body's warmth caress him. The brave woman who'd fought against her attacker and verbally sparred with him earlier tonight, now felt fragile and vulnerable. And with it, Blake's protector instinct surged.

He ran his hand over her hair. "Everything will be fine."

"Thank you," she murmured into his chest, and the vibrations of her voice made his entire body tingle and awaken a desire he knew he couldn't act upon.

With regret, he released her from his embrace. "Let's get you settled. You need to rest."

8

She hadn't told him the entire truth.

Yes, she was scared for her friend, but the reason she'd been shaking was because she was scared of her reaction to Blake. She'd never felt this kind of intense physical attraction to any man, particularly not to one she knew nothing about. There was absolutely no reason whatsoever for her to be drawn to Blake like a moth to the light, especially considering her trust issues.

As she followed him up the stairs into the house, she couldn't help but admire his strong legs and flexing butt muscles. Damn, he filled out a pair of pants like nobody she'd ever seen. He was the epitome of strength and power. And he had a soft side, one she hadn't expected. His embrace had been comforting and gentle. And just about as platonic as it could be. Which drove home another reality: the first man she was interested in since her last relationship two years ago, wasn't interested in her.

Lilo stepped into the hallway as Blake flipped the light switch, illuminating a large entry hall with a mahogany staircase, a long hallway, and an open arch leading into the living room.

"Wow." The word just slipped out.

Stunned, she let her eyes roam. She'd known that San Francisco was famous for its architecture, but she'd never actually been inside one of the gorgeous mansions portrayed in movies and on TV. The period detailing was intricate and beautiful. It lent the house instant warmth. This was a true home.

"You actually live here?"

Setting down her suitcase, he nodded and pointed to the living room. "Sorry, it still looks a little bare. But I only bought the place two months ago and I'm still waiting for a few more pieces of furniture to be delivered."

"It's beautiful. I suppose being a bodyguard pays well." She wanted to slap her hand over her mouth, but it was too late. It wasn't polite to talk about money, but she couldn't imagine how a man of Blake's age—he had to be in his early thirties—could afford a mansion like this.

"Well, my salary didn't pay for this," he said, suddenly looking at his shoes as if embarrassed. "I inherited a trust fund from my family." He took an audible breath. "Well, how about I show you the guestroom?"

"Could I maybe get a glass of water first?" Her throat felt like sandpaper.

"Of course." He motioned to the end of the hallway, when a sound from the front door made him spin around.

Alerted by his sudden reaction, her heart thundered, and she snapped her head in the same direction. A gasp escaped her throat.

A tall bald man stood in the open doorway, a pissed off look on his face, two bags in his hands.

Instinctively, Lilo grabbed Blake's forearm.

"You were supposed to pick up the boys from my house," the stranger growled and set down the luggage.

"Sorry, something came up," Blake replied.

"Yeah, I can see that!" The man glared at her, before stepping aside to let two boys in their early teens enter the house. A young woman followed them.

The boys immediately sauntered toward the living room.

"Nicholas, Adam, didn't I teach you better manners?" the dark-haired woman—who couldn't possibly be their mother, not unless she'd had them when she was ten—called after them.

The younger boy looked over his shoulder. "Sorry!" Then he glanced at Blake. "Hey, Blake."

"Hey, Adam," Blake replied.

The older boy stopped, too, tipping his chin in Blake's direction. "Hey, Blake, okay if we play Xbox?"

Blake grinned and winked at the bald man. "Only if your dad says it's okay. Right, Zane?"

Zane rolled his eyes. "As if you care what my sons are allowed or not allowed to do. Every time they stay with you, they come home acting like they were raised by wolves."

"You exaggerate." Blake walked toward the woman and gave her a quick hug. "Hey, Portia."

The woman looked past him. "Don't you wanna introduce us to your *friend?*"

Suddenly all eyes were on Lilo, and she felt like she was on display.

Blake turned on his heel. "This is Lilo. Lilo, this is my colleague Zane and his wife Portia." He pointed to the living room. "And their sons, Nicholas and Adam."

Zane nodded and grunted a quick hello, while Portia smiled and said, "Nice to meet you, Lilo."

Zane turned to Blake. "If you don't have time to look after the boys, we'll take them to New Orleans with us."

"I said I'd take care of them. So I will."

"Just saying," Zane added, looking as if assessing her. Then he pulled up one side of his mouth into an almost-smile. "Though anybody would be a better influence on the boys than you."

Portia shook her head and put her hand on her husband's arm. "Don't listen to him, Blake. He's just pissed that Nicholas and Adam don't want to come with us. He hates being separated from them."

Zane shot his wife an angry glare. "Damn it, Portia!"

Instead of shrinking back from him, she stroked her hand over his cheek. Before her eyes, the intimidating man softened.

"They'll be safe with Blake," Portia murmured.

Lilo had never seen anything like it. Immediately, she understood their relationship. They were true partners, one incomplete without the other. This was what true love looked like. It existed. And it could last.

Zane nodded before severing the intimate contact with his wife. His eyes met Blake's. "You'd better make sure of that, or I'm gonna crush you with my bare hands."

"Get out of here, and have a great time in NOLA. Give my best to Cain and Faye," Blake said.

"Nicholas, Adam!" Zane called out.

As if the boys knew that this was good-bye, they came running and flew into their father's outstretched arms.

"You guys behave, okay? Or I'll be back to drag you down to New Orleans by your ears." Despite the threat, Zane's voice was soft.

"Yes, Dad," Nicholas said, and Adam echoed it.

The affectionate exchange made them appear younger, and Lilo realized that despite their obvious attempts at wanting to show their independence from their parents by not going on this trip with them, they were still kids who sought their parents' approval and affection.

Portia bent down and kissed her sons. "Time to go." She looked at Blake. "Thanks, Blake. And nice to meet you, Lilo. Don't let the boys drive you crazy."

Involuntarily, Lilo had to smile. She liked the young mother who seemed to have such power over her husband and such confidence in Blake. When the door closed behind them and the two boys were already running back into the living room, Lilo turned and found herself facing Blake.

"It's nice of you to look after two young boys."

Blake shrugged. "They're really no trouble."

She lifted an eyebrow, when she heard one of the boys yell.

"Give me that remote! It's my turn!" It was the younger boy.

"I'm the man in the house when Dad's not here, and you know it."

Blake chuckled and winked at her. "Okay, maybe just a little trouble."

"Blake?" Nicholas called from the living room.

"Yes?" he answered and walked toward the arch, looking into the room.

Lilo followed him.

"I'm going to stay in the guestroom with the turret. Adam can sleep in the room out front," Nicholas announced in a determined voice.

"That's not what we agreed!" Adam ground out and kicked his brother in the shin. "You said we were gonna play for it. And whoever wins the first game gets that room. You're such a jerk sometimes."

"Hey guys, sorry, but you'll have to share the room out front," Blake interrupted.

Both boys stared at Blake, their mouths gaping open. "Why?"

"Lilo is staying in the room with the turret."

Nicholas jumped up. "What? I don't wanna share with Adam. I need my own room. Can't your girlfriend stay in your room? It's not like you have to pretend for us." The teenager puffed up his chest. "I know about these things."

Lilo felt heat shoot into her cheeks. They thought she was Blake's girlfriend? Just like Zane had probably thought so, too. His look had implied as much.

Next to her Blake ground out a low curse. "You're sharing the room out front. No discussion." Then he turned to look at her and said more quietly, "I'm sorry about that. They're just boys. They don't know any better."

9

Blake closed the refrigerator and turned back to Nicholas and Adam who were both stuffing their faces with sandwiches. That was one thing about young hybrids: they were constantly eating. Not only human food, but also blood to keep up their vampire strength. It didn't matter that it was two in the morning.

"And not another remark about Lilo and me. Is that clear?" he said, pinning Nicholas with his eyes.

The boy shrugged and managed to look sheepish. "How was I supposed to know she's not your girlfriend?"

"That's exactly the reason why you don't make assumptions."

"Is she pissed at us?" Adam interrupted.

Blake smiled at him. "I don't think so." Somewhat embarrassed maybe, but not upset. At least that much he'd gathered when he'd shown her to her room in silence. That had been nearly a half hour ago. "Now eat, and then you should go to bed."

Nicholas protested instantly. "It's school holidays. We're allowed to stay up as long as we want."

Blake tilted his head to the side.

"Honestly!" the fifteen-year-old hybrid insisted. "Even Dad lets us keep vampire hours when there's no school."

Adam kicked him under the table. "Shh! You're not supposed to say vampire when there's a human in the house." He lifted his eyes and met Blake's gaze, looking for approval. "Right, Blake?"

"That's right, Adam. Your brother should know better."

Nicholas shrugged, Blake's reprimand sliding off him like oil off a Teflon pan. "So the broad doesn't know what you are, huh?"

"Broad?" Blake asked, shaking his head in disbelief.

Adam rolled his eyes, looking all grown-up, despite his tender age of thirteen. "Nikki's been watching those old gangster movies. You know, Al Capone stuff."

"You're not supposed to call me Nikki! I'm too old for that."

"Enough, guys. If you want to stay up, you'll have to behave. And that means: nobody calls a woman a broad, the word vampire won't come out of either one of your mouths, and there will be no fighting. Do I make myself clear?"

Adam nodded wordlessly, while Nicholas said, "And Adam can't call me Nikki."

Blake sighed. There was just no winning an argument with a teenager. "Remind me why I volunteered to watch you two while your parents visit Cain and Faye."

Adam's face split into a wide grin. "'Cause you love us and we're fun to hang out with?"

Blake threw his head back and laughed. "I guess I can't argue with that. Now go play before I change my mind."

He rose and was about to clear off the kitchen table when he heard a beep from the kitchen's security monitor, and the corresponding sound of the front door opening. He glanced at the screen: Eddie was finally here.

He marched out into the hallway to greet his friend and colleague. As always, Eddie was dressed in his biker gear: leather, and more leather. With his sandy-blond hair and deep dimples, he looked like the kid from next door.

"Thanks for coming, Eddie."

"What can I do?"

Blake ushered him into his office.

"Haven't had time to unpack, huh?" Eddie asked, pointing at the boxes that were stacked up against one wall.

Blake grinned. "Maybe I'll get Nicholas and Adam to give me a hand while they're here."

Eddie chuckled. "Yeah, good luck with that." He sauntered to the desk. "Is that the laptop you wanted me to have a crack at?"

"Yes, it belongs to Hannah Bergdorf. Have at it."

"Do I know her?"

"She works for Vüber and disappeared three days ago."

Eddie nodded and slunk into the chair behind the desk. He pulled out a small electronic device from his pocket and connected it to the computer, then booted up the machine. While he waited, Eddie asked, "Did you check her last Vüber ride to see if a customer could be involved in her disappearance?"

"Finn sent me the info of her last ride, but I have the feeling that's a dead end."

"Why?"

"Her last ride was a Scanguards employee: Roxanne. I left a message for Roxanne to call me, but you know she's solid. I'd trust her with my life."

Eddie nodded and started typing on the keyboard. "Same here." Then he fell silent, focusing on his task.

Blake walked to the window and stared out into the darkness. In five hours, the sun would come up, limiting him in his search for Hannah. While he didn't need much sleep, he wouldn't be able to explore every lead during daytime. He would have to rely on others, mostly hybrids, whom the sun's rays couldn't hurt.

Fortunately, Blake's house was outfitted with several special features, designed by Scanguards' IT expert Thomas, which made it easier to hide his vampiric nature from Lilo. The windows were treated with special UV-impenetrable coating, making it possible for him to move around unimpeded, without the need for heavy, drawn curtains during the day. As long as Nicholas and Adam didn't trip him up, his secret was safe.

"Hi."

The quiet female voice made him turn. Lilo stood in the open door to his office, hesitating. He motioned her to approach, and walked toward her. "Come in, Lilo." He pointed to Eddie. "This is my colleague Eddie."

Eddie lifted his head for a moment and gave a quick nod of acknowledgement. "Hey." Then he immersed himself in his work again.

"I thought you might have gone to sleep."

She shook her blond locks. "I can't sleep. Too much has happened."

"I know. Come, I want to talk to you." He pointed to the Chesterfield couch in one corner of the office.

Lilo sat down, and he followed her. "I want to know more about this Ronny. We need to find him."

"I've told the police everything I know."

"Tell me again. Maybe there was something you missed. Every detail is important." Blake sat on the edge of the couch and turned sideways, leaning toward her. "Tell me everything Hannah told you about him."

Lilo sighed. "It started maybe six to eight months ago. She didn't tell me at first, maybe because she knew I wouldn't approve of him."

"Why?"

"Hannah is too good. She's the kind of person who picks up strays, because she pities them, and then ends up a penniless cat lady."

Involuntarily, Blake had to smile. "She always thinks the best of people."

"Unfortunately," Lilo agreed. "But it never ends well. I knew Ronny was a loser from the moment she told me about him."

"A loser? In what way?"

She huffed. "Well, for starters, he was *in between* jobs." She made air quotes around the words to emphasize her disdain. "I don't think you can be in between jobs, when you've never had a real job."

"So how did he make money?"

Lilo shrugged. "Hell knows. Sponging off girlfriends?"

"You think he used Hannah?"

"Probably. Or he did something illegal. She always made excuses for him when I asked why he hadn't gotten a job."

"What kind of excuses?"

"That he couldn't work the hours they wanted him to work. That there weren't that many jobs that would let him work the nightshift." She threw up her hands. "I mean, who wants to work the nightshift if they don't have to? Particularly if your girlfriend works during the day. That makes no sense at all."

"Hmm." Blake pretended to think about that, but he'd already guessed the reason why Ronny wanted to work the nightshift. "Did Hannah ever mention how she and Ronny met?"

"Through her job somehow."

"You sure?"

"I think he was a customer, and they got to talking one day."

This was the break he'd been looking for. Excitedly, he pulled his cell phone from his pocket. While dialing, he said to Lilo, "If he was a customer, Vüber will have his information. He would have had to sign up for an account."

Lilo's face brightened with hope. She reached for his hand and squeezed it. "Oh, I hope you're right."

The call was answered. "It's Finn, what's up?"

"Finn, it's Blake. Can you please go through Vüber's customer records and find anybody with the name of Ron, or Ronny, or Ronald. Cross-reference anybody you find with the fares Hannah Bergdorf accepted in the last eight months. Can you do that for me?"

"When do you need it by?"

"ASAP."

"Give me about an hour and a half."

"Thanks. Call me as soon as you have something."

"No prob."

Blake disconnected the phone. "We should know more in a couple of hours."

Lilo shook her head, disbelief coloring her features. "I'm amazed at all the things your company can do. I mean, you seem to have more resources than the police. And you work a lot faster than they do."

He grinned. "Don't tell them or they'll get envious."

She hesitated, studying him for a long moment. "What you're doing… it's legal, isn't it?"

"Of course it's legal. The customer records belong to the company. We decide what to do with them, particularly when it means protecting one of our employees. So don't worry about it."

"Hey, I'm in," Eddie interrupted.

Blake jumped up and rushed to Eddie's side. "Let's see. Go to her emails."

Lilo walked to Eddie's other side and looked over his shoulder, too, while he scrolled through Hannah's inbox, scanning the emails. For fifteen minutes they all silently perused her messages, but there was nothing that gave any clue as to Hannah's whereabouts or what she'd wanted to speak to Lilo about so urgently.

"Nothing," Blake said, frustrated. He ran a hand through his hair. "How about her calendar?"

Eddie navigated to her online calendar. A second later, he looked up, surprised. "Not a single entry."

"Hannah was paranoid that her computer would crash and she'd lose all her appointment info." Lilo met Eddie's look. "She always wrote them on paper. She kept a diary."

Blake nodded. "We need to find it." He walked around the desk. "Eddie, can you go through whatever else is on the computer? And the tablet, too. Files, browsing history, etcetera, while I go over to Hannah's flat and search for her diary?"

"Sure thing, just be quick about it." He looked at his wristwatch. "I've gotta be back at the office in a couple of hours."

"No worries. I won't be long. And keep an eye on the boys while I'm gone, will you?"

Blake was about to storm out, when he heard footsteps behind him. He looked over his shoulder. Lilo was following him.

"I'll be able to find it faster than you. I know Hannah's taste. I know what her diary would look like."

"Then describe it for me."

She crossed her arms over her chest, drawing his eyes to those tempting curves. "I'm coming with you."

"Damn it, Lilo. What if that intruder comes back while we're there?"

"In that case it's even more important that you don't go alone."

He did a double take. "Are you trying to imply that *you*'d be protecting *me*?"

From behind him, he heard Eddie chuckle. Without taking his eyes off Lilo, he growled, "Not funny, Eddie."

Yeah, it was so not funny that this woman was getting under his skin with such ease.

Or that he was allowing it.

And possibly even enjoying it.

10

Lilo felt the air sizzle between them when they were back in the car, heading for Hannah's apartment. Blake was clearly not used to a woman ignoring his orders.

"I'm not ungrateful, you know," she started.

He didn't take his eyes off the road. "I didn't say you were."

She scoffed. "You didn't have to."

"I'm just trying to protect you. It's bad enough that Hannah has disappeared. How can I find her, how can I function normally, if I have to worry about you too?"

For a moment she was speechless. Blake would find it hard to function if he had to worry about *her*? Instinctively she shook her head. That was impossible. It would imply that he cared. About her. When he didn't even know her.

"What?" he barked.

She looked at his profile, and she finally understood. "I'm sorry."

"Sorry for what?"

"You're as stressed out about this whole thing as I am, and I'm only causing you more grief." She stared out the window on her side and watched the lights whizz past it. "You're used to doing all this without somebody interfering. You don't need my help to find Hannah." She sniffled. "It's just... I want to help. I want to know that I'm doing something to find my friend. I owe her that." Her voice cracked. Damn it! She wasn't gonna cry, not now when she'd tried to be so brave all night.

A warm hand clasping hers made her whip her head in Blake's direction. She found him looking at her, his gaze kind and understanding.

"We both want the same thing: to find Hannah." He smiled. "And I do need your help. If you hadn't mentioned that Ronny was a Vüber client, we wouldn't have any leads."

He released her hand, making her realize how much the innocent touch had comforted her.

"And you're right: I'm not used to having my orders ignorcd. By anyone." He smirked. "Not just women."

"Or teenagers?" she teased, his words having put her at ease again.

He grimaced. "Particularly teenagers."

Once in the apartment, it didn't take long to find what they were looking for. Lilo pulled a datebook from a shelf. It had a thick, cushioned cover decorated with dried flowers. "Here it is."

"Let's see." Blake reached for it, and together they turned to the week of Hannah's disappearance. "She abbreviates a lot."

Lilo nodded. "She's done that since we were kids." She pointed to an entry the day before her disappearance. "She took Frankenfurter to the vet here. There's a telephone number."

Blake saved it in his cell phone. "I'll call the clinic as soon as they open in the morning and find out whether Hannah kept the appointment."

"Maybe Frankenfurter had to stay there overnight. That would explain why he isn't anywhere to be found."

"Maybe." But the doubt in Blake's voice was audible.

Apart from a few reminders to pay bills, there weren't many entries for the week in question. The weeks before showed a dentist appointment, a note to fire the dog walker, several movie dates, presumably with Ronny, a hair appointment, and a visit to check out a gym.

"Nothing out of the ordinary," Blake said, sounding disappointed. "Let's take it with us, just in case."

Lilo slipped the book into her purse just as Blake's phone rang.

He answered it immediately. "What have you got?"

He listened for a few seconds, then said, "Text me his address. And his photo, too. Thanks, Finn!" He pressed the *end* button. "There was only one man named Ronald who got rides from Hannah." His cell phone pinged, indicating the arrival of a text message. Blake pointed to the display. "And now we have his address and what he looks like."

Lilo tapped on the photo to enlarge it. "That's not the man who broke in." She shrugged. "Doesn't matter. Maybe he sent a friend. Or maybe the two events aren't connected after all. Let's not waste any time. Let's go to his house. Now," she demanded, already heading for the door.

Blake caught up with her. "We're not going without backup. We don't know what we're dealing with. He might not be alone."

"Good idea. Let's call the police." She pulled Donnelly's card from her pocket. He'd handed it to her, telling her to call his direct line if anything else came up.

"No. If the police show up, he'll run. Besides, they have no probable cause to act. We'll check it out ourselves first." He dialed a number on his phone. "I'll get somebody from the company to help us."

"But if he's dangerous, the police are much better equipped to—"

Blake lifted his hand to stop her. "Hey, Wes, I need your help. Can you meet me out in the Excelsior?" He paused for a moment. "Yes, now. I'll text you the address. And, Wes, we don't wanna wake anybody up and alert them to our arrival. Bring your bag of tricks, just in case." He disconnected the call.

"What bag of tricks?" Lilo asked, curious.

"The usual equipment any bodyguard has. Plus, a few extras. In case the guy gives us any trouble."

"You mean stuff to tie him up with? Or are you talking about something to... make him tell us where Hannah is?"

He took her elbow and ushered her out of the apartment. "We're not the CIA."

"Could've fooled me, considering all the resources you have at your disposal," she shot back.

She'd never encountered a law enforcement agency or private security firm that worked as seamlessly and efficiently as the company that employed Blake. And she'd researched the field thoroughly for her mystery series. So why, if Scanguards was so good at what they did, had she never heard of them?

~ ~ ~

Wesley, Scanguards' resident witch, was already waiting for them, when Blake pulled up in his Aston Martin. Wes had parked his black BMW a block away from Ronny's house. The license plate, WTW—Wesley, The Witch—was hard to miss.

Blake parked behind Wes and killed the engine.

"I would tell you to stay in the car, but I'm guessing you'd ignore me." He glanced at Lilo whose hand was already on the door handle.

She stopped in mid-motion, and met his eyes. From somewhere, light reflected in them, and for a moment he was mesmerized by her cornflower-blue irises. They should signify innocence, but in Lilo they accentuated her mysteriousness. She'd told him a lot by her actions, her willingness to fly halfway across the country to look for Hannah, her determination to put herself in harm's way if only it would bring her a step closer to her friend. He admired that in a person. And even more so in a human who didn't even know what she was up against.

But he knew: whatever the reason for Hannah's disappearance, the evidence was mounting that a vampire was behind it. The fact that Ronny was a Vüber client confirmed that he was a vampire, because only vampires were allowed to sign up for the service. So if Hannah was dating a vampire, and had disappeared three days ago, why had her loving boyfriend not reached out to Scanguards? It was an open secret in the vampire community that Scanguards dealt with any vampire-related crimes. Ronny would have been assured discretion and wouldn't have had to hide who or what he was.

"Thank you…"

Lilo's voice pulled him from his reverie. Their gazes locked.

"…for everything you're doing for Hannah. Without you, I don't know what I'd be doing."

He felt himself move closer, drawn to her soft voice and tender gaze.

"She's very lucky to have a colleague like you," Lilo continued. "Somebody who's watching out for her." She lifted her hand as if to touch him.

A knock at the window made Lilo pull her hand back and Blake twist his head.

Wesley stood on the driver's side, his head tilted to the side, his eyes rolling.

Quickly, Blake opened the door and got out.

"If you wanted an audience for your make-out session, you should have told me in advance. I would have brought popcorn."

"That was not a—"

He left the sentence unfinished when Lilo appeared next to him.

"Lilo, this is Wesley. He also works for Scanguards."

They shook hands.

"Hi, Wesley. Sorry to drag you out here," Lilo apologized.

Wes jerked his thumb at Blake. "I'm used to it from him." He shifted his gaze. "So, what's this about?"

"One of our Vüber employees is missing. You might know her: Hannah Bergdorf."

"Pretty redhead?" Wes asked.

Blake nodded. "That's her. She hasn't been seen or heard from in three days. Lilo here is her best friend and flew out from Nebraska to try to find her. We've already searched her flat, and we have reason to believe that her boyfriend has something to do with it. He was one of her Vüber clients." The last sentence he added to make sure Wes understood that Hannah's boyfriend was a vampire.

"Ah, I see."

Blake gestured to the end of the block. "Ronny lives out here. We thought we'd pay him a visit, see why he hasn't contacted anybody about his girlfriend's disappearance."

"Well, what are we waiting for?" Wes grinned. He loved nothing more than driving a little fear into a man who didn't treat his woman right.

Blake suppressed a chuckle. In that respect, they were the same, though they'd started out as competitors when they'd both first joined Scanguards and hadn't always seen eye to eye. Shortly before they'd met, Wesley had found out that he was a witch. In the years that followed, he'd worked diligently to gain back the powers that his mother had robbed him of as a child, and now he was one of the most accomplished witches in the country. And he was on Scanguards' side, though witches had traditionally been the vampires' enemy.

"This way."

He led the way while Wes and Lilo followed close behind. Ronny's house was nothing special, a 1950s ranch-style house with a short driveway in front, a tiny untended patch of grass next to it, and a dilapidated wooden gate that only hung on one hinge.

Silently, Blake marched up to the front door and listened. It was about three hours before sunrise. No vampire would be asleep this time of night, but the house was quiet and dark.

He looked over his shoulder and motioned to Wes. He only had to point to the front door, and Wes knew what he needed to do.

Blake moved to the side to let his friend do his magic. And magic it truly was: a simple spell that unlocked any door. While Wes mumbled the verse as quietly as possible, Blake turned around to Lilo, his broad back shielding Wes from her view.

What is he doing? Lilo mouthed.

Blake shook his head and put his finger across his lips to indicate to her to remain quiet. For once, she complied, though she tried to spy past him to get a glimpse at Wes. The witch, however, was already done. There was a soft click, and the door eased open.

Blake lifted his hand to signal Lilo to remain where she was, while he nodded to Wes and slipped past him into the house. He let his senses roam. It smelled of vampire, but the scent was at least a day old. Nevertheless, he proceeded with caution as he moved farther into the house. There were two bedrooms, a living room, a kitchen, and a bathroom. Every room was empty.

He marched back into the hallway. "You can come in, he's not here."

As soon as Wes and Lilo entered and closed the door behind them, Blake flipped the light switch. He didn't need the light to find his way around, but neither Wes nor Lilo possessed the superior night vision of a vampire.

"He's gone?" Lilo asked, disappointment coloring her voice.

"I'm afraid so. But that's not to say he's not coming back." Blake walked back into the living room. "He's messy, but it doesn't look like he's moved out."

"Maybe he left in a hurry," Lilo suggested.

"Don't think so," Wes said, and pointed to a table. "He left his computer. And that looks like a pretty new Mac. Even if he was in a hurry, he would have taken that with him."

"Wes is right." He exchanged a look with his friend. "Let's put surveillance on the house in case he comes back, and let's take the computer with us."

Lilo stared at him. "You're gonna steal the computer? Don't you need like, a warrant, or something?"

Blake winked at her. "Luckily, we're not the police. Besides, we'll give it back once we don't need it anymore."

"I'll take it back to the office and have IT check it out," Wes offered.

"Eddie can do it." He pulled his cell from his pocket and dialed. The call was answered immediately.

"I was about to call you to tell you I'm leaving," Eddie said, before Blake could say anything.

"I've got another computer for you to check out."

"Sorry, can't stay. Bring it to the office, and I'll have one of my guys do it, but I need to get back to HQ. Thomas just called."

"Fine. I'll send Wes with the computer. Did you find anything else on Hannah's laptop or tablet?"

"Not much. I'll send a list of her web searches to your email so you can go through them and see what might be important. But there was nothing significant in her emails or any of the files on the computer."

"Thanks."

"Oh, and what do you want me to do about Nicholas and Adam?"

"They'll be fine on their own for a short while. I should be back within an hour. Tell them not to answer the door while they're alone, and to run for the safe room if they hear or see anything suspicious." The kids knew the drill. He wasn't too worried.

"Sounds good. Leaving now."

"Thanks, Eddie."

He shoved the phone back into his pocket. "Let's see if there's anything else that could tell us if he took Hannah and where they might have gone. Lilo, why don't you start in the bedroom?"

She nodded and disappeared.

Blake followed Wes into the kitchen. "Wes, another thing," he said quietly, so Lilo wouldn't hear them.

"Yeah?"

"I need you to scry for Hannah." Scrying was a skill only witches had. A skill that helped them find missing people.

"Do you have anything with her DNA on it?"

"Not on me. Go to her flat and see what you can find."

"Will do right after we're done here."

"Thanks."

11

The search of Ronny's house hadn't yielded anything else, but had confirmed what Lilo had always suspected: that he was a loser. He owned nothing of value besides the computer, and he was a slob, judging by the state of his house. What did Hannah see in him?

She recalled the photo Blake had shown her and had to admit that Ronny was good looking. Was that what he was living on? His good looks? Coupled with charm and some skill in bed, she knew only too well how a woman could lose her good sense and stay with a man like that longer than she should. She'd found herself on the receiving end of such an arrangement only a few years earlier. But she'd learned from it. Now she chose her boyfriends with care, in fact with so much care that she hadn't dated anyone for the last two years.

Maybe her break from dating was the reason why Morgan West, her protagonist, had become so lifelike and real to her. He was the personification of what a man should be like: strong, decisive, reliable. A take-charge kind of guy. A man she could rely on. Just like Blake.

The more she saw him in action, the more she was in awe of him. His colleagues seemed to respect him and not question any of his demands. He always seemed to know what to do next; there was no hesitation in his actions.

As she now followed Blake up the stairs from the garage into his house, she couldn't help but find herself admiring his muscled physique. Was it really possible that this man had everything she'd ever wanted? Not just a great character, but also a great body? Not to speak of a kind disposition, which surfaced when he dealt with Nicholas and Adam.

She sighed and entered the hallway. From the living room the TV blared, and Blake headed for it. She followed and watched him snatch the remote control, switching it off. Silence descended on the room.

Adam and Nicholas were asleep on the couch.

Blake looked over his shoulder, meeting her gaze. "Guess it's time for those two to go to bed."

He shook Nicholas gently, until the boy opened his eyes. "Hmm? What?"

"Time for bed."

While Nicholas got up rather sluggishly, Blake scooped the still sleeping Adam up into his arms.

"Do you need help?" she asked.

He smiled and shook his head. "Why don't you rest?" Then he carried Adam upstairs, while Nicholas followed him.

It was only a few minutes before Blake came downstairs again. Lilo still stood in the archway between the hallway and living room, having watched him walk down the stairs. Despite the fact that she'd been up all night, she wasn't ready to sleep. So much had happened in such a short time that her mind wasn't ready to rest yet.

"They're all settled in?" she asked.

Blake stopped in front of her, nodding. "You should go to sleep, too. I'm sorry I kept you up for so long. It'll be morning in a couple of hours."

"It doesn't matter. I can sleep when we've found Hannah."

"There's no need for you to stay up. I'll take care of what needs to be taken care of. We'll check if Ronny has a car, and if he does, we'll find it. I'm still waiting to hear back on whether they've found Hannah's car. Eddie should have emailed me Hannah's web searches by now. I'll go through them and—"

She lifted her hand to his cheek, touching him, surprising herself with the impulsive gesture. "You're doing so much. I just hope it will lead us to Hannah."

She was about to pull her hand away when he captured it and held it against his cheek. Surprised, she sucked in a breath of air. His lids lifted, and the blue of his eyes was suddenly more intense as he pinned her with them. Mesmerized, she was unable to move or look away. Her heart pounded in her chest, and her pulse raced.

"Lilo…"

"I should…" She swallowed nervously. "…go to bed." Yet she made no attempt to move. Instead she eased closer, comforted by his nearness. She'd been through a lot tonight. Perhaps she deserved just a few moments of tranquility, of peace, of the kind of comfort only a man's arms could give. Was it so wrong to want that?

"Yes, you should…" Blake agreed, but didn't release her hand.

He turned his face now and pressed a kiss into her palm.

"Blake…" She suppressed a moan when his lips brushed her fingertips. "It's probably better if I go upstairs…"

"Better?" He shook his head. "Smarter for you, for both of us, yes, but not better."

She knew exactly what he was implying. And what she wanted. To let herself go. To accept the comfort he was offering, even though she barely knew him. He'd helped her today, done everything he could to find Hannah. He wasn't really a stranger anymore. He was somebody she could rely on. More than she'd ever been able to rely on any of her previous lovers or boyfriends. Didn't that make him a friend? And friends could give each other comfort, hold each other for a moment. That was all it would be. Just a short embrace at the end of a long night.

Whether she stepped closer to him or whether Blake leaned in, she wasn't entirely sure, but suddenly her face was only inches from his, and his arm was coming around her waist, bringing her hips flush to his, her body connecting with his.

The first thing she felt was the heat emanating from him, from every part of him: his hand on her lower back, his pelvis brushing against hers, and his breath ghosting over her face. Then he drew her closer and his heartbeat seemed to reverberate in her body, echoing the rapid drumming of her own.

"I should let you go," he murmured, his mouth coming closer.

"Don't." She slid her hand onto his nape, feeling him shiver. "Please don't."

~ ~ ~

Her tender plea sank deep into him, settling in his groin, adding fuel to the fire that raged there. He'd promised himself not to act on it, but when she'd touched his cheek, he'd thrown all his good intentions out the window.

"As if I could." He whispered the words against her red lips, lips that had tempted him all night. Lips that parted now in invitation.

Damn it, he had no chance of resisting now. She held all the cards. And she was practically begging him to kiss her. He wasn't the predator in this game; wasn't coercing her into something she didn't want. He wasn't even seducing her; Lilo was seducing *him*. And while he held her in his vampire arms, arms she wouldn't be able to escape unless he allowed it, she was the one who held *him* captive.

"As if I could escape you now," he corrected himself and brushed his lips over hers.

The touch was electrifying. Her lips were warm and soft, yielding to him. He was hesitant at first, not wanting to spook her in case he'd interpreted her signs incorrectly.

"You want that?" he murmured.

She hummed, and the sound vibrated on his skin, making him shiver. Her fingers on his nape pulled him closer. There was no doubt now: she wanted him as much as he wanted her. All hesitation gone, he captured her mouth fully, dipping his tongue between her parted lips and stroking it against hers.

A spear of white-hot heat shot through him, sending blood rushing to his groin. Fuck, this was worse than he'd expected. Worse, because at the rate he was getting aroused he'd have her flat on her back in about sixty seconds, thrusting into her in the middle of the hallway where the boys could surprise them at any moment.

But not even that thought could stop him from delving deeper into her, exploring her, tasting her. And, damn it, she tasted good. Felt even better. He angled his head to get better access, and she obliged him and did the same. She now lapped her tongue against his, demanding he kiss her harder.

For a moment, he tore his lips from hers. "Damn it, Lilo!" But despite the fact that her kiss was teasing the vampire inside him to emerge, he couldn't stop. Crushing her mouth with his, he pressed her against the wall and pinned her there. Passion and lust surged within him, seeking an outlet. Breathing hard, he claimed her mouth more fiercely than he'd planned. Planned? Hell, he hadn't planned this at all. It had just happened. One look into those cornflower-blue eyes, and he was lost.

Too late to do anything about it now.

He thrust his pelvis against her, feeling his hard-on rubbing along her stomach, cradling him with her warmth and softness. Tempting him to unleash the beast within him.

Lilo kissed him back with a passion he hadn't expected, especially not from a woman who barely knew him. She was pure fire and unrestrained hunger. She was positively wanton. He felt her heartbeat reverberate in his chest, her soft breasts crushed against him. Gentle moans escaped from her throat whenever he gave her occasion to breathe. But the reprieve never lasted long. A mere second, and she would seek his lips again, demanding more, a deeper connection, as if she couldn't get enough of this kiss, of him. Just like he couldn't get enough of her.

His cock ached now, desperate to plunge into her heat and find release. He let his hands roam over her body, exploring her luscious curves, caressing her, seducing her. Yes, he knew what he was doing. Using her vulnerability to get what he wanted: a taste of this beautiful and brave woman. He should be ashamed of himself for giving into his baser needs and stop this madness now. He'd brought her to his house to protect her, not to maul her like a hungry animal. But his cock cared nothing about that. Didn't know what honor was. Only wanted to feel her. To be with her.

And she did nothing to stop him. There was no resistance. He didn't have a snowball's chance in hell of stopping this, of doing the honorable thing and letting her go to bed—alone. All he could think about was how to maneuver her upstairs to his bedroom where they could continue this folly with some privacy. Where he could strip off her clothes and feast his eyes on her, while he brought her to ecstasy.

But he knew that wouldn't be enough. Even finding release inside her wouldn't suffice. No, he knew with a certainty he'd never felt before that only when he tasted Lilo's blood would he be truly satisfied. Sated. Happy.

But this would mean exposing himself. Showing her who he was. What he was. How would she react? Would she still rub her sexy body against him and allow him to touch her? Would she still want to touch him? The way she touched him now? With her warm fingers sliding underneath his shirt, her fingernails clawing at his back, while he tunneled underneath her top and touched the smooth skin of her abdomen? He slid higher, slowly, gently, waiting for her to stop him. But no protest came from her lips, lips that were busy devouring him.

Only a few more inches and his hands would be on her breasts, cradling those perfect globes in his palms, teasing those nipples with his fingers...

"Blake, luvvie, are you h—?"

Blake spun around, breathing heavily, glaring at the person coming through the front door.

"Rose?" He ran a shaky hand through his hair. Fuck! It was his 4th great-grandmother, walking in on him practically fucking Lilo in the hallway. Just fucking perfect! "I thought you were in Carmel…"

Rose looked past him. "Oh…"

From the corner of his eye he saw Lilo nervously rearranging her clothing. "I'm sorry." Her voice cracked. She looked at Rose, then back at him. "I need to go." She dashed past him to the stairs, running up to the second floor.

"Lilo!"

But she didn't stop.

"I guess I came at a bad time," Rose said.

"You could say that."

12

How could she have been so stupid?

Lilo shut the door to the guestroom behind her and lifted her suitcase onto the bed. She rushed into the ensuite bathroom, and grabbed the few things she'd unpacked earlier, tossing them back into the suitcase.

Blake had a girlfriend! His stunned words had confirmed as much. *I thought you were in Carmel.* Apparently he hadn't expected her home so early. So he'd thought he could mess around while his girlfriend was out of town. Damn it! He was just as bad as all other men. Only Morgan West wasn't like that, because she'd written him differently: at least Morgan never committed to one woman and let his various bedmates know that he wasn't exclusive. He didn't lie.

Well, technically Blake hadn't lied, he'd simply *forgotten* to tell her that he had a girlfriend. A very beautiful one at that. She looked no older than twenty-five and was as stunning as any model. Blonde, petite, delicate features. And a British accent. Clearly, Blake went for blondes. Maybe a few days without his girlfriend had made him randy. Maybe he'd needed to get a fix from another blonde, and she'd been the willing victim.

How could she have let herself go like that? She'd been about to undress him, throwing all caution to the wind. A few more minutes and she would have been sleeping with a complete stranger, a man she knew nothing about. A man who was cheating on his girlfriend.

A knock at the door made her stiffen.

"Lilo, please, we have to talk."

She scoffed. She had nothing to say to him. "Don't worry, I'm leaving. Tell your girlfriend—"

The door opened, making her spin around. Blake stood there, his eyes immediately darting past her to the suitcase on the bed, his surprise evident.

"You can't leave." He marched into the room and closed the door behind him.

Instinctively, she took a step back, the back of her legs bumping against the bed. "Please tell her I'm sorry. If I'd known…"

"You think Rose is my girlfriend?"

"She shows up here at five in the morning and calls you luvvie."

Blake had the audacity to chuckle. "Rose is English. She calls everybody luvvie. Or dear."

"Please don't make any excuses. It's embarrassing enough. I shouldn't have kissed you…"

He shook his head, a smile on his lips. "There was nothing wrong with what we did. I wanted it as much as you did. And more. I still do."

At his last words, she shivered. "Stop!" She pointed to the door. "Your girlfriend is down there. How dare you say these things to me?"

"Rose isn't my girlfriend. She's my cousin."

Lilo frowned. "Cousin?" She didn't believe it for a second. What cousin stopped by at five in the morning and didn't even ring the doorbell? She shook her head. "Your cousin visits you at this time of night?"

"She's helping me decorate my house. She found some antique barstools in Carmel that she wanted to bring over."

"At five in the morning?"

He shrugged. "She gets very excited when she has a find like that and couldn't wait to show me." He stepped closer. "You might not believe me, but you'll believe Rose. Or do you really think my girlfriend would lie to you and pretend she was my cousin?"

Of course no girlfriend would do that. "No, but—"

He put his finger over her lips, lips that still felt swollen from his passionate kiss.

"Come downstairs with me. We'll clear this all up. I'm sorry that I came on so strong. But I wanted to kiss you from the moment I saw you in Hannah's flat. And I'm not an impulsive kind of guy. And just so you know: I would never have kissed you if I were in a relationship with another woman. I don't play the field. Not anymore. Life's too precious to waste it on things that mean nothing."

She noticed how his eyes homed in on her lips, and saw him swallow hard.

"I'd rather spend my time differently." He smiled. "What I felt when I kissed you… that's something that only happens once in a million times."

She sucked in a breath of air.

He clasped her hand, intertwining his fingers with hers. "Now come and let me introduce you to Rose. Curiosity must be killing her by now."

Lilo had no choice but to go with him as he led her down the stairs, not letting go of her hand until they'd reached the hallway, where Rose was waiting for them.

The young woman smiled at her, stretching out her hand in greeting. "I'm Rose, and please, let me apologize. If I'd known that Blake wasn't alone, I would have never barged in like that."

Lilo shook her hand. "I'm sorry I gave you the wrong impression…"

"Oh, luvvie, please don't apologize. I've known this guy here all his life and he can be a bit much to handle. Let's just blame him, shall we?"

"Thanks a lot, Rose," Blake interjected.

Lilo stumbled over something in Rose's words. "You mean you've known him all *your* life? Not *his*. You're clearly younger than Blake."

"Oh, yes, of course, dear." She made a dismissive gesture. "Now I'll get out of your hair in a moment, but I have two barstools in my car, and I'll need a hand with them."

"I'll take care of that. Give me your keys," Blake offered immediately, as if glad to escape for a moment.

Rose tossed him the keys, and a moment later he stalked outside into the dark, and Rose turned back to her.

"Well, that gives us some time to get to know each other."

Lilo nodded and shifted from one foot to the other. "I'm sorry, I just have to ask. He said you're his cousin, but you don't look alike at all, and your accent is British."

Rose took her hand. "Blake and I are family. And I know how it looked when I came in, but he just caught me by surprise. I haven't seen him with a woman in a long time. He doesn't do *casual*."

Lilo swallowed. "Casual?"

"You know: casual sex. He's too busy for that. And he never mentioned you to me before." The question in Rose's words was implied.

"We only met tonight." Immediately she wanted to take the words back. "I'm sorry. You must think I'm easy. I don't normally do things like that…" She wanted to sink into the ground, wanted to crawl into a hole and hide. "It's not how it seems…"

"Oh, dear." Rose suddenly sounded like an elderly aunt about to give advice.

Lilo lifted her lids and met Rose's eyes. Concern was etched deep into them.

"Then you don't really know him yet." Rose leaned in and lowered her voice. "Blake is a good man. Trust in that, no matter what happens. If he cares about you, he will protect you with his life."

Surprised at the other's strange words, Lilo wanted to ask what Rose meant, but Blake appeared at that moment carrying two barstools. He set them down.

"Everything alright here?" he asked, his gaze bouncing between her and Rose.

"Of course, luvvie," Rose replied. Then she walked to the door, accepting her car keys from Blake. She looked over her shoulder. "I should go home. Quinn is waiting for me." She smiled. "It was very nice meeting you, Lilo. I hope it won't be the last time."

"Nice meeting you, too, Rose," she managed to reply before the beautiful blonde breezed out of the house.

Slowly Blake approached. "Are we okay?"

"I should go to sleep. It's been a long night." She avoided his gaze. Before she could walk past him, he stopped her and put his fingers under her chin, making her look at him.

"I'm not going to do anything you don't want. You have my word… No matter how hot it got earlier." He kissed her gently on the cheek. "Good night, Lilo. Get some rest. Perhaps we'll have a few leads on Hannah by tomorrow."

She smiled at him, at ease again. Rose was right. Blake was a good man. But even good men turned into hungry predators when teased. And she had teased him, tempted him. Though she didn't regret it. No, not a single second of it. But she also knew she had to take things slower. The incident with Rose had shown her that she knew next to nothing about the man who made her pulse race like a bullet train and her blood sizzle like an egg on the hood of a hot car. And as much as she wanted to continue where they'd left off before Rose had interrupted them, she knew it was better to resist that urge and try to get to know Blake better before she did something she couldn't undo.

13

Wesley dropped the crystal pendant on the map of Northern California and sighed in frustration. He'd gone to Hannah's flat, but he hadn't found much. It turned out that Hannah was pretty neat and tidy. He'd taken her toothbrush in the hopes enough of her DNA was on the bristles, as well as her hairbrush, which only contained a few strands of her hair. Using those two things he'd scried for her, but come up empty.

"Fuck!" he grunted.

Scrying was one of the most basic magical skills, and he was more accomplished than most. He was aware that scrying didn't work on vampires, but Hannah was human, so he should have found her by now. There were two reasons why he wouldn't—the first was that the amount of DNA on the toothbrush and the hairbrush weren't sufficient, the second that she was dead. And the latter reason he wasn't ready to accept. Because Blake wouldn't accept it.

So he clung to the first reason. After all, the toothbrush had looked rather new and clean, and he'd found only a half dozen hairs in Hannah's brush. Probably not enough to get a reading on her, particularly not if she was far away.

His phone rang, interrupting him.

"Yes?"

"Wes, it's Matt. I've got the results for you."

"Coming down now."

He needed to clear his head anyway. Maybe he would come up with something later.

Wesley marched down the hallway of one of the basement floors of Scanguards' Mission headquarters, heading for the IT lab. Both Thomas and Eddie had left shortly after Wesley had brought the suspect's laptop to the office, so the task of hacking into it and examining the information on it had been given to Matt, one of their trusted human employees.

It was quiet as he walked down the corridor. Mostly humans and hybrids manned the offices during the day. Few vampires were around, most of them having gone home to sleep. It was midday. As soon as the winter sun set, headquarters would be buzzing like a beehive again. But during the day, this was his domain: he was the highest-ranking Scanguards employee on site. And he liked it that way.

Without knocking, Wes entered the IT lab.

Only a few people were sitting in front of the many computer workstations dotted around the large room. Including one person he hadn't been expecting.

"Isabelle? What are you doing here?"

Samson's twenty-two-year-old hybrid daughter looked up from the computer and smiled. "Hi, Wes." She jerked her thumb at the man next to her. "Clark is teaching me programming and stuff."

Wes raised an eyebrow. "I didn't know you were interested in IT."

She shrugged, tossing a strand of her long dark hair over her shoulder. She was as beautiful as her mother, as ambitious as her father, and as smart as both of them. "I'm not. But I figured if I want to run the company one day I should know as much as possible about how everything works."

Wesley couldn't help but chuckle. "You wouldn't by any chance be competing with your brother again?"

"Which one?" she shot back.

"Both, actually," Wes said.

Though Grayson, one year Isabelle's junior, was the more ambitious of her brothers. Patrick, who'd only just turned nineteen was a little more laid back and wasn't yet thinking of how to position himself to take over his father's company, should Samson ever decide to retire. Which, considering how much Samson loved his job, would probably never happen.

"All Grayson wants to do is go on patrol." She scoffed. "If that's how he plans to prove to Dad that he's a grown-up, then let him. It takes more than brawn to run Scanguards." She tipped her finger to her temple. "It takes what's up here."

Wes shook his head. "You should be out having fun like other young women your age, and instead you sit in here and work. When I was your age, I had fun."

Isabelle laughed. "Oh I've heard all about the fun you had when you were younger. Haven is quite a storyteller."

"My brother likes to distort the truth."

She winked mischievously. "Your brother is standing right behind you."

"Really, Isa? You think I'd fall for such an old trick?"

A heavy hand landed on his shoulder, making him whirl around. His heart nearly stopped.

"Shit, Hav! Why the fuck do you have to sneak up on me like that? You're not even supposed to be here."

His vampire brother grinned from one ear to the other. "You know you should never talk bad about me behind my back."

"I wasn't. If you want, I can talk bad about you right in front of you."

He wasn't afraid of his older brother. Hadn't been since his brother had saved him and their sister from certain death. Ever since then he'd idolized Haven, though he would never tell him that. Too much admiration was bad for a man's character.

"That's my brother," Haven said.

Wes tipped up his chin. "Shouldn't you be sleeping in the arms of your beautiful wife?"

"I would be if John hadn't called me to come in and take a look at this guy they brought in."

"What guy?"

"A suspect in one of the recent robberies. Donnelly transferred him over to us."

"So he's a vampire."

Haven shook his head. "Human."

"Then why is Donnelly sending him to us? Does he want us to handle human crime now, too?" He glanced at Isabelle. "Maybe you should add renegotiating contracts with the city to your curriculum while you're at it."

"Something is off with him. Donnelly asked us to take a look at him. And boy, is he messed up. John can't figure out what's wrong with him. He's running some tests, but he won't have the results for a few hours."

"What kind of tests?"

"Blood tests. We could use your help."

"Why's that?"

"Seems he's under the influence of something. Could be a spell, or drugs, or mind control. You're better equipped to figure it out."

Wes grinned. "Aren't you lucky to have a witch for a brother?"

Haven turned toward the door. "I'm lucky to have a brother. You coming?"

"I'll be there in two minutes." He marched to one of the computer stations, where another human was sitting. "Hey, Matt, what have you got for me?"

Matt stared up at him through his John Lennon glasses. "I'm afraid it's not much." He reached for a few sheets of paper. "I printed out what I thought was important, but I can also send you the electronic file, which is a little more comprehensive."

Wes motioned to the pages. "Give me a quick summary. I'll look at the details later."

"I found the usual: shopping, YouTube stuff, online gaming. But I'm a little stumped by this." He pointed to a spot on the sheet. "I can't pronounce it, sorry. Seems to be some herb."

Wes leaned closer. "Höllenkraut?" Fuck! "Where did you find this?"

"In what looks like an online cookbook he'd saved. Which is odd—"

"—given that this guy is a vampire, and doesn't eat or drink." He patted Matt on the shoulder, cutting him off. "Well done. Send the entire file with all the links to my email. I'll check into it."

"Will do."

Wes had already turned away, heading for the door, when Matt added, "What is that stuff? That Höllenkraut?"

He looked over his shoulder. "If I'm right, and I hope I'm not, then it's one of the most dangerous plants in the world."

And if Ronny had used it on Hannah in some way, all rescue efforts might already be too late.

A moment later, he was marching toward the interrogation room. Inside, Haven and John hovered over a human who was slumped over in a plastic chair.

John glanced up and acknowledged him with a nod. "Let's see if you have more luck with him than I," he said in his Louisiana accent.

Despite the fact that he'd moved to San Francisco and joined Scanguards four years earlier, he'd lost nothing of his Southern drawl.

Wes joined his colleagues and perused the suspect. "What do we know about him?"

"His name is Michael Thorland. He got picked up for possession a few times, but all the charges were dropped. No criminal record until he got caught robbing a liquor store two days ago. At first they threw him in a cell in the hopes that he'd sober up so they could question him, but when he didn't, Donnelly figured something wasn't right and transferred him over to us." John put his hand underneath the guy's chin and lifted his head. "He's been like this ever since he arrived."

Wes looked closer. The suspect's eyes stared at him blankly. "Catatonic?"

"Looks like it, doesn't it?" John said. "And he doesn't respond to mind control either."

Wes lifted an eyebrow. "I thought every human responds to mind control." He motioned to the suspect. "Even in a drugged state."

"That's what I thought, too."

"Maybe you're just tired," Wes suggested.

John instantly flashed his fangs at him. "I'm not fucking tired!"

"Just saying…"

"I'll try it," Haven interrupted, but a moment later had to concede, too. "John is right. He doesn't respond to mind control. Very odd."

"Something is wrong. Seriously wrong," Wes murmured.

Mind control worked on all humans. And this man was clearly human.

"He might be under a spell," Haven mused. "It's a possibility, right, Wes?"

"We'll find out. Somebody get me my black bag from my office." It contained basic tools for witchcraft. While he kept a more comprehensive collection of tools, books, and herbs at his home, he always had the essentials in his office. "And then clear the room. It won't be safe in here for any of you."

Because not even vampires had any protection against spells.

14

Blake got out of the shower and dressed quickly. It was mid-afternoon and he'd only slept a few hours, but he'd gotten a call from Scanguards twenty minutes ago that they'd found Hannah's car and were transporting it to headquarters for examination. He wanted to take a look at it, in the hopes that Hannah had left a clue as to her whereabouts.

He opened the door to leave his bedroom, when he heard sounds from the guestroom Nicholas and Adam were occupying. The boys were stirring. He knew he couldn't leave them to their own devices, particularly since he didn't know how long he'd be gone.

He pulled his cell phone from his pocket and dialed Wesley's number. It took three rings before Scanguards' resident witch finally replied.

"Yeah?"

"Hey Wes, how did the scrying go?"

"It didn't."

"You didn't find anything with Hannah's DNA on it?"

"I did, but it didn't work. The crystal couldn't pinpoint her location. I can't find her."

"What does that mean? I thought you could find any human."

"I thought so, too." He sighed. "Listen, I've gotta get back to what I'm doing."

"One more thing." Blake stopped him from disconnecting the call. "I need your help."

"I'm really busy right now."

"It's important. They found Hannah's car. I need to check it out. Can you look after Nicholas and Adam, and keep an eye on Lilo, too?"

"Can't you find somebody else? I'm examining some files right now."

"Can't that wait?"

"No!"

Blake sighed. "Then why don't you bring the files with you to the house? You can work in my office. Come on, be a good sport."

"Why is it that your work always takes precedence over mine?"

He heard the edge in Wesley's voice and knew to tread lightly. "It doesn't. But this is about Hannah."

There was a short pause, then Wes replied, "Blake, I don't want you to panic, but… there's something we found on Ronny's computer."

"What did you find?" His heart was suddenly hammering as loud as a locomotive.

"It's possible that Ronny has been experimenting with potions."

"Potions? You mean like your kind of potions?"

"Not exactly. More like drugs."

"Doing what?"

"I don't know yet. There's something else: today Donnelly transferred a human into our custody. It looked like he was under a spell or something. But when I examined him I couldn't find any sign of witchcraft. Which leaves us with something physical."

"Physical?"

"Yeah, as in drugs. Something mind-altering. And it just happens that I came across an herb today that scares the shit out of me."

"An herb scares the shit out of you? You're exaggerating."

"I found the name of the herb on Ronny's computer. That's why I'm going through these files. I need to find out what he's been up to. If he's been using this stuff, this Höllenkraut, on humans…"

"What does it do?"

"Not sure exactly. There were other ingredients, too, that have strange effects on humans. I'm not sure exactly how he's combining them and what the point of all this is. But I don't like it."

Blake blew out a breath. "Neither do I. Any leads on Ronny's car?"

"Donnelly and his team are keeping their eyes and ears open, but nothing so far. Have you spoken to the vet?"

"The office wasn't open yet when I went to sleep. I left Ryder a message to stop by the clinic during office hours and find out whether Hannah kept the appointment she had for her dog."

Ryder was Gabriel and Maya's son, and a hybrid, which meant he could be out in sunlight without the rays damaging his skin. But he and his brother Ethan and sister Vanessa were different from the other hybrids in his care. Their parents were very special vampires: before they'd been turned they were satyrs. Their species' DNA was so dominant that even as vampires they retained some of their satyr traits and had passed them on to their children. And while their parents' ability to tolerate sunlight had been extinguished at their turning, as born vampire-satyr-hybrids, just like as born vampire-human-hybrids, Ryder and his siblings were able to be out in sunlight without being turned into ash.

"I'm waiting to hear from him," Blake now added.

"Good." There was a short pause, before Wes added, "You're doing everything you can."

"It doesn't seem to be enough." Because Blake still had no lead on Hannah's whereabouts. And with every hour that passed, the chances of finding her alive and well, dwindled.

A sigh on the other end of the line. "I'll be there in half an hour. But you'd better tell those boys that I need to work and am not there to hang out with them."

"You've got it. You won't even notice that they're here."

"Yeah, right."

Blake disconnected the call and walked to the guestroom. He knocked briefly, then opened the door and walked in, pulling it shut behind him.

Nicholas sat up in his bed and rubbed his eyes. Adam turned beneath the duvet and mumbled something.

"Hey, sorry guys, but I've gotta go to the office. Wes will be over shortly; he's going to stay with you until I'm back."

Adam shot up to a sitting position. "Wes is coming? Cool!"

Blake raised his hand. "Now, just so you know, Wes is bringing his work with him, so I don't want you to disturb him unless there's an emergency."

Adam grimaced. "Then what's the point of him coming over at all?"

"To watch us, dummy," his brother replied. "As if we were little kids who needed a babysitter." He huffed.

"Wes isn't your babysitter, he's your bodyguard," Blake corrected him. "You should be used to it by now. You've had bodyguards since you were born."

Nicholas rolled his eyes. "Yeah, and it's getting old."

"You won't be saying that when your bodyguard saves your life."

"We're not in danger," Nicholas protested. "I don't know why everybody is constantly making such a fuss."

Blake sighed. He'd had similar conversations with some of the other hybrids, who at some point or other, had rebelled against their parents' over-protectiveness. He took a few steps forward, and sat down on the edge of Nicholas's bed.

"There's always danger, even if you don't see it. You and your brother are hybrids; you're precious not only to your parents, but to the entire vampire community. You can do things an ordinary vampire can't. You're stronger and less vulnerable. But there are many in the vampire world who consider your very existence an abomination. Your parents are right to protect you."

For a few seconds there was silence in the room. Then Nicholas sighed. "Fine. We'll just ignore Wes." He swung his legs out of the bed. "But it's not fair. If I'm really stronger than you and less vulnerable, then why do I need protection?"

With a few skilled movements, Blake lifted Nicholas off his feet and pinned him down on the floor, before the kid even had occasion to blink. "That's why. You might be stronger, but I'm smarter and more skilled. Once you're able to defeat me, I'll gladly resign from protecting you. But until then, my dear boy, you'll have to tolerate me or somebody else from Scanguards as your bodyguard."

From the other bed, Adam chuckled.

Nicholas raised his head and glared at his brother. "Not funny, Adam!"

15

Lilo hesitated before walking down the stairs. She'd slept surprisingly well—and long—despite all the things that had happened the night before, the good and the bad. In the end, she'd been so tired that she'd fallen asleep the moment her head hit the pillow. Now, as she slowly descended the stairs, she felt apprehensive about seeing Blake again. Would the sizzle that had flared up between them last night still be there today? Or had it been only a reaction to the stress they'd both been under?

When she reached the hallway, she heard a sound coming from Blake's office and walked toward it. The door was open.

"Hi, Blake, I—"

She stopped herself. The man looking up from behind the desk wasn't Blake. It was Wesley, his colleague whom she'd met the night before. He was casually dressed, a light gray polo shirt complementing his dark hair and bronzed skin. Dark stubble showed around his chin, as if he hadn't shaved in a while. The two-day growth looked good on him.

"Hey, Lilo," he greeted her. "Sorry, Blake's not here. He had to go into the office. They found Hannah's car."

Instantly her heart beat faster, and her legs carried her into the office until she stood right in front of the desk. "And Hannah?" She was scared to hear the answer, but she knew she needed to find out.

Wesley shook his head. "Sorry, no sign of her yet. Blake's having a forensic team comb through the car to see if there's any evidence of—" He hesitated, then made a dismissive movement with his hand. "Anyway, they're trying to figure out where the car has been, so they can possibly try and retrace her steps."

Lilo nodded. "I understand." She sighed. It had been unrealistic to hope they'd found Hannah so quickly.

He pointed to her hand. "What have you got there?"

She showed him the book in her hand. "Hannah's appointment book. I thought I'd go through it again to see if I can find anything that might lead us to her." She doubted it, but last night she'd been too tired to go through it again, and today she had fresh eyes. Maybe she'd find something.

"Good idea."

She gave a faint smile. "Anything on Ronny's computer yet?"

Wesley pointed to the laptop in front of him. "The IT department sent me everything they found on it. I'm analyzing it right now."

Curious, she stepped around to look at the screen, but Wesley stood up and blocked her view. "You must be hungry. The boys are in the kitchen, getting some food. Why don't you join them?" He winked. "And if they start getting rowdy, give me a holler and I'll set them straight. They know I'm the boss around here when Blake's out."

Hesitantly she nodded, feeling a little taken aback by his obvious attempt at preventing her from looking at what they'd found on Ronny's computer. She motioned to it. "You'd tell me if you found something bad, wouldn't you?"

"Promise." He smiled a kind, warm smile. "Now, go eat something, before Adam and Nicholas empty the fridge. I'll let you know when I have something concrete."

With a nod of acknowledgement she turned and followed his suggestion.

Lilo pushed the door to the kitchen open, feeling a little awkward about roaming the house while her host was absent, but now that Wesley had brought it up, she did feel hungry. Her last meal had been before she'd boarded the plane in Omaha.

Nicholas and Adam were both sitting at the kitchen table.

"Morning," Nicholas chimed and immediately turned back to the plate in front of him, shoving an overly full fork of scrambled eggs into his mouth.

Adam, who sat opposite him, nodded shyly and mumbled, "Hi. It's not really morning anymore."

"Hi," she replied, forcing herself to sound cheerful. She pointed to the refrigerator. "I was just gonna make myself something to eat."

Adam pointed to his plate. "We already finished the scrambled eggs Wes made. But there are more eggs in the fridge."

He attempted to rise, but she raised her hand, stopping him. "No, no, eat, please. I'll find something."

Lilo placed Hannah's appointment book on the counter and opened the refrigerator. It was well-stocked for a bachelor's fridge, and not just with junk food. Staples like milk, eggs, and orange juice greeted her. As did yogurts and cheeses, cold cuts and vegetables.

She took out everything she needed for a healthy omelet and got to work.

"Lilo, do you want to play videogames with us later?" Adam suddenly asked.

She looked at him. "Oh, I'd like to, but I'm not very good. I'm afraid I'd just be holding you back."

"That doesn't matter."

Nicholas shook his head, motioning to his younger brother. "Don't give in. He's just looking for somebody he can beat, 'cause he's got no chance against me."

"That's so not true!" Adam piped up.

Lilo tossed the omelet mixture into the hot pan, before looking back at the two teenagers. "I'm sure you're both very good. But I never got into playing videogames."

"So what did you do then?"

"Read."

"Sounds boring," Nicholas commented.

"Not really," Lilo said, flipping the omelet in the pan, so it could brown on the other side. "Some books can take you on quite an adventure."

Nicholas shrugged, disinterested. "Okay."

Adam's eyes widened a little, showing that he wasn't quite as blasé about books as his older brother. "What kind of books?"

"I like mysteries and thrillers."

Adam grinned. "You mean with lots of blood and gore?"

She laughed out loud. Figured that a teenager would be interested in that. "Not necessarily. But with lots of suspense."

"Oh, yeah, well." Clearly, Adam had lost interest now, too.

But she loved a challenge. And maybe there was a way of sparking Adam's interest again.

She tossed her omelet on a plate and walked to the table, joining the two boys. After the first bite, she said casually, "You know, I write books for a living."

Both boys' heads snapped up.

"You're an author?" Nicholas asked, suddenly all ears. "You write, like, real books?"

"What do you write?" Adam wanted to know, his eyes now even wider than before.

She smiled to herself. One nil for Maxim Holt! Of course, she couldn't tell the boys what her pen name was. It was a closely-guarded secret, particularly because she wrote under a male pseudonym, a necessity in order to be taken seriously in the male-dominated thriller genre. If it came out that the writer behind the Morgan West Bounty Hunter series was a woman, millions of male readers would feel betrayed.

"I write thrillers and mysteries. You know—" She winked at Adam. "—with barely any blood and gore, but with lots of suspense."

"Wow, that's cool," Nicholas said. "So, can we have one of your books? I mean just to see what they're like."

"I don't have any on me right now."

"You can probably order them online somewhere, right?" Adam tossed her a hopeful glance.

"Sure." What had she started? All she'd wanted was to show the boys that reading didn't have to be boring, and now they were eager to find out about her books. She'd have to stall them. "I'll check on that later."

Adam pointed to a nook where a laptop was sitting. "You can use that computer. There's no password on it."

Lilo shoved another forkful of her omelet into her mouth, buying herself a moment before answering. It turned out she didn't have to, because the door suddenly opened. A young Asian woman with a boy entered.

She stopped, looking surprised. "Oh, hi!"

"Hey, Sebastian!" Adam called out and jumped up. "You wanna play videogames?"

Lilo rose from her chair and walked up to the woman, stretching her hand out and perusing her. Her black hair was straight, and shimmered when she moved, and her eyes were dark and mysterious. She looked exotic, graceful, and gorgeous.

"Hi, I'm Lilo. I'm just visiting."

"She's Blake's friend," Nicholas interjected. "She stayed overnight."

At Nicholas's words, Lilo felt like cringing. This wasn't the impression she wanted to give everybody: that she was some one-night stand Blake had dragged in.

The woman smiled and took her hand, shaking it briefly. "I'm Ursula, Blake's sister-in-law." Her eyes followed her son who was heading for the refrigerator now. "Sebastian, you just ate."

He looked over his shoulder. "Yeah, but I'm growing." He ripped the refrigerator door open.

Ursula rolled her eyes. "Can't argue with that, can I?" She smiled at Lilo. "So, you're visiting Blake. He didn't mention that he was expecting anybody."

"Oh, uh, it was very last minute. I, uh…"

Ursula made a dismissive hand movement. "Don't worry. I'm not prying. I just wanted to drop off Sebastian. He likes hanging out with these hoodlums here."

"Ursula, you shouldn't call us hoodlums," Adam said in a strict tone. "We're very well behaved."

"With a father like Zane, who wouldn't be?" She winked at the boys, then turned back to Lilo. "Don't tell me you got roped into watching them."

"No, Wesley is here while Blake is at the office."

Ursula's eyebrows snapped together. "At this time of day?"

Lilo tossed her a surprised look. It was afternoon. Why would she find it strange that Blake was at the office?

"I mean," Ursula added hastily, "I thought he was on the night shift."

"Oh, yeah, he is, but we're looking for my friend. Hannah. She disappeared. That's why I'm here. I flew in from Omaha yesterday, and Blake is helping me find her."

"Ah, I see. I didn't realize you were a client. Well, your case is in the best hands." She looked at her wrist watch. "I'd better go. I have some shopping to do. I'll be back in a few hours to pick up Sebastian."

A howl of disappointment came from Sebastian, who turned a pleading look at his mother. "I thought I could spend the night. *They* are." He pointed to Nicholas and Adam.

"Yes, because they somehow managed to convince their parents to go to New Orleans without them."

Nicholas snickered. "It was a stroke of genius to suggest to Mom that this could be like a second honeymoon for her and Dad."

Ursula turned her eyes to the ceiling. "How manipulative." Then she looked back at her son. "How about I pick you up at midnight?" She opened the door and stepped through.

Surprised, Lilo followed her. "How old is Sebastian?"

"Twelve. Why?"

"At his age, I was lucky to be allowed to stay up till nine."

Ursula shrugged. "It's the school holidays. I'm much stricter when he has to go to school. But he's a boy with lots of energy, and he needs to hang out with his friends. He's an only child, you know."

At the front door, Ursula stopped. "I hope you find your friend."

"That's very kind of you to say."

A moment later, the door fell shut behind Blake's sister-in-law. For a while, Lilo just stood there, lost in her own thoughts. She'd only just met Blake, but she practically knew his entire family already: Rose, his cousin, Ursula, his sister-in-law, and Sebastian, his nephew. Not to speak of his friends and colleagues and their kids. Her last boyfriend had taken several months before reluctantly introducing her to his brother, and by the time he was ready to introduce her to his mother, Lilo had been ready to break up with him.

Surprised at the direction her thoughts had taken, she shook her head. One kiss didn't make a boyfriend. It was best that she be realistic about that and concentrate on what was important: finding Hannah.

A loud noise interrupted her thoughts. It originated in the kitchen, where, judging by the shrieks, the slamming of doors and drawers, and the three boys talking over each other, something was getting out of hand.

16

Lilo pushed the door to the kitchen open and stepped into chaos. Nicholas was yelling at the two younger boys as they fought over the half-gallon carton of orange juice.

"There's enough for both of you!" Nicholas ground out. "You idiots!"

Instantly both boys glared at him.

"You're the idiot!" Adam let out.

Nicholas suddenly growled like an animal. "Don't talk to me like that!" He lunged at his brother.

"Stop it!" Lilo screamed, rushing toward them.

All heads turned to her, and several things happened at once. Nicholas crashed into Adam, and Adam released his hold on the orange juice, knocking his elbow into Sebastian's stomach. Sebastian gasped, and also let go of the carton, his hand instinctively flying to his stomach to protect himself.

The carton tipped over, and the orange liquid spilled over the counter, soaking everything on it.

"Oh shit!" Adam cursed in a tiny voice, his eyes darting to the counter.

But Lilo was already rushing toward it, trying to save what could be saved. She was too late: Hannah's appointment book sat in a puddle of orange juice, its padded cover soaking up the liquid, the decorative dried flowers dissolving into a gooey mess.

"Oh no!" she cried out.

"Sorry," Sebastian said, stepping away from the counter to let her pass. Then he pointed his finger at Adam and Nicholas. "But those two started it."

"It's okay, it's okay," she said to the boy. Reprimanding him wouldn't help now that the proverbial milk was spilled. Instead, she quickly reached for a kitchen towel and lifted the appointment book up, wrapped it in the towel and soaked up as much of the liquid as she could, hoping the pages weren't ruined.

Lilo stepped aside to the kitchen island, where it was dry, and grabbed a fresh towel, still trying to salvage the book. Behind her, Nicholas took charge of the clean-up efforts.

"It dripped on the floor, too," he said. "Adam, get me another towel."

His brother voiced no protest, but Lilo wasn't paying much attention to the boys now. Her focus was on saving the pages of Hannah's appointment book, and preserving the writing inside. Carefully, she dabbed the sides of the book with the dry towel, hoping that the orange juice hadn't damaged it too badly. When it looked like she'd soaked up all the liquid, she set the towel aside and opened the book in the middle.

Some of the liquid had bled about an inch into the book, but hadn't done any damage to the writing. She leafed through the book and sighed in relief, before closing it again. That's when she saw it: the padded back cover was starting to peel away. She turned the book over and suddenly noticed a bump underneath the cover. Delicately she peeled the damaged padding away.

A gasp escaped her.

There, affixed to the hard cover of the book, hidden underneath heavy padding, sat a thin USB stick. On its shiny casing, the letter H was written with a pink Sharpie.

"Hannah," she murmured to herself. Only Hannah could have put it there.

Nicholas was suddenly standing next to her, staring curiously at the appointment book. She met his gaze, but didn't say anything.

After a moment of silence, he looked over his shoulder. "Hey Adam, Sebastian, how about we play some videogames?" Then he ushered the two younger boys into the living room.

When the door fell shut behind them, Lilo took a deep breath. Maybe now she'd find out what had been troubling Hannah. For her friend to hide a USB stick in her appointment book, something serious had to be going on.

She reached for the USB stick. It was a little damp, so she dried it. Remembering Adam's comment that she could use the laptop in the kitchen, she walked to the nook and sat down in front of the computer. She jiggled the mouse, and the screen woke up.

While she inserted the stick into a USB port, all kinds of ideas as to what data she would find coursed through her head. Had Hannah come across some government corruption or witnessed a crime? Had she come into possession of important documents that had inadvertently put her in danger? Was she involved with some kind of organized crime, like the Mafia, Russian or otherwise?

Finally, a window opened, displaying the contents of the memory stick: one single file. A video. She double-clicked it, then extended the picture to full screen.

She recognized the setting immediately. It was Hannah's apartment. The angle at which the recording was taken suggested that the camera had been sitting on the bookshelf. Almost as if she'd had a baby-cam. Or a dog-cam. Hadn't Hannah mentioned a few months earlier that she'd wanted to keep an eye on Frankenfurter during the day while she was out working? Had she bought a hidden camera to do just that?

Well, it didn't matter. What mattered was what the video showed. There was no audio. Nevertheless, it was evident that the two men in Hannah's living room were arguing. One of them was Ronny—she recognized him from the picture Blake had shown her. The other one stood with his back to the camera, preventing her from seeing his face.

Why had Hannah hidden this USB stick, when all it showed was her boyfriend arguing with another man? Without sound, she couldn't even make out what they were fighting about. Maybe a lip reader could decipher some of the things Ronny was saying, but the other man's replies remained unknown.

With a frustrated sigh, she focused on the video again, just as Ronny moved toward the door. The other man grabbed his shoulder, turning toward the camera and jerking him back. Now she could see both men's faces. And she recognized the other man now: it was the man who'd attacked her in Hannah's apartment. Ronny and he knew each other!

She had to tell Blake. In her mind, this practically confirmed that Ronny and this stranger had something to do with Hannah's disappearance.

She was about to jump up, when something on the screen drew her attention back to it. The two men glared at each other, their eyes like red beams.

"What the—" She choked on her next word. What was happening in front of her eyes wasn't possible. No, she had to be hallucinating. She blinked, trying to clear her vision. What she was seeing was impossible, was against all laws of nature.

Ronny and the assailant were turning into creatures that couldn't possibly exist: creatures with red glaring eyes and sharp white fangs that they flashed at each other in a show of aggression.

Vampires.

No. It couldn't be.

She moved the progress bar back a few seconds to the point where the stranger grabbed Ronny's shoulder and watched the entire sequence again, this time focusing on any inconsistencies in the video that might indicate that it had been manipulated. But it was seamless. These weren't two videos that had been spliced together, no, this was one continuous recording.

Which could only mean one thing: the two men in the video were vampires. Real vampires.

Her heart beat into her throat, and her hands began to shake. This was what Hannah had been afraid of. She'd found out that her boyfriend was a vampire. And to protect his secret, he had…

"Oh God," she murmured, slamming her hand over her mouth to stop herself from crying out, when a gasp behind her made her whirl around, sending her heartbeat into the stratosphere.

"Wesley," she choked out.

But he wasn't looking at her. He was staring straight past her at the screen. "Where did you get this?"

Automatically, she pointed to the ruined appointment book on the kitchen counter. "Hannah's appointment book. She hid it in there."

Tears welled up in her eyes. "This can't be true." She looked back at the picture which had frozen on the last frame. The white of the two vampires' fangs fairly leapt off the screen. "But it must be. Wesley, they are vampires. The man who attacked me. And Ronny, Hannah's boyfriend." A tear she couldn't stop rolled down her cheek. "What are we gonna do now? Hannah found out about them. They must have hurt her to protect their secret."

The secret that vampires existed. That they weren't just fictional.

Wesley slid onto the seat next to her. "Let's look at it rationally." He pointed to the screen. "This is probably a fake. It has to be. There's a lot you can do nowadays with video editing software."

"This isn't edited. This is one continuous recording. Wesley, they're transforming into vampires right in front of my eyes. Don't you see that?" As hard as acknowledging this fact was, she couldn't deny what she saw with her own eyes.

Wesley sighed. "I know it looks like it, but we have to weigh up all the possibilities first, before we jump to conclusions."

She shook her head, slamming her fist on the table. "But I'm looking at it. It all makes sense now. That guy—" She pointed to the stranger in the video. "—when he attacked me, I thought I saw his eyes glare red. At first I thought it was just some light reflecting off his irises. But that's not what it was. He was about to show his vampire side. If Blake hadn't shown up when he did, he would have bitten me!"

"Lilo, calm down. You can't know that!"

"I'm not crazy, Wesley!"

"I'm not saying you're crazy."

"You're implying it." She huffed. "Damn it, why don't you look at it?" She pointed to the screen once more. "Ronny and his friend are vampires. And this is how Hannah found out. She accidentally recorded them. She was afraid for her life. That's why she hid this in her appointment book, so if something happened to her, we would find it and figure out who hurt her." She closed the window and ripped the stick from the port. "I'm going to take this to the police."

"No," Wesley protested.

She shot him a glare.

"I mean, they're just gonna look at you like you're crazy. They'll never believe that this is real and not just some video some kid put together for Halloween. Think about it for a moment, before you do anything."

"The police need to see this." She jumped up.

"At least wait until Blake is back. Maybe he can make sense of this."

"There's no time. I can't wait. Every second counts. If Hannah is still alive, and I pray she is, then I could never forgive myself if I waited even one minute when this information could help us find her." She shoved the USB drive into her pants pocket.

She took a few steps toward the door, and Wesley followed her. He grabbed her arm, making her look over her shoulder.

"Some random policeman isn't gonna believe you. It's a waste of time."

Lilo shook her head. "Call Blake and tell him I'm on my way to the police station. Tell him what we found. But I've got to go. Officer Donnelly already has a report about Hannah's disappearance. He's already working on this. When he sees this video, he'll know what to do."

At least she hoped so, because she didn't know what else to do. She'd never had to deal with anything like this in her life.

Vampires!

Not only was their existence a shock she couldn't begin to grasp, the horror of knowing that Hannah was in their hands filled her with pain to the point of paralyzing her. She needed help. She couldn't wait for Blake. Who knew when he would be back? Besides, he was following up on other leads about Hannah's whereabouts. No, the police would have to help her with this. They would have to use all their resources now to get Hannah back and protect the rest of the city from these monsters.

17

It had taken Lilo nearly a quarter of an hour to hail a taxi. She'd had to walk two blocks to get to a busier area where more cars were circulating. Only now, in the late afternoon light, did she realize what an exclusive area Blake's house was located in, away from the hustle and bustle of the city. But right now she couldn't feel any appreciation for her surroundings, because her entire belief system had just collapsed.

Vampires! How could they possibly exist?

Guilt blasted through her once more. She'd failed Hannah. She hadn't been there when her friend needed her most. How much her friend had needed help was only now becoming evident. And what had she done? She'd been concerned about the deadline for her book! As if that mattered now.

The video flashed in front of her eyes again. How would she ever forget what she'd seen? Monsters. Vile creatures, out to kill. The thought sent a chill through her bones. What if it was already too late for Hannah? What if they'd sucked her dry and killed her?

Lilo pushed the tears back. No, she couldn't allow herself to cry. She had to keep up the hope that Hannah was alive.

"This is it," the taxi driver announced, coming to a stop in front of the police station she'd visited only last night.

She paid the driver and got out. Her knees were shaking when she walked up the stairs to the front doors. For a brief moment she stopped there, taking a deep breath.

Inside the police station, she looked around. Several people were waiting, one female officer was talking to one person, and several others were crowding around them, talking excitedly. Behind the counter, several policemen in uniform and in plain clothes were milling about.

She craned her neck to look over the people in front of her to see if Officer Donnelly was sitting in one of the cubicles.

"Officer Donnelly?" she called out.

The policewoman at the counter cast her an annoyed look. "You'll have to wait your turn, ma'am. Take a seat."

"But I just need to talk to Officer Donnelly. He knows me."

"Be that as it may, as you can see, we're busy here."

"Donnelly isn't on shift till tonight," a policeman from behind the counter said, as he walked by.

"Oh, no!" She caught the policeman's eye. "This is urgent. I filed a missing person's case with him last night. And I have a lead on who might have kidnapped my friend."

The policeman stopped and looked back at her. "Listen, ma'am, just wait your turn, and somebody will be with you shortly."

She squeezed through to the counter. "Please, Officer, I can't wait. Every minute counts. The longer my friend is missing, the less likely it is that we find her alive. Please!" This time, she allowed the tears to well up in her eyes.

The police officer sighed. "Fine." He waved to the door on the other side.

As she made her way there, several of the people in the waiting area grumbled about her jumping the line. But she ignored them. If only they knew what she'd found out.

The policeman opened the door for her and let her in. "I'm Officer Carter. What's your name, ma'am?"

"I'm Lilo Schroeder. I was here last night."

He motioned to one of the cubicles. While he took the chair behind the desk, Lilo slunk into the one next to it.

"So, what can I help you with?"

Lilo leaned forward. "I think I know who took my friend."

"So we're talking about a kidnapping?" His gaze was steady and almost disinterested.

"Yes, well, I filed a missing person's report last night, but now I'm pretty sure she was taken."

"How's that, Miss Schroeder?"

"I saw the man who attacked me in her apartment."

"You were attacked in your friend's apartment?"

She nodded eagerly. "Yes, yes, I told Officer Donnelly all about it last night. He's got it in his report." She pointed to the computer. "It's all in there."

"Hmm, well, let's check then." He put his fingers on the keyboard. "You don't happen to have the case number?"

She shook her head.

"No worries. How about the name of the missing person?"

"Hannah Bergdorf."

He started typing, then glanced at the screen. "Hmm." He looked back at her. "Hanna with an *h* or no *h* at the end?"

"An h."

He typed again, pressing his lips together. "Hmm. That's odd. There's nothing in here. Maybe it was entered under your name."

"Lieselotte Schroeder."

He entered her name, then shook his head. "Nothing. You said you were here last night and you filed a report?"

"Yes." She leaned forward to look at the monitor. "There must be something. I also reported the break-in."

"A break-in?"

"Yes, in my friend's apartment. By the guy who attacked me."

The policeman tossed her a skeptical look. Did he not believe her?

"Please, you need to help me. I think I know who took my friend." She dug into her pants pocket and pulled out the USB stick, showing it to him. "It's all on here. It's on video. It's horrible." She looked toward the counter, where civilians were getting impatient. "But you have to look at it somewhere in private. If people see what's on there, there'll be panic."

He reached out his hand, taking the memory stick from her. "Mm-hmm." His voice was a little softer than before, as if he was trying to calm her down.

Suddenly a hand swooped in and snatched the USB stick. "Why don't I take it from here?"

She whirled her head to the man, who'd spoken and sighed with relief. "Officer Donnelly."

"Miss Schroeder."

"Donnelly, what are you doing here?"

Donnelly shrugged. "Thought I'd come in early. Heard it was busy."

"Yeah, you can say that again." The police officer paused for a moment, then pointed to the screen. "Couldn't find the missing person's report Miss Schroeder here was talking about."

Donnelly cleared his throat. "Yeah, my system crashed after I entered it. Gotta reenter all the data." Then he turned away from his colleague. "Now, Miss Schroeder, why don't we go to my office. It's way too loud out here to have a proper conversation."

Relieved, she dropped her shoulders, relaxing a little. Donnelly would help her.

When Donnelly closed the door to his office behind them, shutting out the voices from the waiting area, it felt soothing.

"So, what's going on, Miss Schroeder? Has something happened since last night?"

He pointed to the chair next to the desk and she sat down, while he leaned against the desk.

She pointed to the USB stick in his hand. "I found this in Hannah's appointment book. I think she was hiding it in case something happened to her."

"What is it?"

"A video. It shows her boyfriend arguing with the man who attacked me last night."

He straightened. "Oh. That's quite a find. And you recognize the man with one hundred percent certainty?"

"Yes. It's him. There's no doubt. But there's something else. It's horrible. At first, I couldn't even believe my own eyes. But there's no doubt."

"About what?"

She pointed to the stick. "Watch it for yourself."

He walked around the desk and inserted the memory stick into a USB port, then concentrated on the screen.

Lilo wrung her hands, waiting eagerly. If she had told Donnelly outright that the video showed two vampires, he would have probably dismissed her as crazy and ushered her out of the police station as quickly as possible. But if he saw it for himself, without her suggesting anything, then he'd have to believe it.

The snapping together of his eyebrows indicated that he'd gotten to the part in the video where both men showed their glaring red eyes and sharp white fangs. Seconds later, he looked away from the screen and met her eyes.

"This is impossible," he said. "I know what it looks like on the screen, but I think we're both being tricked here."

"But you see it, too, don't you? Those two men are turning into vampires. Right there."

"I'll take this into evidence and have our IT experts look at it to see if the file has been doctored or if it's genuine."

"But we don't have time. My friend Hannah is in their hands. They're hurting her. We can't waste time." She pointed to the screen. "And now that you know what my attacker looks like, you have a better chance of finding him. He has Hannah. He and Ronny, they have Hannah."

"We don't know that for sure." When she tried to protest, he lifted his hand. "But I'll run the picture of both men through our system to see whether we can identify who they are."

"Thank you." Then she remembered something. "The one guy, I know who he is. Ronny Clifford. He lives out in the Excelsior district."

Officer Donnelly raised an eyebrow. "And you know this how?"

"My friend, Mr. Bond, found out," she said quickly. Then she realized that this might look as if she'd been withholding information from the police. "I was gonna tell you and give you all his information so you could look for him."

Donnelly's cell phone pinged and he pulled it from his pocket, typed a few words, then put it back.

"We'll do everything we can, I can assure you, Miss Schroeder." She noticed him glancing to the clock on the wall. "But let's go over all the details once more. I don't want to miss anything that might help us find your friend." He underscored his request with a warm smile.

Lilo felt some of the tension ease from her body and sighed.

18

"And you didn't try to stop her?" Blake growled.

If Wesley had been standing in front of him, he would have had him by the throat. But as it was, Wes was reasonably safe at the other end of the line.

"I tried, but your new girlfriend is pretty determined."

"She's not my girlfriend," Blake grunted.

"Oh, my bad. I thought because she's sleeping at your house… It's not like you invite every client to stay with you."

"She had no place to stay. I couldn't very well let her stay in Hannah's flat, where the lock's busted."

"'Course not."

Blake turned away from the forensics team that was examining Hannah's car in one of the subterranean levels of Scanguards' headquarters. "Where is she now?"

"With Donnelly. He'll stall her until you can get there."

Blake looked at his watch. "It's still daylight for over half an hour."

"He knows that. Text him when you're outside. It'll take you a half hour anyway to make your way through traffic."

He disconnected the call.

Wesley was right, of course, but that didn't diminish the feeling of helplessness that rose in him. The one thing about being a vampire he didn't like was how limited he was during daytime.

He hit the elevator button and waited impatiently, slamming his fist against the frame for good measure.

"Come on!"

He couldn't even imagine what Lilo was thinking right now. Every human reacted differently when confronted with the knowledge that vampires existed. He'd seen both sides of the spectrum, from calm and efficient acceptance to downright I-must-be-hallucinating denial. He had no idea what camp Lilo would be in. But no matter what, he had two options: come clean and explain everything to her, or wipe her memory, so she would never know what she'd seen on the video.

The elevator doors suddenly opened and he nearly collided with John, who was rushing out.

"Blake," John greeted him, shoving a hand through his hair. "Couldn't get a hold of Wesley. Line's busy all the time. So I was looking for you."

"I just spoke to him. He's at my place." Blake darted into the elevator and pressed the button for the level where his car was parked.

"We got the results from the blood tests back."

"Blood tests?" The doors were already starting to close.

"Yeah, from a human Donnelly transferred over to us. Wes is gonna wanna know right away."

Blake extended his arm and stopped the elevator doors from closing. "What did you find in his blood?"

John did a one-shouldered shrug. "Some strange herbs. The lab tech said only Wes would know. It had a foreign name. Something German sounding."

"Höllenkraut?"

John gave him a surprised look. "Yeah. How did you know?"

"Just a gut feeling. Call Wes, you should be able to reach him now. And send Ryder to my house to watch the hybrids. Wes will want to head back to HQ and his lab."

"Will do."

Blake removed his hand to allow the doors to close. "Thanks."

Moments later, he was in his car and speeding out of Scanguards' underground garage, merging onto busy Mission Street. The sun was hanging low over the horizon, but the specially designed windows of his Aston Martin protected him from its burning rays. The glass was covered with a UV-impenetrable film. In addition, the glass had been strengthened so that in case of an accident occurring during daylight hours, the windows wouldn't shatter and expose the vampire inside.

This improvement had been necessary after an incident four years ago, when a damaged rear window had nearly cost him his life. But thoughts like this only distracted him from the task ahead: to make sure Lilo didn't—whether on purpose or not—announce the existence of vampires to anybody who wasn't authorized to handle this information. Once he'd contained that threat, then he'd have to make the decision of whether to tell Lilo the truth or wipe her memory.

The thought of doing the latter knotted his stomach uncomfortably. He'd never taken somebody's memories lightly—he'd only ever used his skill to protect himself and his family: Scanguards. But today he was reluctant to even entertain the idea. Lilo was a brave woman, coming to San Francisco to look for her friend. And with her help alone, they'd already made progress: finding out about Ronny, and now having a visual of the guy who'd broken into Hannah's flat and attacked Lilo. As soon as he could get his hands on the memory stick, he'd get Thomas to run it through facial recognition to identify the assailant.

Could he really punish Lilo for having seen something she shouldn't have seen? Punish her by taking away her memories? Was such treatment warranted?

Blake gripped the steering wheel tighter. Maybe it wouldn't have to come to that. Maybe she was reasonable and would take it all in stride. And eventually accept the facts: that not only were Ronny and her assailant vampires, but that he, the man she'd kissed the night before, was one, too.

Maybe it was that kiss that now helped him come to a decision.

He pulled to a stop in the parking lot and immediately texted Donnelly, while the sun set behind him. By the time he was finally able to get out of the car, Lilo was already exiting through the double door of the police station. He rushed toward her, meeting her halfway up the stairs.

"Blake!" She practically threw herself into his arms.

"Lilo. I came as soon as Wes told me." He wrapped her in a tight embrace, feeling how her body was trembling. Instinctively he pressed a kiss on the top of her head and rocked her in his arms. "It's gonna be all right."

She lifted her head, looking up at him, her eyes full of doubt and fear. "Did he tell you what's on that video?"

He nodded. "Do me a favor, Lilo, wait in the car for me, while I quickly talk to the police officer."

She sniffled and nodded. "Yes, see it for yourself. If I hadn't seen it, I wouldn't have believed it myself." She eased herself from his embrace.

Blake motioned to the car. "I'll only be a minute."

He watched her walk to his car and get in, then hurried into the building. Donnelly was already waiting for him, and ushered him into his office in the back. When the door closed behind him, Blake let out a breath.

"Fuck!"

Donnelly nodded. "That was close. You guys were lucky that I wasn't far away and managed to get to the station before she could show that video to one of my colleagues."

"I know. I owe you." Then he pointed to the computer. "Show it to me."

They both walked around to look at the screen, and Donnelly replayed the video. It was as Wes had described: two men arguing and then turning into vampires. Aggressive vampires. Shit! This wasn't the kind of introduction to vampires he'd want any human to face. Let alone Lilo. First impressions were hard to forget. This would make it even harder to gain her acceptance once he revealed the truth about himself.

"At least we now know what Lilo's attacker looks like. I can have IT run it through facial recognition."

"I already sent a copy over to Thomas for you. I figured you'd want to find out who this guy is," Donnelly said.

"You're the best."

"I know," Donnelly replied dryly and pulled the USB stick from his laptop. "You'd better take this. It's not safe at the station."

Blake took the memory stick from him, shoved it into his pants pocket and turned to leave.

"What're you gonna do now?"

Blake hesitated at the door and glanced over his shoulder. "Try to make Lilo understand that we're not all bad."

"You're gonna tell her the truth about Scanguards and about yourself?"

"Do I have a choice?"

Donnelly sighed. "We always have a choice. The question is what's less painful? Coming clean or erasing what she's seen?"

"Painful for whom?" Blake murmured to himself and left the office.

19

They'd barely spoken in the car. He'd told Lilo that they would talk once they were home. After all, the car wasn't the right place to confess to her that vampires truly existed, and that he was one of them. What if she panicked and jumped out of the car, trying to run away? No, he had to get her home first, calm her down, and then gently tell her the truth. He could only hope that she would understand.

Blake opened the door leading from the garage to the hallway and ushered Lilo inside ahead of him. The voices of the boys were coming from the living room.

"Ryder?" he called out.

The twenty-year-old hybrid appeared almost immediately. He was mature for his age, one of the more serious and responsible of his hybrid charges. Ryder was less wild than Amaury's twins, and less stubborn than Grayson, Samson's eldest son. "You're back."

Blake pointed to him, while looking at Lilo. "Lilo, this is Ryder, one of our bodyguards-in-training."

Lilo nodded, her "Nice to meet you" sounding automatic and distracted.

Ryder smiled. "Same." He came closer. "I checked with the vet like you told me. Turns out Hannah did indeed keep her appointment for the dog. Wanna know what she had done?"

Blake raised a curious eyebrow. "What do you mean?"

"She had a GPS chip implanted in her dog. You know, one of those you can trace in case the animal gets lost."

"Good work," he praised the young hybrid. "Let's see if we can find the dog. Maybe he's with her."

Next to him, he noticed Lilo draw closer, hope lighting up her features.

"I've already put a request in to get the info for the chip. We should have it soon, and then IT will trace it," Ryder reported.

"Thanks, Ryder, I really appreciate it." Then he motioned to the living room. "Can you do me a favor?"

"Sure."

"Take the boys out for pizza. I need to talk to Lilo alone."

Ryder cast a quick look at Lilo, then nodded. "Not a problem." Then he called out, "Nicholas, Adam, Sebastian, we're going for pizza."

While the boys came running, Blake asked, "Sebastian is here, too?"

"His mother dropped him off earlier," Lilo said.

Sebastian was already coming toward them. Blake pulled him into a quick hug. "Hey, buddy. Good to see you."

The boy beamed back at him. "Hey, Uncle Blake."

"We'll hang out later, okay? I've just gotta do a few things first, while you guys go for pizza, alright?"

"Yeah, sure."

"Okay, guys, let's go," Ryder commanded. "I'll take the van?"

Blake nodded. "Keys are inside."

Moments later, the house was quiet. He looked at Lilo. She was shivering now, and there was a watery sheen to her eyes.

"Come, let's talk."

She sniffled, drawing up her shoulders. "They're ugly, evil monsters." She raised her face to look at him. "They've hurt her. I know they have."

"Lilo, please, you need to calm down."

"Calm down? I can't. Don't you see what's happening? Our very existence is being threatened by these... these vile creatures. They're abominations! They shouldn't even exist. Blake, why is this happening?"

Tears dislodged from her eyes, and he couldn't bear seeing her like this. Without a second thought, he pulled her into his arms and cradled her. "Oh, baby, everything will be all right. I promise you."

"How can it?" she wailed. "How can anything ever be all right again when awful creatures like that exist? Vampires! Bloodsuckers! Out to kill us all."

The words stabbed into his heart like blades. It wouldn't be easy to convince her that not all vampires were bad. That in fact the majority of vampires he knew were good and decent people. People who'd vowed to protect humankind.

Blake pressed a kiss into Lilo's hair. "Let's look at the evidence first. We don't really know what they've done." Though he was certain they were behind Hannah's disappearance. "Why don't we talk?"

She shook her head and wrapped her arms tighter around his torso. "I don't want to talk. I want to forget. I want to not think about what I saw. I wish I'd never seen it. How will I ever sleep again? How will I ever be able to feel safe again?"

"Some things aren't always like they appear at first," he said, trying to pacify her.

"We're not safe, Blake. We'll never be safe again." She looked up at him, her eyes round and brimming with tears.

To see fear etched so deeply in her features hurt him to the core. "You'll always be safe with me."

She lifted one hand and reached for his face, stroking her fingers over his cheek. "When I'm with you, I can almost believe it." She brought her face closer. "When you hold me, the nightmare seems to be less real."

He felt his blood heat at her nearness, his vampire side registering the change in her demeanor. Where fear had reigned only moments earlier, hope was blossoming, and arousal was growing.

"Maybe if you hold me closer, we can make this horror disappear. Maybe then I'll wake up from this nightmare."

Her lips beckoned, looking more enticing than ever. He already knew what they tasted like, and that fact made resisting even harder.

"Lilo, it's not going to make this go away. I have to tell you—"

"Please, Blake, I know you don't find me unattractive…" She sniffled. "I felt it when you kissed me."

He sighed. "That's not the point, Lilo, but you're vulnerable right now. It wouldn't be fair if I took advantage—"

"You're not taking advantage." She lifted herself on her toes, bringing her head level to his, her lips even closer now. "I'm taking advantage of your goodness. Please make love to me. I need this now. I need to forget."

Blake's heart thundered out of control. "Lilo, please, you don't know me. You might regret this."

"Regret going to bed with a man who's done everything in his power to help a friend? No, I won't regret that." She brushed her lips over his.

"Lilo," he murmured, still trying to hold onto his control.

"Unless you don't want me…"

"Of course I want you!" he ground out. "But I'm not who you think I am." But he was a man, one who couldn't deny that the sexual attraction between them was burning like a wildfire now. One he wouldn't be able to douse.

"Then make love to me. Because tomorrow we could all be dead. Killed by those evil things."

Despite his better judgment, he yanked her to him. "We shouldn't do this," he said before capturing her mouth in a searing kiss.

No, they wouldn't be dead tomorrow, but by tomorrow Lilo would know that he was a vampire, and then she'd never allow him to touch her again. And the thought that he might never find out what it felt like to lose himself in Lilo's body and find ecstasy with her, was something he couldn't bear. And though he knew it was wrong, he lifted her into his arms and carried her to his bedroom, not for a single second letting go of her hungry lips.

He knew he would pay for this sin in short order, but right now he didn't care.

Right now he was all man, all vampire, hungry for a woman who tempted him like no other.

20

Blake kicked the bedroom door shut with his heel and carried her to his bed. He knew he was beyond stopping now. Soon, Lilo would hate him for what he was about to do. The least he could do at this point was give her more pleasure than she'd ever experienced. Then maybe, just maybe, once she found out the truth, she would remember how gentle his touch had been. Not like a vampire, but like a man worshipping her.

He laid her on the sheets and released her mouth. A disappointed mewl came over her lips, and she pulled him back with a hand on his nape.

"Don't stop," she murmured.

He brushed a blond lock from her forehead and gazed into her heated face. "I won't stop until you and I are both completely satisfied, trust me on that." Nothing less would do. But he also wanted to establish one thing first. "But I'm not going to rush this."

He pulled back a little farther, shifting on the bed so he wasn't crushing her with his weight, and let his gaze travel down her torso. She wore a long-sleeved tightly-fitting jersey top with buttons down the front. Beneath the soft fabric, the outline of her bra showed. When he lifted his eyes back to her face, he noticed that she was pulling her lower lip between her teeth, sucking in a breath.

Not breaking eye contact, he moved his hand lower, letting his fingers slowly trail down her front until he reached the peak of her left breast. There he stopped and began to circle her nipple. A sharp intake of breath confirmed that his touch had the desired reaction.

"Yes!" she let out.

Male pride blooming, he captured her breast in his hand and squeezed the responsive flesh, feeling her hard nipple brush against his palm. If she responded with such enthusiasm to this tame touch, she'd be screaming in ecstasy as soon as he laid her bare and was caressing her in earnest.

Now he was even gladder that he'd sent Ryder away with the hybrids. What was about to happen in this room wasn't suitable for the ears of impressionable teenage boys. Their sensitive hybrid hearing—as sensitive as that of a vampire—would pick up every sound. And he didn't want or need anybody witnessing him making love to Lilo. This was just for the two of them. Private and intimate.

"I'm going to undress you now." He wanted her to know what he was doing at every turn. There would be no misunderstandings between them, not when it came to making love. "Are you sure you want this?"

God help him if she said no. Because even if she did, he wouldn't be able to release her now. Already, his cock was pumped full with blood, aching for release. If they weren't both still dressed, he would already be inside her, thrusting toward his first orgasm. But he had to think of Lilo, her needs, her desires. And she didn't need fast and hard. She needed gentle and loving. She needed a dream, one that would make reality easier to bear. He read it in her eyes. In her tears.

"Blake…" She lifted her leg and curled it around his upper thigh, pulling him closer. "I want you."

"Oh, you've got me, Lilo."

What that meant she couldn't possibly begin to imagine. Nor could he explain it to her, because he barely understood it himself. But he knew that if he took her now, there would be no going back. He wouldn't be the old Blake anymore. He would change irrevocably because of the woman in his arms. He'd never before believed in fate or that things happened for a reason. But he knew now that even his car accident four years ago had happened so that he could meet Lilo.

"You have all of me, baby," he repeated and sank his mouth onto her parted lips, soaking in her intoxicating scent as if Lilo were the only nourishment he needed. And perhaps one day she would be just that.

Slowly he began to open the buttons of her top. With each button that popped open, more of her skin was revealed, until he could finally peel the top away from her torso, then pull it off her completely. He swept his eyes over her then, drinking in the beauty of her glistening skin, her firm stomach muscles and her lush breasts. Her hard nipples pushed through the black lace bra, inviting him to come closer.

He dipped his head to lick over the protrusion under the fabric, wringing a stifled moan from Lilo's lips.

"You've seen nothing yet," he promised, and got to work on the front clasp of her bra.

When it snapped open, he peeled back the cups and let her breasts spill into his waiting hands. "Oh, baby."

He buried his face in her bosom, reveling in the softness of her warm skin. He inhaled deeply and felt his fangs itch in response. Oh God, this was worse than he'd thought. He would have to use every ounce of his strength to fight against his transformation. He had to keep the beast in check and make sure it didn't slip past his defenses. The vampire in him would find no satisfaction tonight, because the man in him needed Lilo to trust him.

Blake lifted his face and slid his lips around one hard nipple, sucking it deep into his mouth. The temptation to sink his fangs into her soft flesh and taste her blood was strong, but he pushed it back. Instead, he licked the hard bud with his tongue, swiping over it again and again, enjoying how Lilo writhed beneath him in obvious delight.

Her hand on his nape clawed into him, and he welcomed her fingernails digging into him, sending shivers down his spine and into his tailbone. A corresponding bolt of adrenaline shot into his balls and his cock, making him grind out a curse. Fuck, he should have more control than this! Why was his body reacting as if he'd never been touched by a woman?

"Oh, Blake, that's good," Lilo murmured, her other hand sliding to his butt to grip him there.

Instinctively he thrust his pelvis, rubbing his iron-hard erection against her center.

Lilo gasped, the sound so thrilling that he couldn't help himself and thrust once more, while sucking harder on her nipple.

He lifted his head and met her gaze. "You want that inside you?"

"Yes." Her voice was a mere echo, but it sent a tantalizing shudder through his body.

"Soon…"

Carefully, he now peeled her out of her bra, tossing the garment to the foot of the bed. Then he continued caressing her breasts, exploring every inch of her torso, the deep ridge between her breasts, the high peaks crowned with rosy, hard nipples, and everything in between: the valley of her navel and the curves where her waist tapered before flaring out to her hips again.

Such perfection. Such beauty. He couldn't get enough of touching her, of listening to her heartbeat as it began to gallop toward the inevitable climax, of smelling her blood as it raced through her veins like a torrent following the carved-out path of a stony river.

All the while, his own blood was thundering in his body, taking sides in the silent war that raged inside him: the battle between man and vampire. For now, the man was winning.

Blake caressed Lilo's breasts, kissed and sucked and licked every exposed inch of her delectable skin, but it wasn't enough. He slid one hand down her body, heading for the waistband of her pants.

"I'm going to touch your pussy," he warned and opened the button.

He felt her hold her breath, her pelvis tilting toward his hand. The invitation unmistakable, he lowered the zipper and slid his fingers underneath her bikini panties. He was greeted by a light dusting of hair and a heat so blistering it nearly scorched him.

Lilo bucked toward him, moaning.

Gently he moved lower, his fingers finding the spot where warm moisture dripped from her. Greedily, he bathed his finger in her arousal, closing his eyes to let himself fall deeper into the enchantment that Lilo was weaving around him. A man could lose himself forever in the web she wove so easily.

"You feel so good," he murmured against her breast, planting kisses on her flesh as he worked his way higher. He kissed alongside her neck, sensing the drum of her pulse underneath his lips. Like a beacon it was calling to him, tempting him to extend his fangs so he could still the hunger that ravaged his body. But he couldn't give in. Gaining Lilo's trust by showing her that he was a selfless lover, that her pleasure came before his, was more important.

Carefully, he began to caress her wet folds, stroked along her slit, and teased moan after moan and sigh after sigh from her red lips. At her ear, he whispered, "Imagine it's my cock."

She gasped and lifted her pelvis up, her hands suddenly coming to aid to push her pants and panties lower to give him better access. He allowed her to move the garments to mid-thigh, then stopped her. It was better that she couldn't open her legs too wide for a while, or this would be over far too quickly.

"Not yet, baby." He pressed a kiss below her earlobe. "Just take this for now." He slid his middle finger deep into her tight channel, until it could go no farther.

"Ohhhh!" She arched off the bed, and her muscles clamped down on his digit.

"Easy, baby, relax," he coaxed.

Lilo eased back into the sheets, then pulled his head down to her. Her lips were hungry when they slid over his. God, how he loved a woman who took charge and wasn't afraid to show a man what she expected from him.

Slowly he pulled his finger back, then moved higher to her center of pleasure. When he rubbed over the swollen bundle of nerves for the first time, Lilo moaned into his mouth. He swallowed the intoxicating sound and did it again, gently drawing small circles around the precious organ. He sensed her need to move with him, to rock against his hand, but he swung his leg over her thighs to restrain her. When she wanted to protest, he ripped his lips from hers.

"We've got to go slow, baby, or this isn't going to last."

Without giving her time to answer, he took her mouth again and continued his passionate kiss, while farther below he caressed her with more tenderness, easing off her clit whenever he felt her pulse become erratic and her breath come in pants, denying her the release she craved only to prepare her for a more massive one.

Every time he drew back, Lilo moaned in frustration, but the moment he continued his heated caresses, she purred like a kitten. There was no sight more beautiful than a woman in ecstasy.

Blake released her lips and kissed his way along her jaw, then to her neck. She was ready now to experience her first taste of what he could give her.

"You wanna come, Lilo, don't you?"

"Yes!" she cried out.

He planted open-mouthed kisses along the slender column of her neck and continued his ministrations. But this time he didn't stop when he felt her body tense. Didn't withdraw his hand, didn't deprive her of what she needed. This time he increased his tempo, caressed her with more pressure, listening to her body to know when it was time.

The shudders that went through Lilo's body when she climaxed were the purest thing he'd ever been part of. His hand stilled over her sex, allowing the tremors that shook her to extend to him and send tiny shockwaves through his body and into his cock.

Soon, he promised himself. Just as soon as Lilo was truly ready for him.

When he lifted his head from her neck and looked at her, her eyes were closed. She opened them, meeting his gaze. Her hand came up, and she ran it through his hair. He captured it and pressed a kiss into her palm, before lifting himself off her.

Before she could sit up, he was already at her feet, freeing her of her shoes and socks, then pulling her pants and panties down completely, until she lay naked in front of him. He noticed how she lifted her head and reached for the duvet as if wanting to cover herself, but he was already positioning himself between her legs, spreading them apart.

"Don't hide from me. You're beautiful." Then he lowered his head to the juncture of her thighs. "I want to taste you." He met her stunned gaze. "Tell me you want that."

"But... you just made me come," she said, her voice a little shaky, and a dark red blush spreading on her cheeks.

He couldn't suppress his grin. "Yeah, and now I'm gonna make you come with my mouth. Something wrong with that?"

She took a few uneven breaths, but finally shook her head. "No, nothing wrong. Nothing at all."

21

Lilo stared at Blake's dark hair as he dipped his head to the juncture of her thighs and buried his face in her heat. His hot breath ghosted over her flesh, and a moment later, his tongue licked over her sex, soothing her.

"Oh, Blake."

She couldn't believe what he was doing. Not only had he touched her so patiently and skillfully that she had firmly exploded, but even now he still took no pleasure for himself. Instead, he sucked her with such fervor that she wasn't sure she wasn't dreaming—because no man was this selfless. Maybe she'd passed out.

But the strong hands on her thighs, keeping her legs spread, and the warm tongue licking her were too real to be a dream. She reached for him, running her hands through his thick dark hair and feeling him shudder under her touch.

For a moment he lifted his head, their gazes colliding. In his eyes she read the promise he was making her: to shower her with pleasure.

She felt safe now. With Blake by her side, the fear was retreating, fading into the background. Whether it would stay there, she didn't know, but for now, for the next hour or two, she could breathe again.

She reveled in the sensations Blake unleashed in her. The euphoria. The lust. The pleasure. Already, her arousal was spiking, all thanks to Blake's skilled tongue and masterful mouth. There was nothing mechanical or perfunctory about his caresses. No, every stroke, every nibble, every lick appeared to give him as much pleasure as her, if the guttural moans coming from his throat were anything to go by.

Did he lavish every woman with such tender passion? For some selfish reason, she wanted to believe that she was the only one he touched, made love to this way. She'd never met a man like him. Not even Morgan West was like this: a selfless lover with boundless energy and skill. She couldn't invent a man like Blake if she tried. Nobody would believe her. But Blake was real.

Already he was coaxing her toward another orgasm, but she knew she needed more this time. She wanted to experience this high with him inside her. It was the only way to truly share how he made her feel.

Lilo put her hands on his face and lifted it up.

He looked at her, surprised. "You don't like it?"

"I love it," she hastened to assure him. "But I want you inside me. I want to feel you."

He lifted himself up to sit. "You sure you want that?"

She sat up and nodded, then reached for the buttons of his shirt, undoing the first one, then the second, until she could slide it over his shoulders and rid him of it.

There was only a mild dusting of dark hair on his chest, a chest that attested to his fit state. He was muscular and well-toned, his skin a beautiful bronze tone. Fascinated by so much male perfection, she ran her hand over the hard ridges of his chest and abdomen and felt him inhale. His skin was smooth and soft. Beneath it, his muscles flexed. She loved the way he reacted to her touch, sitting entirely still while his heart thundered under her palm.

"Lilo…"

She lifted her lids, tearing her eyes away from his naked chest. "Yes?"

"Undress me."

She smiled at the request. Blake turned to the side, kicking his shoes off so they fell down next to the bed, before lying down on his back.

Without hesitation she bent over him. Her eyes fell on the bulge that had formed beneath his pants. An involuntary gasp escaped her before she could stop herself.

A chuckle came from Blake, making her meet his gaze. "I'm not sure whether to apologize or thank you for the compliment," he said with a smirk. His hand came up and he stroked his knuckles over her cheek. "Don't worry, I'll be very gentle."

She felt her cheeks flush with heat. "I know that." Just like he'd been gentle when he'd touched her. Though maybe she didn't want gentle. Maybe she wanted something more.

Boldly, she opened the button of Blake's pants and lowered the zipper. She gripped the waistband and pulled, while Blake lifted himself up so she could free him of his clothing. She threw his pants onto the floor in the middle of the room, before helping him with his socks. When she looked back at him, he lay there in only his boxer briefs. The fabric stretched tightly over his groin. Slowly she pulled it down completely. Only now, the true size of his erection became evident. Her chin dropped, and involuntarily she licked her lips. He was the most amazing specimen of aroused male she'd ever seen.

A groan bounced off the walls of the bedroom. "Fuck, Lilo, don't do that, you're gonna make me come before I'm even inside you."

"Do what?"

"Look at me like you want to devour me."

"I'm not…"

Blake sat up and put his hand on her nape, pulling her face to him. "You are. And ordinarily I'd love for you to look at me like that. But when you lick your lips like that, my mind imagines all kinds of things… and all kinds of ways I want to take you."

"And that's a bad thing?" she teased, feeling her confidence grow at the knowledge that Blake desired her.

"Yeah, very bad. Because it means that I won't be able to make love to you for nearly as long as I want to."

"Ever heard of seconds?"

He laughed out loud. "Thank God for that!" Then he captured her lips and shifted to press her back into the sheets and roll over her.

Her legs fell open, making space for him. His hard cock nudged against her center, sending a spike of adrenaline through her core at the contact of skin on skin. Flames seemed to ignite inside her.

Blake tilted his pelvis and adjusted his erection.

Lilo ripped her mouth from his. "Condom," she panted. In the heat of the moment, she'd almost forgotten about it.

He froze in mid-movement, pulling back a few inches. He expelled a breath, before moving his head from side to side. "I'm sorry. I don't have any." He hesitated, then pulled back farther. "I don't… I'm healthy. The company… they test us regularly."

She tried to make sense of his explanation. He was talking about STDs. But that wasn't her only worry. "I'm not on the pill." There hadn't been any need. She hadn't been with a man in a long time.

He seemed to relax a little. "If you're worried about a pregnancy, don't be. I'm sterile."

"Sterile?"

He shrugged. "Happens to the best of us."

"Oh." Was it true? She hesitated, letting the words sink in.

Blake sat back on his heels. "Maybe this was a bad idea." He reached for the duvet, pulling it halfway over her. "I don't even have condoms in the house. What was I thinking? Of course you don't wanna sleep with me without proper protection. You don't know me." He ran his hand through his hair. "You have no reason to believe a single word I'm saying."

He jumped up from the bed. "I'll let you get dressed."

She watched him turn, giving her a view of his toned butt. "Blake!" She got out of bed and reached for his arm, her decision suddenly clear.

He turned, giving her a regretful smile.

"If you say you're healthy and you can't get me pregnant, I believe you." She drew him closer to her. "Make love to me. Let me feel you."

"Are you sure?"

There was a wild glint in his eyes, and it sparked something primal in her.

"Yes. Any way you want to." She'd never given any man carte blanche, but Blake made her want to do anything and everything.

In the next instant, Blake lifted her off her feet, and a few seconds later she found herself with her back against the wall, her legs spread, suspended in the air, only held up by Blake's strong hands. But she had no time to marvel at his strength, because he was lowering her onto his cock, seating himself deep inside her with one continuous thrust.

"Ohhhhh!" she cried out in surprise. She closed her eyes, overtaken by the sensation of how he filled her so completely. Her channel stretched to accommodate him, and all her nerve endings tingled pleasantly.

"Too much?" he mumbled.

She opened her eyes and looked at him. He was clenching his jaw, and the cords in his neck protruded, pulsing under the strain, a golden rim around his irises from the light reflecting off the wall.

"It's perfect," she managed to say. "You're perfect."

As if he'd been waiting for her approval, he pulled back his hips, letting his cock slide from her so only the bulbous head was still submerged, before plunging back into her. His powerful thrust robbed her of the air to breathe. She sucked in some oxygen. "Yes! Oh, Blake, yes. Just like that."

Why she'd suddenly turned into a woman who liked to be fucked hard and fast against a wall, she had no idea. But as Blake was taking her like this, thrusting into her with powerful moves, she couldn't imagine ever wanting anything else. She'd never in her life felt so desired.

"Baby," he ground out against her lips, while he plunged so deep she thought he was touching her womb. "You feel so good."

He took her lips as if wanting to eat her alive. His tongue dipped between her parted lips, exploring her, taking possession of her, making her submit to his wishes.

She surrendered willingly, opening up her body to him, giving him what he wanted. And she took what she needed, too. She soaked up all he was willing to give her. The spark that had ignited between them the night before was now burning like a wildfire. Out of control. Hot. Untamed. She'd never felt anything like it before. Never known what making love could be like. How every cell in her body could hum with pleasure.

Blake released her lips, looking at her, as if to reassure himself that she was fine.

He was panting heavily, but he wasn't slowing down. His body was glistening with perspiration now, and his muscles were flexing with every move he made.

"So close," he murmured.

He dipped his face to the crook of her neck and kissed her there. She shivered at the contact and tilted her head to allow him better access. "Yes."

Blake's moan went through her like a shudder, while his lips caressed the sensitive skin of her neck. He trailed open-mouthed kisses along her heated flesh, simultaneously soothing and igniting her again. Then she felt his teeth rub against her skin, and a corresponding shudder go through Blake's body.

"Fuck!" he cried out and delivered several more thrusts, his pelvic bone hitting her clit, just as she felt the warm spray of his semen fill her.

Her climax followed his within a second, and she felt herself relax against the wall, Blake still holding her up. For several seconds, all she could do was catch her breath. He didn't seem to be faring much better.

Slowly he lifted his head and leaned his forehead against hers, exhaling. "This was much more than I'd ever expected." He pressed a gentle kiss to her lips. "You're amazing, Lilo. Truly amazing."

She had to smile. He thought she was amazing? She hadn't done anything. He was the one who'd turned this into an out-of-this-world experience.

She ran her hand through his hair. "Blake, I've never felt anything this good. You are—"

He chuckled. "I wasn't fishing for compliments." He pinned her with his eyes, the blue in them more vibrant than ever. "And I truly hope that this isn't the last time you let me make love to you."

His comment seemed a little out of place, considering he was the most confident man she'd ever met—even more confident than her cocky fictional character, Morgan West.

"Seconds, remember?" she teased.

"Yeah, seconds." He slid his lips over hers, and kissed her. This time, his kiss was slow and gentle. The tenderness with which he worshipped her mouth was unexpected, but she soaked it up, just as she'd gobbled up his passion earlier.

An eternity seemed to pass before he finally withdrew his cock from her and set her back on her feet.

"How about I get the shower running?" he asked.

"I'd like that."

He released her from his arms and crossed the room toward the ensuite bathroom. "It's an old house. The hot water takes a couple of minutes."

She watched him disappear in the bathroom, admiring his muscular physique. Few men looked great both in clothes and out of them. Blake was one of them.

Still in a state of bliss, she peeled herself away from the wall and slowly crossed the room, when her gaze fell onto the nightstand. There, on the middle shelf, lay a book. She smiled to herself. It was a Morgan West bounty hunter novel, one of her books. If only Blake knew that she was the author who'd penned the novel he was currently reading. Perhaps she should tell him. They would both get a chuckle out of it.

"Water is getting warmer," Blake called from the bathroom.

She turned and continued walking, but with her next step, her foot landed on something sharp, and she involuntarily cried out, "Ouch!"

She lifted her foot and saw what she'd stepped on. She froze, then slowly bent down. Was this what she thought it was? No, it couldn't be.

But there was no doubt. A pink H was scribbled on the small shiny item and it fairly stared her in the face.

"Are you coming, Lilo?"

She collected the item that lay next to Blake's pants. Had it fallen out of his pocket when she'd tossed them on the floor while undressing him? Lilo rose, turning toward the bathroom, where Blake now appeared in the doorframe.

"What is this?" She held up the USB stick, the one she'd given to Officer Donnelly. "Why do you have this? What's going on?"

Blake stared at the memory stick in her hand, his eyes wide. "I'm sorry. I was gonna tell you."

"Tell me what?" In her own ears, her voice suddenly sounded shrill. He'd lied to her.

"The truth."

22

Blake had grabbed his clothes and gone downstairs to let Lilo get dressed in private.

Now he was pacing in front of the fireplace in the living room, guilt blasting through him. He'd screwed up. Major. Why on earth had he not told her everything the moment Ryder had left with the hybrids? He knew exactly why: because his dick had done the thinking for him.

"Fuck!" He slammed his fist against the mantle.

By sleeping with Lilo he'd made things a hundred times worse. Not only would she feel betrayed, but he was also sure now that he couldn't let her go. He'd never felt such ecstasy in his life as when he'd come inside her and felt her interior muscles clamp around him as if she'd wanted to imprison him. But the chances of ever holding her in his arms again had just dropped to zero.

The hurt look she'd tossed him before he'd left the bedroom had said as much.

Coming clean now, laying himself bare before her, was his only chance at redemption in her eyes. But even if he could make her understand why he'd had to keep secrets from her, there was no way of knowing how she would react to finding out that he was the very creature she found so disgusting.

His ears perked up when he heard footsteps on the stairs. Taking a deep breath, he prepared himself. This was the moment of truth, and so much depended on how he handled the next few minutes.

When he heard her at the open archway, he turned slowly. She stood there between the hallway and living room, fully dressed, her cheeks still flushed, her hair unruly.

He motioned to the couch. "Why don't you take a seat?"

"I'd rather stand."

"Believe me, you'll want to sit for this. What I'm going to tell you isn't easy to swallow."

She lashed a glare at him. "Why? Because it's another lie?"

He flinched. "I deserved that. But what I'm going to tell you now is the truth." He sighed. "I wanted to tell you earlier. That's why I sent Ryder and the boys away, but things…" He cleared his throat. "…things happened. And I'm not proud of how I behaved."

He ran his eyes over her.

"But I'm only a man. And it's hard to resist something that you want so damn much."

She ignored his comment and walked to the sofa, sinking into one corner of it. He remained standing near the fireplace, sensing that she didn't want him to come any closer.

"Lilo, I want you to understand something. It wasn't my intention to take advantage of you, but I never had a chance resisting you. You're brave and smart. And so damn beautiful."

She didn't buy it. Instead, she pressed her lips together.

"You might not believe everything I've got to say. But there's one thing that you *have* to believe: I will never hurt you. I will protect you with my life, if it comes to that."

She made an abrupt movement with her hand, cutting him off. "Get to the point." She tossed the USB stick on the coffee table. "I gave this to the police. How did you get it?"

He nodded, trying to find the right way to start. Maybe the easy things first. "What I told you about myself is true. I'm a bodyguard for Scanguards. But what I didn't mention is that Scanguards has a consulting contract with the police department. They rely on us to solve cases they can't."

She narrowed her eyes in suspicion. "What's that supposed to mean?"

He pointed to the stick. "The video that's on there. It's real. Vampires exist, and I've been aware of it for a long time. As is the police chief and a few select police officers who act as our liaisons."

"Like Donnelly?"

"Yes. He's one of the few who know what they're dealing with, and whenever a case in which vampires appear to be involved crosses their desks, they contact Scanguards, and we take over."

He could see her mind processing the information he gave her. Her forehead furrowed. Suddenly she shook her head. "You pretended not to know Donnelly when you brought me to the police station that night. And he played along. I take it that it wasn't a coincidence that you drove me to that particular station?"

Blake shook his head. "You insisted on going to the police, and I couldn't let you go to just anybody. Public knowledge about vampires has to be contained, or there will be panic everywhere. So I texted Donnelly."

"No, no, no! Don't try to confuse me. You couldn't have known back then that we were dealing with vampires. I found the video only today."

He took a few steps closer and lowered himself to sit on the coffee table a few feet away from her. "Lilo, I knew immediately that night that the man who attacked you was a vampire."

"How?"

He shrugged, not ready to give away his secret yet. He needed to explain a lot more before she was ready to hear this. "I can identify vampires. But I couldn't tell you. You were scared enough. I needed you to remain calm."

"So you lied to me?" Her lips quivered.

"I didn't lie. I just withheld things from you. I had to." He shoved a hand through his hair and threw his head back. "But you've earned the right to hear the truth now. Without your help we wouldn't know who your attacker was. But with the video we'll be able to find him in the database, I'm certain."

"Database?"

"Scanguards has built up a database of known vampires."

She shook her head again and again. "I can't believe this. A company that consults with the city? That hunts vampires? This is crazy."

"I know it sounds like it at first. But that's what Scanguards does."

"And the database? Why? I mean, if you know who's a vampire, then why not kill them right away?"

As if she'd physically driven a knife through his ribs, pain seared through him. "Lilo, it's not all black and white."

"I don't—"

"Not all vampires are bad. In fact, most are upstanding citizens with families and—"

"No, no, that's not possible. They're vile creatures. They suck humans dry. They kill them."

"No, the vampires I know are honorable people. They protect humans."

"They bite humans and drink their blood!"

If only she knew what a euphoric feeling a vampire's bite could cause. But the way things stood right now, she'd never find out for herself. "Please listen to me. I want to tell you about the vampires I know."

"How many do you know?" she spat.

"Many. They have families, children, dogs…"

"Children?"

"Hybrids to be exact. Half-vampire, half-human."

He could see her mind working.

"But that would mean…" she started, her eyes widening.

This was his opportunity to tell her about his species, and that they needn't be feared. "Yes. That's exactly what that means. Vampires can bond with humans. For life."

"Why would a human agree to that?"

"Many reasons: love being the strongest. And the advantages for the human are without equal: through their blood-bond the human feeds off the vampire's immortality."

"The human becomes immortal? No. You mean the human is turned into a vampire."

"No. The human remains human. Who would the vampire feed off if he turned his human mate into a vampire? No, he needs her to remain human, because he can only take nourishment from his mate. He will only ever feed off his human mate."

"I don't understand. He won't bite another human?"

"He couldn't, even if he wanted to. The blood-bond is so strong that he would get sick from drinking another human's blood."

"That still leaves all those other vampires." She pointed toward the door indicating the world outside their four walls. "The ones who're not that tame. Those who don't have human mates." She shivered visibly, as if the thought disgusted her. "Vampires like Ronny, and the one who attacked me."

Slowly Blake nodded. "Yes, there are those." He looked at her, searching her eyes, making sure he had her full attention. "That's why Scanguards came into existence. To protect humans from evil vampires."

She waved her hands nervously. "But how? I felt how strong that vampire was. How could a human possibly have a chance against something like that?"

"A human wouldn't." He waited, letting the words sink in.

"But if not a human then…" Her eyes moved, her irises widening, swallowing up most of the white in her eyes.

"Scanguards was founded by a vampire named Samson Woodford. He still runs the company today, over two hundred years later. Many of the employees are vampires who've pledged their lives to protect the humans in their care."

Lilo's head moved from side to side, her chin dropping. "No, no, I can't hear anymore of this. This is crazy. This can't be true. Please tell me none of this is true."

He met her pleading look. "I wish I could. But there's one more thing. Something I wanted to tell you before we ended up in bed." He hesitated, but there was no way back now. She deserved to know.

"Lilo, I'm one of them. I'm a vampire."

23

Lilo's heart stopped. Her lungs stopped working. Her muscles froze. Paralyzed, she stared at Blake, sitting on the edge of the coffee table, hands clasped. His words still echoed in her ears, but they couldn't be true.

Her mouth could only form one word. "No."

Maybe if she said it often enough, it would become true, and the nightmare she found herself in would end.

"I'm sorry, Lilo, but it's the truth. I became a vampire fourteen years ago."

She continued shaking her head, not wanting to believe his words. Because believing them would mean she'd have to admit that she'd kissed a vampire, touched him, slept with him.

Blake leaned closer, and she involuntarily shrank back into her corner of the sofa. Immediately he made a calming gesture with his hand, easing back again. "I have no intention of frightening you or hurting you in any way. On the contrary. I want you to know everything about me. I want you to understand me, and why I had to keep this from you. I need you to trust me."

"Trust?" She laughed hysterically. "Trust a vampire? Like Hannah trusted Ronny?" She expelled an angry breath. "See where that got her! She's probably dead already!" Tears welled up in her eyes now, but she forced them back. No, crying wouldn't help now. She had to remain strong. "Hannah would have never gotten involved with a vampire, had she known what Ronny was. Never!"

"Hannah met Ronny through her job. She knew what he was."

"No! He lied to her, just like you lied to me!"

"Hannah works for Vüber. Scanguards created Vüber for the sole purpose of providing vampire-safe transportation during daylight hours. Every single client is a vampire. The human drivers know that. We retrofit their cars to make them vampire-safe. Hannah knew who she was transporting. She knew what Ronny was even before they started dating."

Lilo pressed her hand over her mouth to prevent herself from screaming.

"Hannah went into this relationship with her eyes open. Ronny didn't lie to her." He sighed. "I'm afraid I can't claim the same for myself. But I knew, from your reaction when I picked you up from the police station, that you'd never let me make love to you if you knew what I was." He ran a shaky hand through his hair. "Hell, by telling you this I'm probably making things even worse for myself." He shot her a pleading look. "But I can't lie to you any longer. I want you, Lilo. The thought of never again touching you, kissing you, making love to you, is killing me."

"Like Ronny wanted Hannah?" she ground out. "As if I don't know what that means. You know how many times Hannah complained about Ronny's possessiveness? His demanding nature? His jealousy? It all makes sense now. He's a vampire, an animal. Just like you."

He flinched, and quickly closed his eyes, but she'd seen it nevertheless: a red flickering in his irises, as if he was about to lose control.

"You're right, Lilo." He rose and turned his back to her. "I'm an animal. And I'll tell you why: I love my family, and I would do anything to protect them. That's why I asked my fourth great-grandfather to turn me. So I could protect those I love. Scanguards is my family. The boys you met here—Sebastian, Adam, and Nicholas—they're my charges. They're hybrids. The sons of Scanguards' senior management. Thirteen half-vampires, ten boys and three girls, rely on me for their security when their parents are otherwise occupied. Yes, I'm an animal, because I'll protect them to the death."

The words shocked her to the core. Such passion. Such devotion. Such honor.

Could a vampire really possess those traits? Could he really live by such a code?

"I'm also an animal," he continued, "because of my need for blood. I can't deny that. But it doesn't make me a beast, and it doesn't make me evil. Because I can control that need. I did earlier."

Her breath hitched, and he slowly turned, looking at her.

"When you were in my arms, I didn't only want to make love to you, though, by God, that was my greatest desire. But I also wanted to taste your blood. I wanted to sink my fangs into your skin and drink from you."

His eyes suddenly began to shimmer golden, and she now realized that it was the same shimmer she'd seen earlier when he'd taken her against the wall.

"Oh, God," she whimpered.

His gaze dropped to her chest. "Yes, I wanted to sink my fangs into your breast and drink from you there, while I brought us both to an earth-shattering climax. But I didn't do it, because you didn't give me permission. And I would never violate anybody like that."

Her heart pounded up into her throat. "As if anybody would give a vampire permission to bite them! Why would anybody allow that?" she cried out. Only a crazy person would do that.

"Once we find Hannah, you can ask her why."

"Hannah would never…"

A slow shake of his head silenced her.

"She's been dating Ronny for several months. I can guarantee you that she allowed him to bite her. Maybe not right away, but eventually." He paused for a moment. "A vampire's bite is virtually painless. The host feels no more than a pinprick. But once a vampire draws on the human's vein, the human will feel a sense of euphoria, of pleasure so intense it eclipses any orgasm. And if a vampire chooses to bite his lover during sex…"

He didn't finish the sentence, and he didn't have to. The look on his face told her everything she needed to know.

"That's why a human will give her vampire lover permission to bite her," he murmured. "So they can experience that ultimate ecstasy together. A special connection."

Lilo pressed her hand to her chest. This was all too much. She couldn't process all the information he'd given her. How could she know what was true and what wasn't? She had no proof of anything. Only his words.

"I want to see." The words were out before she realized she'd made the decision.

"See what?"

"You. I want to see the real you." Then at least one question would be answered once and for all, and she could panic in earnest.

"I guess you have a right to it after all that's happened." He stood up and put several feet of distance between them. "I don't want you to be scared of what you're about to see. I'll be in control of myself the entire time. I could never hurt you."

Had Ronny said those words to Hannah, too? Had he, too, professed that he'd never hurt her, and then done it anyway?

She swallowed, bracing herself for what was about to happen. Her palms felt sweaty, and she rubbed them on her pants. Her heart was beating out of control, but there was nothing she could do to calm it down.

"I'm ready."

Her eyes were trained on Blake's face. At first nothing happened, then his eyes started to shimmer golden. It took several seconds before the golden hue turned orange, and then red, until his irises were finally glowing scarlet, like two alarm beacons.

She held her breath, as her gaze was drawn to his mouth. His lips parted slowly, revealing his pearly white teeth. He opened wider and exhaled visibly, while at the same time one canine to each side of his jaw lengthened into a razor-sharp fang.

"Oh my God," she murmured to herself, her hands holding onto her thighs as if her life depended on it.

But evidently Blake wasn't done, because he now lifted his arms and made her look at his hands, while his fingers turned into sharp claws, claws that could rip an elephant to shreds.

She gasped. He'd touched her with those hands, when he could have easily ripped her throat out with one single swipe. There was no denying it any longer. Blake was a vampire.

And she was caught in the middle of a battle in which the various sides hadn't even been identified yet. She didn't know who was good and who was bad. And she didn't know whose side she would find herself on. If she lived long enough to take sides.

"Lilo, it's still me," Blake said softly. "I'm still the man who made love to you. The man whose touch you enjoyed, whose kisses you responded to. I'm still that man."

She lifted her eyes to his face, and watched him turn back into a man. His eyes were of a vibrant blue again, and his teeth were a beautiful row of white perfection. Nothing gave away what lay hidden beneath that beautiful facade. Which made him even more dangerous.

She scraped together all her courage and lifted her chin. "What are you planning to do with me, now that I know?"

He tilted his head to the side. "Do with you?"

"Yes, now that I know your secret. Yours and Scanguards. How are you going to make sure I won't talk?"

To her surprise, he let out a soft chuckle. "Oh, Lilo. You really think I'd have it in me to kill you?" He shook his head. "I could wipe your memory, of course."

She jolted. "What?"

"It's a skill every vampire possesses: to wipe a human's memory of an event so the vampire's secret remains hidden. I could do that. But I'm not going to. I want you to know the truth about what's going on. I don't want you to be in the dark any longer. You're much more use in helping me in my search for Hannah if you know everything."

"You're truly looking for her?"

"From the moment I found out she disappeared, I've done everything in my power to find her. And I won't rest until we've got her back, safe and sound," he vowed.

"Why? She's just a human. She can't mean anything to you."

"I don't distinguish between human and vampire when I choose my friends. And Hannah is my friend."

The sincerity in his voice was undeniable, as was the honest look in his eyes.

Slowly she nodded. "And once we find her. What then?"

"That's up to you, Lilo. It'll be your decision. To go home and pretend nothing has happened, or to accept this new world and make it yours. I already know what I would choose, if I had a say in it." He ran a searing look over her that made her shiver involuntarily. "But whatever you decide in the end, you'll be safe. Nobody will hurt you as long as my heart beats."

Lilo could only stare at him in disbelief. Was she really listening to a vampire making her a promise, a promise she was inclined to believe? She searched his eyes to find the truth in them. Would he keep his word?

The chiming of a cell phone cut through the silence of the room. Blake pulled it from his pocket and looked at the display.

"Sorry, I have to take this." He connected the call. "Wes?"

Lilo couldn't hear Wesley's words, only Blake's reply. "We'll be there shortly. Thanks."

He disconnected the call and looked straight at her. "Wesley is calling a meeting at headquarters. He's figured out what Ronny's been up to."

24

Blake slowed the Aston Martin and entered Scanguards' well-lit underground parking garage, while tossing Lilo, who sat in the passenger seat, a quick glance.

"We're here."

She nodded. "Good."

While she'd gotten in the car without protest, knowing he couldn't leave her alone at his house, Lilo had carefully avoided touching him, always keeping distance between them. Her eyes had been vigilant at all times, watching him for a sign that he would pounce. Without a doubt, he'd rattled her with his confession, though he was pleased to see that she wasn't hysterical and had accepted his revelations with stoic grace. And a pinch of apprehension, though not fear. Fear was too strong a word; he didn't think that Lilo feared him. She was too smart and too brave for that.

But just because she didn't fear him, didn't mean that she welcomed him with open arms. How he could ever regain her trust, he didn't know. But he was willing to try anything, because never making love to Lilo again wasn't an option.

Blake pulled into his assigned parking spot, and switched off the engine. Lilo was already reaching for the door handle, but he put his hand on her forearm.

Lilo shrieked and whirled her head to him, shock lighting up her eyes.

"I didn't mean to startle you." He eased his hand off her arm, regretting the loss of physical contact. "When we're in the office, I want you to stay close to me. Don't wander off. The building is crawling with vampires, and without an employee badge they'll assume you're an intruder. I'm breaking a few rules by taking you inside. Some people won't like that."

"Okay."

Blake got out of the car and watched Lilo do the same. At the elevator, he turned to Lilo, who'd followed him.

"Most of my colleagues are like tame lambs once you get to know them."

"Well, excuse me if I take that with a grain of salt," she said and tossed him a you're-shitting-me look.

"Fine, maybe not like lambs, but real laid-back guys."

She tilted her head to the side. She wasn't buying it.

He shook his head. "Okay, you've got me. Every single one of my colleagues is an alpha. Including the female bodyguards."

For the first time in the last half hour, Lilo's face lit up with genuine interest. "Female bodyguards? Are they vampires?"

"Yes. Does that surprise you?"

The elevator doors opened and he ushered her in.

"I just thought… I mean you said vampires bond with human women to have children." She suddenly froze. "You told me you were sterile. But you admitted that vampires can father children with human women. Does that mean you—"

"Lied about being sterile? No. I am sterile. For now. Every unbonded vampire is. Only once he's blood-bonded he's able to impregnate a woman—and then only his mate. Not that a bonded vampire would ever want to touch a woman other than his mate."

"I understand."

But he wasn't done talking yet. This was his opportunity to tell her about his world. "Vampire males can of course also bond with vampire females. And have offspring."

"You mean children born as vampires? But would they grow up?"

He understood where she was coming from. "Well, actually, they would still be hybrids, half vampire, half human."

"I don't get that. Where would they get their human part from, if not from their mother?"

"That's where science comes in. By nature, vampire females have always been sterile, and they still are. But Maya, the wife of Scanguards' second-in-command, Gabriel Giles, was a doctor before she was turned. And she'd made it her mission to find a way for vampire females to bear children. She succeeded."

"How?"

"By implanting human stem cells into the vampire's uterus so she could get pregnant and carry the child to term."

"I'm surprised."

"Why? Maya is a brilliant doctor."

Lilo shook her head. "Not about that. But about the fact that a vampire female would go through so much trouble to have children."

He smiled. "Vampire females are just like other women. Some of them want a family as badly as human women. They're no different in that respect."

"Mmm." She nodded. "I think I would like to meet a female vampire. I can't quite imagine what a woman like that must be like."

"You met one the other night: Rose."

"Your cousin?"

Blake made a grimace. Another lie he had to set straight. "Rose isn't my cousin."

Lilo's eyes narrowed in suspicion.

"Rose is my grandmother," he hastened to say.

"Grandmother?"

"My fourth great-grandmother to be exact. In 1814, when Rose was still human, she gave birth to my third great-grandmother. Rose was turned shortly after that and from then on watched over her human line from afar, until she had to reveal herself to me to save my life."

Lilo stared at him in stunned silence. "Oh my God, she must be over two-hundred years old!"

Blake winked at her, smiling. "Granny doesn't look it, does she?"

When Lilo chuckled unexpectedly, he added, "Don't tell her I called her granny, or she'll stake me."

He noticed Lilo swallow hard. "So the legend is true: a stake through the heart will kill a vampire."

He nodded slowly. Should he be careful about revealing how a vampire could be killed? What if she used this knowledge against him? But when he looked into her eyes he didn't see a woman scheming, but he saw the writer in her, the person who wanted to understand the process.

"A stake isn't the only thing that can kill us. Silver can do that, too."

"How?"

He welcomed her eagerness to learn. It would only help her understand him better. "A silver bullet will burn a vampire from the inside. Shot into the brain or the heart, it's fatal almost instantly, in other parts of the body it leads to the silver eating its way through flesh and bone. But if the bullet can be extracted in time, there's a good chance of recovery. Given sufficient human blood and sleep, a vampire will heal in a few hours."

"So when you get injured, you can heal yourself?"

He smiled. "Our bodies are made that way. Any injury will be healed during our restorative sleep cycle. Major injuries need human blood to help the healing process along."

"So human blood is your cure-all?" There was no accusation in her tone. It was a simple question a researcher would ask.

"The same way vampire blood can heal a human, human blood can heal a vampire."

Suddenly she shifted her eyes and stared at the shiny elevator wall. "A perfect symbiosis…"

He'd never thought of it this way, but now that she'd uttered the word, he couldn't deny that the lives of the human and vampire races were intertwined to the advantage of both. He didn't get a chance to agree with Lilo though, because the elevator doors opened on the executive floor.

He stepped into the hallway, quickly ascertaining who was milling about, before looking over his shoulder at Lilo.

"If you can bear my touch at all, I'd like to take your hand. It'll make it clear to everybody that you're with me.

The faint smell of sex that still clung to her—as well as to him—would equally make it clear to any vampire or hybrid that Lilo was his. But he wanted to have a physical connection to Lilo, just in case one of the young pups they were likely to encounter didn't have his hormones under control, and he needed to maneuver her out of a delicate situation quickly.

When Lilo finally slipped her hand into his, he released a silent sigh of relief. At least she wasn't so disgusted with him that she couldn't even hold his hand. It was a step in the right direction.

"The conference room is this way."

"It looks like a real office," she said, pointing at a niche with a photocopier.

"It *is* a real office." He smiled at her. "We all take our work seriously. Without us, people die."

She looked up at him then. "I'm beginning to understand that."

"Hey, Blake, wait up!" At hearing Amaury's voice, Blake stopped and turned, releasing Lilo's hand in the process.

Amaury, one of Scanguards' directors, marched toward him. As so often, he was dressed in a loose shirt and cargo pants. Built like a tank, the Frenchman with the long dark hair and the gravely voice was one of the strongest vampires he'd ever encountered.

"Amaury."

Amaury's gaze shifted to Lilo and a flash of recognition filled his eyes for a moment. He stopped a couple of feet away.

"I hope you have a good explanation for this."

His superior didn't need to clarify what he was referring to. Blake knew the rules well enough: no humans were allowed on the executive floor. Well, no humans other than the human mates of Scanguards' upper management.

"I know: no humans up here." Blake bent to Lilo. "Lilo, this is Amaury LeSang. He's one of Scanguards' directors. A vampire, in case you were wondering."

Amaury sucked in a sharp breath. "What the f—"

"Lilo knows the truth. She's vital to this case. Without her, I doubt very much that Wesley would have been able to figure out what's going on in this city."

Amaury ran his eyes over Lilo, assessing her. "The drug case?"

"Yes."

"Drugs?" she squeezed out.

Blake looked at her. "Hannah's disappearance involves drugs."

He caught Amaury raising his eyebrows. "I didn't realize you were on that case. I thought you were in charge of Nicholas and Adam for the week."

"Ryder is watching them right now."

"Why don't I call the twins? Let them do their share and help Ryder out."

Blake nodded. "Appreciate it. I sent Ryder out to grab some pizza with the boys. Have them call him to see where he is now."

While Amaury pulled out his cell phone, Blake ushered Lilo toward the conference room.

"What twins?" Lilo whispered.

"Amaury's got two boys. They're in training to become bodyguards."

"So he's blood-bonded. To a human or a vampire?"

"You learn fast. He has a human mate, Nina. She's one hell of a woman." He smiled. "A lot like you. Blond. Lots of spunk. And she's got Amaury wrapped around her little finger so tightly the poor guy has no chance of ever denying her anything."

Lilo looked over her shoulder. "He doesn't look like a pushover to me."

Blake chuckled. "As I said earlier: tame lambs."

She turned her head back to him and rolled her eyes, but her lips quirked into the beginnings of a warm smile.

25

Lilo stopped at the open door to the conference room, Blake next to her.

She knew exactly what he was doing: he was making small talk to put her at ease. She had to admit that it was working. Blake's sudden willingness to answer all of her questions, not just with a perfunctory yes or no, but with a full explanation helping her understand the vampire species better, helped calm her nerves.

Despite the fact that she was now in the lion's den, or the vampire's lair, if that's what they called it, she felt oddly safe. The building they were in looked like an ordinary office building, and this almost sterile environment helped give the impression that Scanguards was truly just another security company.

So far none of the people they'd encountered on their short walk to the conference room showed any outward signs of being vampires: no fangs, no glaring red eyes, no claws instead of fingers. Everybody looked… civilized.

She peered into the conference room. By her estimate it could hold around thirty people, and it was currently half full.

"Ready?" Blake whispered from next to her.

"As ready as I'll ever be."

She felt his hand at the small of her back, gently guiding her forward. The touch wasn't unpleasant, just as it hadn't been unpleasant when he'd taken her hand earlier. Even though she'd seen what his hands could turn into, right now she could only feel the softness of his fingertips as he ushered her to an empty seat around the oval table.

"Here, take a seat. I need to have a quick word with Wes." He pointed to one corner of the room where Wes stood talking to another man.

Instinctively she reached for his arm. "I don't know anybody else here."

"I'll be just a moment." He bent closer, dipping his face to her ear. "I'll let you in on a secret: a vampire is the fastest animal on this planet. It would take me only a second to rush to your side if you needed me."

Her heart suddenly hammered out of control. Could he hear it? Was the legend true that a vampire had more sensitive hearing than a human?

"Okay."

She watched Blake walk to Wes and pat him on the shoulder. They exchanged a few words, and Wes looked in her direction, lifting his hand in greeting. She nodded to acknowledge him, then looked around the room once more. She couldn't help but catch the furtive stares the men and women in the room gave her, though nobody approached her to confront her about her presence here.

More people entered the room, taking up more of the empty seats, while others continued to stand. Amaury was now coming in. He spotted her and walked toward her. Instinctively, she froze. He let himself fall into the chair next to her.

Nervously, she clasped her hands in her lap.

"So Blake told you about us," he started without preamble.

Her throat was suddenly as dry as the Sahara. "He did."

"Did he explain to you that we won't tolerate anybody spreading our secrets?"

She lifted her chin. "He didn't have to. I got that when he showed me his fangs and his claws."

"Ah, you got a demonstration. Did you like it?"

"What are you doing, Amaury?"

She took a relieved breath at the sound of Blake's voice behind her.

"Just chatting with your girlfriend," he said casually.

"She's not my—"

"I'm not his girlfriend," Lilo ground out.

"—girlfriend," Blake finished.

"Whoa!" Amaury lifted his hands in a show of surrender and got up. "My nose hasn't betrayed me yet. And it sure isn't lying now either." He grinned triumphantly and turned away.

Lilo swiveled in her chair and faced Blake, who now sat down in the chair on her other side. "What did he mean by that?"

Blake ran his hand through his dark hair, an expression of embarrassment on his face. "A vampire's sense of smell is ten times better than that of a dog. Amaury could smell me on you, and you on me. He knows we had sex."

Lilo felt like sinking into the floor. "Oh, crap!"

"Do you really regret it that much?"

There was a touch of pain in his voice that made her meet his gaze. Their eyes locked. Did she regret having slept with him? If she could turn back time, would she make it undone? If she knew everything she knew now, would she still allow him to make love to her and surrender in his arms? Would she be the sensible one and stay away from him, or would she—just like Hannah—fall for a vampire, even though she knew that nothing good could come from it? That one day she, too, might disappear.

"Welcome!"

Wesley's voice coming over the loudspeakers in the room saved her from having to come up with an answer, for both Blake and herself. She tore her gaze away from Blake and looked to the front of the room, where Wesley was standing at a lectern, speaking into a microphone. Behind him the desktop of a computer was being projected on a screen on the wall.

"Let's all settle down. We need to get this started. I have to bring you all up to speed on a lot," Wesley urged. He craned his neck toward the door, where more men streamed in. "Is everybody here?"

She recognized one other person now: Eddie, the man who'd analyzed Hannah's computer was strolling in, a blond guy walking next to him. When they both went to the other side of the room, Lilo noticed the other man's hand resting on Eddie's lower back.

A moment later, she felt Blake's breath near her ear. "You want me to tell you who everybody is?"

She nodded automatically.

"The blond man with Eddie is Thomas, his blood-bonded mate."

"Two guys?"

"They were human once; their turning didn't change their sexual orientation." Then he pointed to the dark-haired man who she'd seen talking to Wesley when they'd entered the room. "That's Samson, the founder of Scanguards."

Lilo perused him. He was tall and handsome. And he oozed authority. So that was what an over two-hundred-year-old vampire looked like.

Blake directed her gaze to a man who looked like a younger edition of Samson. "That's his son, Grayson. A hothead. Thinks he's invincible." He pointed to the young woman sitting next to him. "His older sister, Isabelle. One of them will run the company one day. My money's on Isabelle."

"Okay, settle down," Wesley said, tapping the microphone. "I called this meeting because we have a serious problem on our hands."

Silence fell over the room, and everyone's eyes were on Wesley.

"First of all, before you all die of curiosity, Blake has asked me to make a quick introduction. The human woman sitting next to him is Lilo Schroeder. Why she's here will become evident shortly. Just let me say this: you may speak freely in her presence. Blake has told her who and what we do." He nodded toward Blake, then continued, "Now, let me start with this."

He shifted the mouse and opened a file for all to see on the oversized screen on the wall. It showed a map of San Francisco. Dozens of red dots were spread all over it.

"John, who's been working with the SFPD on this case, will start."

From one of the seats in the front, a tall man with long dark hair rose and marched to the lectern. Wes stepped to the side, making space for him.

"Thanks, Wes," he said. Lilo detected a slight Southern accent. "So, here's the gist: over the last few months the crime rate in San Francisco has spiked. Home invasions and robberies, both commercial and residential, have increased over 200%. That's astronomical. The odd thing, however, is that the spike occurred during daytime, suggesting that the crimes aren't vampire-related. However, Donnelly, our liaison at the SFPD, begged us to look at it. I'm glad he did."

He exchanged a look with Wesley. "At the beginning I couldn't make heads nor tails of it, but then the police caught one suspect in a recent liquor store robbery. He was completely zonked out. We figured he had to be under the control of a vampire to be so out of it."

Lilo shot Blake a questioning look. He leaned in and whispered to her, "Mind control."

But before she could ask more, John continued.

"We were right, in a way. But I'll let Wes explain those details to you." He stepped aside and returned to his seat.

Wesley clicked on something on the screen, and a picture of an herb appeared. "When I examined the suspect of the liquor store robbery, I found traces of Höllenkraut in his blood. What you're seeing on the screen is the herb in question."

"Höllen-what?" one man asked.

"It's German, it means herb from hell."

Lilo leaned closer to Blake, getting just as impatient as some of the assembled vampires. "What does all this have to do with Hannah?"

"Patience," Blake urged.

"I did a little research," Wesley continued. "In one of my old books I found some interesting information. Turns out that Höllenkraut when combined with a few other herbs turns into a quite potent drug that will render the user highly susceptible to suggestion. In other words: mind control. Now this wouldn't be anything new, since any vampire already has this power. However, with this drug, the vampire can control the human without being anywhere near his victim. This is how we think a group of vampires has been executing these crimes: by using humans who don't even know what they're doing as minions. When they come out of their drug-induced state, they have no idea what they've done. Or who made them do it."

Several men cursed.

"There's more," Wes continued. "We have a lead. Or rather two. This is where Miss Schroeder was instrumental." He opened an image file, and suddenly Hannah's face was right there on the screen. "Some of you may know Hannah Bergdorf, one of our Vüber drivers. She went missing several days ago. Both Blake and Miss Schroeder have been looking for her. Thanks to their efforts, we know the following." He opened another image file: Ronny now grinned at them from the wall. "This is Ronny Clifford, Hannah's boyfriend. He's a vampire, one of her Vüber clients. We raided Ronny's home and on his computer we found evidence that he's been researching or working with Höllenkraut, the same substance that renders a human pliable. Considering how rare Höllenkraut is, and how dangerous, we believe that these two cases are related."

He clicked on the play button of a video file. Lilo's eyes widened. It was the same video that she'd shown to Donnelly. She turned to Blake, and he leaned closer.

"Donnelly sent a copy to our IT guys the moment you left the station," Blake explained, anticipating her question.

Surprised to see how attuned he was to her, she just stared at him, but Wesley was already continuing with his explanations.

"Miss Schroeder found this video hidden among Hannah's personal items. It appears that it was taken in secret in Hannah's flat. And for some reason that we're not quite sure of yet, Hannah hid it. The man on the right is Ronny, her boyfriend. The other man we've identified as Steven Norwood. He's in our database. And listen to this." He switched to another application. A man's face appeared on the screen. "Luther, you're on."

"Hey guys," the rugged-looking man on the screen said. He was wearing black riot gear, as if he worked for the military or a bomb squad.

Greetings echoed through the room.

"Steven Norwood was released from the Grass Valley vampire prison eight months ago," Luther continued. "According to his file, he was no trouble. Served his time in peace and quiet."

Was she hearing correctly? There was a vampire prison?

"I've sent his file to Thomas. There's an old address in San Francisco, but I doubt Norwood returned there. I would lend you one of our trackers, but we've got our hands full here right now and can't spare any."

Samson rose and took the microphone from Wes. "No worries, Luther, thanks. Anything else you can tell us about the guy?"

Luther leafed through the file. "Nothing really. He's got ordinary written all over him." He motioned to somebody off camera. "Sorry, guys, gotta go. We've got a situation here."

"Thanks, Luther," Samson replied and turned back to the assembled, while behind him the screen went dark. "Let's talk about how we're gonna find these guys and put a stop to their operation. Tactical teams, get together your best and brightest. I want suggestions presented to me in two hours."

"What about finding Hannah?" Lilo murmured to herself.

She felt Blake's hand on her shoulder. "That's my first priority. I promise you."

26

The moment the assembled Scanguards employees dispersed, Samson made a beeline for him. Blake had expected as much.

"My office, now. Both of you." Though Samson's voice carried no menace, but his tone was firm.

Blake noticed Lilo shiver and immediately gripped her elbow. She shot him an apprehensive look, but allowed him to guide her out of the conference room. He wanted to reassure her that nothing bad would happen to her, but he was within Samson's earshot and knew better than to say anything before he found out what his boss wanted. So he remained silent and instead stroked his thumb along Lilo's arm where he was holding her and hoped she would find comfort in his touch.

Samson entered his office, and Blake followed him with Lilo. When the door fell shut behind them, Samson turned and ran an assessing gaze over Lilo.

"Miss Schroeder, as you may or may not be aware, Blake bringing you here was against our rules."

Blake opened his mouth to explain, but Samson silenced him by lifting his hand.

"I understand why Blake did this. Obviously he cares about you. That being said, I want to make sure that you understand the rules we live by."

Lilo nodded wordlessly.

"We've operated in this city for many decades without exposure. Our secret has been kept by not only our own species, but also by members of yours. The humans who work for us and know our secret are loyal to us. They've sworn an oath to protect our secret. However, there have been circumstances, where we've been forced to accept that not every human can keep a secret. When that happens, we take action."

Blake felt Lilo stiffen next to him and reached for her hand, clasping it. It was icy.

"So you kill them. I understand," she murmured, her voice shaky.

"Kill?" Samson furrowed his brow and shifted his gaze to Blake. "What the hell have you been telling her about us?"

"I'm afraid Lilo only found out about vampires a few hours ago. I've not been able to fully convince her yet that we don't kill people."

"Ahh." Samson pulled in a breath, his nostrils flaring now, his gaze meeting Blake's. "Very well. I see you have your work cut out for yourself." With a smile, he addressed Lilo, "What I want to say is: we don't kill. Not innocents anyway. But if a human can't keep our secrets, we have to wipe his or her memory. It's a painless process, and it will make life easier for all involved. I want you to know that this option is open to you."

"No!" Blake protested, drawing both Samson's and Lilo's stunned looks onto him. "I mean, I'm sure that won't be necessary." He didn't want Lilo's memory erased. It would mean she wouldn't remember him. And he wanted her to remember him. Hell, he wanted her to know everything about him, to trust him.

"You know the rules, Blake. Every human who accidentally learns of our secret is given a choice, should the circumstances warrant it. I think in this case, Miss Schroeder should be given a choice. If she wants her old life back once all this is over and we've found her friend and dealt with the guilty party, you'll have to let her decide."

"Thank you for telling me." Lilo's voice was firm and determined. "I know so much now. I don't know whether I can go back to being ignorant. To not see what's right in front of me. But no matter what I decide eventually, I'm no danger to you or your secrets."

"I hope you're right, Miss Schroeder," Samson said.

"Is there anything else, Samson?" Blake asked.

"Not for now. I'll see you both when we reconvene in two hours." He walked to his desk and sat down.

Blake turned around and ushered Lilo to the door.

"Oh, and Blake," Samson added. "Get your girlfriend a visitor badge so she won't be harassed."

"She's not my g—"

"I'm not—"

"'Course not." Samson silenced them with his sardonic comment. "My mistake."

Blake maneuvered Lilo out of the office and pulled the door shut behind them. "I'm sorry, Lilo. I know it must be embarrassing for you to constantly be reminded of what happened between us."

She sighed. "It's fine. But I guess since your colleagues don't seem to believe that I'm not your girlfriend, maybe we should just save our breath and let them think what they want."

He felt his lips curve upward into a smile. "I don't have a problem with that. They'll come to their own conclusions anyway." Conclusions that, when it came down to it, were probably closer to the truth than his and Lilo's protests that they weren't dating.

"Hey, Blake!"

Blake turned his head in the direction of the voice and saw Yvette, the dark-haired beauty who was blood-bonded to Haven, Wesley's vampire brother, coming toward him. She was dressed in tight-fitting leather pants and a pink top that accentuated her perfect boobs. Haven was one lucky son of a bitch.

"Yvette, what's going on?"

Yvette nodded at Lilo, then addressed him, "Haven wanted me to tell you that the human we have in custody has come out of his drug-addled state. I'm going down there now if you want to interrogate him."

"Absolutely." He motioned to Lilo. "Lilo, this is Yvette, Wesley's sister-in-law. She's one of our best bodyguards. She's been with Scanguards for decades."

Yvette cast him a sideways glance. "You make me sound old." She smiled at Lilo. "Nice to meet you, Lilo. I know your friend. She's driven me a few times. I pray she's all right."

"Thank you." Lilo sighed and looked at him again. "Where's that interrogation taking place?"

Yvette and Blake exchanged a quick look, then Blake shook his head. "I'm sorry, but for security reasons I can't allow you inside the interrogation room. Why don't you wait in my office for me?"

A disappointed look spread on her face. "But I—"

Her protest was cut off by Yvette. "The V lounge might be a better idea. Nina and Delilah are down there right now. I'm sure they'll be happy to entertain Lilo while we take care of this." She arched an eyebrow at him.

"Excellent idea." He smiled. Since both Nina and Delilah were human and blood-bonded to vampires, they were the ideal conversational partners for Lilo. They could answer whatever questions she might have and give her a different perspective. That of a human who loved a vampire. "I'll walk you down there." He nodded at Yvette. "I'll meet you in the interrogation room in five minutes."

~ ~ ~

After introducing her to two women in a lounge that looked like it belonged in a five-star hotel, Blake left.

Delilah, a very pretty dark-haired woman with curves, patted the sofa cushion next to her. "Why don't you take a seat? It's gonna be a while before the men are done with their work."

"Thank you."

Lilo sat down and glanced at the other woman, who sat opposite. So this was Nina, Amaury's mate? The woman who had her man wrapped around her little finger. She had short blond hair and an athletic figure.

"You must be exhausted," Delilah said and waved to one of the waitresses circulating. "What would you like to drink?"

The waitress approached. "Ma'am?"

"A glass of red wine maybe?" Lilo asked hesitantly, glancing at the glasses in front of Delilah and Nina.

"From Samson's private collection," Delilah instructed the waitress.

The woman nodded and left.

"Your husband drinks wine?" For some reason she'd assumed that vampires didn't consume human food or drink.

Delilah chuckled. "No, he doesn't, of course." She winked at Nina. "Though Amaury, I'm sure wouldn't mind an occasional glass."

Nina grinned. "Amaury would like a lot of things." She winked at Lilo. "Most of which he gets anyway. He's really got nothing to complain about. But no, our men don't eat human food or drink anything but blood."

Instinctively, Lilo's gaze drifted to Nina's neck. "How often do they… you know, feed?"

"Daily," Delilah said, next to her.

Lilo swallowed. "Blake mentioned… I mean is it true…?"

"Is what true, Lilo?" Delilah asked.

"You don't have to be coy with us," Nina added. "I'm sure your questions aren't any different from the ones I had when I found out Amaury was a vampire."

"Ahem," Lilo said, shifting on the couch. "I don't want to pry or anything."

Suddenly she felt Delilah's warm hand on hers. "Dear, I've been with Samson for about twenty-three years, and there's nothing I don't know about vampires. Same goes for Nina. We've been there. I bet you we've had the same doubts and worries."

Was that why Blake had brought her here? So these two women could alleviate her worries about vampires? About having been intimate with one?

"What is it like? The bite?" she finally choked out.

Delilah and Nina exchanged soft chuckles.

"Do you want to, or shall I?" Delilah asked Nina.

Nina motioned to her friend, a sparkle in her eyes. "You go ahead. I really don't know how to describe it."

A warm smile playing around her lips, Delilah turned halfway toward her, angling one leg and resting it on the sofa to be more comfortable.

"There's nothing comparable in the human world. To say that it's like an orgasm isn't doing it justice. It's more than that. Not just physical pleasure, but bliss that touches your soul, that fills your heart and warms it. It's a connection on a deep level." She sighed. "Of course, it's more intense when it happens between a blood-bonded couple, like in our cases." She pointed to Nina and herself. "But even a casual bite is something out of this world. And during sex..." She left the sentence unfinished.

Blake had said as much, but hearing it from a woman, a human, who'd experienced the bite, the words had so much more weight.

"And your husband, he bites you every day?"

"Yes, he needs to. See, he can only drink my blood, no other human's. It would make him sick."

"Mmm," Lilo murmured, contemplating her words. "But if he can only drink your blood because you're blood-bonded, how does that work when two vampires are blood-bonded? Can't they drink human blood anymore? How do they survive? By drinking from each other?"

Delilah laughed quietly. "That's a lot of questions, but let me see if I can explain all that without boring you."

Boring her? This was fascinating.

"So, when two vampires are blood-bonded, like Yvette and Haven, or like Eddie and Thomas, they will of course need to drink human blood to survive. The change that happens in a vampire when bonding with a human, doesn't happen when two vampires bond. Don't get me wrong, their bond is just as strong, their devotion just as deep, but they are physically able to drink blood that doesn't come from their mate. Which of course doesn't stop them from biting each other." Delilah winked. "Mostly during sex…"

Fascinated, Lilo listened. But Delilah wasn't quite done yet.

"It's different for a vampire bonded to a human. He's entirely dependent on her for his survival. He needs her. Of course, during my pregnancies, Samson was restraining himself to drinking from me just once every few days. He wanted to make sure I kept my strength."

Nina huffed. "Yeah, 'cause Samson is a gentleman. Amaury? Not so much! He was randier than a sailor while I was pregnant with Damian and Benjamin. He said I had a glow about me. Wouldn't give me a moment's rest."

Though judging by her flushed cheeks, Nina hadn't objected much to her husband's advances.

When Delilah started to laugh, Lilo couldn't help herself and chuckled.

"Well, we all know Amaury," Delilah said and winked at Lilo. "Have you met him yet?"

"I ran into him in the hallway up on the top floor. He wasn't too pleased to see me. He said no humans were allowed up there."

Delilah shrugged. "Yeah, well, that rule's been broken more often than I can count on both of my hands. He'll get over it."

Lilo moved her head from side to side. "You both seem to be so unafraid of them. Aren't you worried that one day they'll turn around and lash out? They're so much stronger than you. So much more powerful."

"They're just like every other man," Nina claimed. "They want the same thing. A woman who will love them and will never look at another man again. Once they're certain of that, they'll grant her every wish in their power." Nina smirked mischievously. "It's really quite empowering."

Lilo's chin dropped. "Are you telling me that you manipulate Amaury?"

Nina laughed. "I wouldn't call it that. All I do is give him what he craves, and luckily that coincides exactly with what I crave, too. And if he showers me with gifts on top of that, who am I to complain? I've got two smart, beautiful sons, and a husband who'd kill to protect me. Who could want more out of life?"

"Don't forget the not aging part," Delilah interjected.

"Oh, yes, that's not too bad either. I was twenty-seven when I met Amaury." She swept her hands down her body. "And look at me now, twenty-two years later. Not too shabby for a cougar."

"Nina, I don't think you're a cougar. You'd have to date a younger man for that. And despite his youthful looks, Amaury has long passed the four-hundred-year mark."

Lilo gasped. "Four hundred?"

Nina winked at her. "And before you wonder. No, a vampire's sex drive doesn't diminish with age."

Lilo felt her cheeks heat.

"Now, now, no need to be shy," Delilah said. "Scanguards is like a small town where everybody knows about everybody else's business, and rumors are circulating fast. I spoke to Rose a while ago. She mentioned she met you at Blake's house. So as you can imagine, everybody is curious about you. Blake isn't the kind of guy to indulge in casual things."

"Not anymore anyway," Nina added. "He sowed his oats when he was in his twenties, but then he got serious."

"For him to have a woman stay with him, well…" Delilah hesitated. "He must care about you."

"I'm just staying with him to make it easier to work together finding Hannah. You must have heard…"

Delilah made a dismissive hand movement. "We've heard. And if anybody can find your friend, it'll be Scanguards."

Nina nodded. "But your staying with Blake has nothing to do with that. He has you stay with him, because he wants you around."

"And you're staying with him," Delilah added, "because you want to be around *him*. Or would you have accepted his invitation if he weren't quite as good looking and charming?"

Lilo opened her mouth to respond, but the lie wouldn't cross her lips. Delilah was right: she'd accepted Blake's invitation because she enjoyed his company and she was attracted to him.

Delilah smiled knowingly. "And now, dear? Do you still feel the same now that you know what he is?"

She met Delilah's green eyes, and contemplated the question. But she wasn't ready to answer it, for Delilah or Nina, or for herself. Too many conflicting emotions warred inside her, and she was too exhausted to analyze them.

27

They'd stayed longer at Scanguards' headquarters than Blake had anticipated, and now, as he drove toward Presidio Heights, it was close to sunrise.

The interrogation of the human in their custody had yielded no results. As Wesley had reported, a human drugged with the Höllenkraut concoction—of which Wes had yet to find the formula—had no memory of his actions. Not even Gabriel's ability to delve into a person's memory, and see what they'd seen, had been of help. Apparently the human brain couldn't form clear memories while drugged, and thus could not replay them for Gabriel.

When the meeting had reconvened, several good ideas had been shared as to how to find Hannah and the vampires behind the dangerous drug. Teams were formed, and when the night had drawn to a close, all the vampires had made their way home, leaving the hybrids and humans in charge of executing those parts of the plans that couldn't be delayed.

Blake turned into his street. Next to him, on the passenger seat, Lilo sat with her eyes closed. He couldn't blame her. It had been a long and stressful night, and she wasn't used to the hours vampires kept. He couldn't deny that he too needed some rest.

When he slowed down as he reached his house, he noticed the trashcans that stood in front of the driveway, blocking access to his garage.

Blake ground out a curse. His neighbor's housekeeper was getting sloppy and had clearly not considered that she was blocking his garage. One trashcan had overturned, maybe from a gust of wind, and the contents had spilled on his driveway.

Lilo jerked up. "What's wrong?"

"Nothing to worry about. I just can't park in the garage right now." He pulled in front of his house, parking the car at the curb. "It'll be fine here."

He could always have Ryder or the boys remove the trash and the cans later and then park the car for him. But with only fifteen to twenty minutes left until sunrise, he wasn't in the mood to spend any time outside.

Blake switched off the engine and got out. He walked around the car and reached the passenger side, before Lilo had a chance to slide out of her seat. Reaching for her, he helped her out and closed the car door behind her.

"Thank you."

She smiled gratefully and didn't seem to mind when he put his hand on the small of her back and guided her up the stairs. When they reached the landing, a motion-sensor switched on the light outside the front door. Blake took a step toward the scanner, the same type that was installed at the garage, but before he could reach it, a sound from across the street made him snap his head to the side.

There was a flash, followed by a loud bang.

His reflexes kicked in instantly. Blake whirled around and lunged for Lilo, covering her with his body as he went down. Simultaneously, a searing pain shot through his shoulder.

He cried out in agony. This kind of pain could be caused by only one thing: a silver bullet.

Another bullet whizzed past his head and hit the door.

Beneath him, Lilo was trembling.

"Are you hurt?"

He heard her mumbled *no* and breathed a sigh of relief. But the danger wasn't over. The shooter was still across the street. If he couldn't get Lilo and himself into the house, they'd be as good as dead. He didn't carry a gun on a regular basis, but inside the house, in the hallway, behind one of the wooden panels, he kept various kinds of weapons for emergencies.

"Stay down," he cautioned Lilo, and turned his head slowly in the direction of the shooter.

And there, across the street, hidden behind a tree, he stood. A vampire, no doubt.

"Coward!" Blake cursed.

The insult did what it was supposed to: for just a split second, the shooter peeked past the tree trunk.

"Ronny," Blake ground out.

Lilo gasped, and he sensed her fear rising.

"Stay down, no matter what," he whispered to her and jumped up, twisting his body so he could lunge for the scanner. His hand hit the smooth surface and he pressed his thumb onto it. But before the scanner could even recognize him, the front door was ripped open, and somebody shot into the dark.

Blake sank to the ground and rolled toward where he'd left Lilo, but she was gone. His heart stopped.

"I've got her," Ryder yelled, reaching for him with one hand while Damian raced past him, a small caliber handgun in his hand. Amaury's son knew where Blake hid his weapons, and reacted quickly. But Blake wasn't going to let the hybrid hurtle headfirst into danger.

"No, Damian, get inside! It's too dangerous," Blake yelled.

"I've got him covered," Benjamin, who now came running, a gun in his hand, assured him. He followed his brother in pursuit of the shooter.

"Let 'em go," Ryder advised, dragging him into the hallway and slamming the door shut behind him.

Inside, Blake didn't even look at his wound, despite the pain it was causing him. Instead, his eyes searched for Lilo.

"Lilo!"

She was just getting up from the floor, most likely having been pulled in by Ryder or one of the twins to get her out of harm's way. Blake tried to move toward her, but he couldn't pull himself up. The silver was already taking its toll on his body, doing severe damage.

"Are you okay?" he asked her.

Instead of an answer, she ran to him, crouching down next to him, her gaze homing in on his shoulder wound, her expression horrified. "Oh my God, he got you!"

"Better me than you."

Lilo met his eyes, and for a moment time stood still. Lilo was safe.

"Let's get this off you." She helped his good arm out of the sleeve of his jacket, then eased it off his injured side. "Oh my God!" She pulled his shirt aside, ripping one button clear off the fabric, before dipping her head past him. "No exit wound."

When she looked at him, he nodded. "I know. The silver bullet is still inside me." That's why vampires preferred small-caliber handguns to anything more powerful: the likelihood of a bullet remaining stuck in the victim's body was higher with a less powerful weapon.

"We've gotta stop the bleeding." She pressed her hand against the wound.

Footsteps on the stairs suddenly alerted him and he lifted his head. Nicholas and Adam came running, their eyes wide.

"Blake?" Nicholas cried out in horror. "You're hurt!"

Blake snapped his head to Ryder. "Get the boys into the safe room. Now!" Then he looked up toward the second floor, a cold hand clamping around his heart. "Where's Sebastian?"

"Ursula picked him up," Ryder said quickly.

Relieved, Blake nodded, when another wave of searing pain wrecked his body. He gritted his teeth. "Ryder, now! Get them to safety."

"Boys, move it!" Ryder ordered and ushered them to a door at the end of the hall.

Knowing his charges would be safe, Blake looked at his shoulder for the first time, trying to assess the damage. "Let me see," he told Lilo, and she removed her hand from the wound.

The entry wound wasn't large, but when he saw little bubbles rising with the blood that gushed from it, he knew it was bad.

"You're bleeding too much." She pressed her hand back on the wound, unafraid. His brave Lilo.

He tried a smile and failed, the pain increasing with every second. "The bullet has to come out." As soon as possible.

"We've gotta get you to the hospital. Right now," she urged.

He shook his head, meeting her concerned look. "By the time we reach a hospital, I'll be dead."

He had maybe ten or fifteen minutes until the silver had eaten away enough of his flesh and bone to poison his blood and send dissolved silver particles straight to his heart.

A choked breath that almost sounded like a sob came from Lilo, and she pressed her lips together.

"Get a butcher knife and a towel from the kitchen."

Lilo stared at him, her mouth gaping open. "Oh my God, you can't be serious. You can't just cut it out like that."

"No, I can't." He swallowed. "But you can." He panted through another wave of pain, trying without success to hold back the scream that was building in his chest. "Uuuughhhh! Get the knife, Lilo, please." He removed her hand from his wound and pressed his own over it. "Please!"

Finally, Lilo jumped up and rushed in the direction of the kitchen, and he let go of his control. Everything before his eyes turned red, and he felt his mouth fill with his fangs as they extended to their full length. His fingers turned into claws, razor-sharp and deadly.

The pain paralyzed him, rendering him unable to move. He could only hope now that Ryder and Lilo knew what to do. Or the silver would eat him alive.

28

Lilo was running on pure adrenaline. Panic gave her wings. If she'd thought that she'd been through the wringer in the last two days, then she'd been wrong. The danger was only just beginning. And now it had reached Blake's doorstep.

She was grateful that he'd told her what silver did to a vampire. His words had sent a chill through her veins: *By the time we reach a hospital, I'll be dead.*

She couldn't let that happen. She owed him too much. He'd pushed her out of the path of the bullet. It was her fault that he was injured.

Lilo pulled a sharp knife from the wooden block on the kitchen counter, then snatched a couple of clean-looking kitchen towels from their hooks and rushed back out into the hallway, just as Ryder was dragging Blake into the living room, Blake's good arm draped over Ryder's shoulder, and Ryder's arm around Blake's waist, supporting his weight. She followed them and watched Ryder deposit Blake on the sofa, where his head slumped back against the cushions.

A gasp escaped her when she saw Blake's face. He was all vampire now: glaring red eyes, extended fangs, and fingers that had turned into claws. To her own surprise, the sight didn't scare her, because she saw something else in his face: pure agony. Her heart bled for him. Nobody should be feeling such pain, not even a vampire.

"I've got the knife," she said.

Ryder turned to her. "Give it to me."

Glad that he was taking charge, she handed it to him and slid next to Blake on the couch. She ripped the already damaged shirt wider, so there was clear access to the wound. It looked larger now than before, evidence that the silver was consuming his flesh.

"Make a deep incision," Blake gritted out.

Ryder nodded in silence and set the knife to the wound. Lilo turned her face away. She couldn't watch this. She gripped Blake's hand, not caring that his fingers were sharp barbs that could slice her into pieces. She squeezed his hand, when Blake whirled his face to look at her, staring at her in grateful surprise.

A scream dislodged from his throat.

"I'm sorry, Blake!" Ryder let out. "But I'm not done."

Lilo held onto Blake's hand while cupping his cheek with the other. He met her eyes then.

"I don't regret it," she confessed, answering the question he'd posed many hours earlier. "I could never regret it."

For a brief moment, the red in his eyes subsided, making space for the golden shimmer she'd seen before.

"Lilo," Blake murmured.

"I can't see the bullet. It's too deep," Ryder interrupted.

Lilo released Blake's hand and leaned over the wound. "There's too much blood." She snatched the towel she'd brought and pressed it against the wound, trying to soak up as much blood as possible, before removing it again. From the corner of her eye she noticed Blake clenching his teeth.

"I'm so sorry."

"I think I can see it," Ryder said. "I'm gonna have to use my fingers." He was already sticking two fingers into the wound.

"No!" Blake protested, jerking away. "Not you! The silver... it'll hurt you."

Lilo understood immediately. Silver wasn't only toxic to a vampire, but also a hybrid. "I'll do it. Move aside."

Ryder didn't protest.

"Hold him immobile," she instructed.

Ryder followed her command and held onto Blake's shoulder and arm with both hands. With an apologetic look at Blake she brought her hand to the open wound. It was all torn skin and damaged muscle, covered in copious amounts of blood, and more spilling from the wound every second. She saw the bone, too, and right there, in Blake's rotator cuff something shone through. The silver bullet.

Choking back the rising nausea at the sight of so much blood, she willed herself to remain calm. She had to do this. One hand she placed at the edge of the wound, pulling it open a little more, while she stuck the index and middle finger of her right hand into Blake's flesh.

He cried out simultaneously, but she forced herself to ignore it. She mustn't be distracted.

She felt for the various different textures: sinew, muscle, blood, now that she had no clear line of sight anymore. It was warm, and the stickiness of the blood as it coated her fingers made her stomach lurch. But she foraged on. There, her fingers had struck something hard. Bone? It had to be. She explored with her fingertips, rubbing along the hardness until she found a bump.

"That's it!" she called out in triumph. "I found the bullet."

"Grab it!" Ryder encouraged her.

Lilo caught Ryder's concerned look, then gazed past him to Blake. His face was distorted from the pain, his mouth open, fangs bared as if ready to attack.

"He can't hold on any longer," the hybrid murmured to her. "Do it!"

She concentrated and curled her middle finger, then pushed her index finger toward it, trying to create human pliers to grip the silver bullet. She yanked at it, her fingers pulling free of the wound. But there was nothing between her fingers, no silver bullet, just more blood and sinew.

Blake howled with pain.

"It slipped," she cried out, sweat beading on her brow, her pulse hammering. Her hands were shaking now. How much time was left? What if she couldn't do it? "Oh God!"

"Again, Lilo!" Blake ground out. "You've gotta scoop it out."

"Scoop?" That was it! "Just a sec." She jumped up and ran to the kitchen, pushing the door open and charging toward the counter. She ripped several drawers open, until she found what she was looking for and raced back into the living room, prize in hand.

Ryder stared at the item in her hand. "A spoon?"

Lilo eagerly nodded. "It'll work. Hold him still."

Ryder pressed a panting Blake back into the cushions, immobilizing his shoulder so Lilo could continue. Swallowing hard, her hand shaking, she dipped the spoon into the wound, guiding it to the spot where she'd felt the bullet. The spoon knocked against something.

"I heard it," Ryder said. "You've got it. Easy now."

She nodded to herself and guided the spoon until it was aligned with the bone, where the silver bullet had embedded itself. "I'm there. Hold him now. This is gonna hurt."

Using the spoon's handle for leverage, she applied weight to it and shoved the round portion of the spoon underneath the bullet. It dislodged, and with it all pressure eased and the spoon ripped from the wound, it catapulted the bullet into the room. It landed on the coffee table, hitting the ornamental Chinese bowl that stood there.

She'd never heard a sweeter sound than the clanging of silver as it settled in the middle of the bowl.

Breathing hard, she looked back at Blake's face. His eyes were closed. Her heart stopped. "Blake, no!"

"He's alive," Ryder assured her, wrapping the dish towel around his wound. "But we can't let him sleep yet."

Before Lilo knew what Ryder was planning, he was already slapping Blake's face. "Wake up, Blake! You can't sleep." He slapped him again, this time harder.

Blake's eyes opened, and his head jerked forward, fangs bared.

"That's it, look at me, Blake! It's me, Ryder." He turned his head to look at her. "Lilo, in the pantry, all the way in the back, there's a fridge. Get me two bottles of the blood that's in there. Quickly."

She didn't question him, didn't ask why there would be blood in bottles, but ran as fast as she could and found the refrigerator just like he'd said. She opened it. Rows and rows of pint bottles filled with red liquid stood there.

Her chin dropped. This was unreal. The bottles were labeled with short codes like *AB-Neg* or *O-Pos*. All the different blood types. She snatched two bottles, not caring about the labels, and raced back into the living room, where Ryder was still restraining Blake.

"Here." She twisted the cap off one bottle and handed it to Ryder.

The young hybrid shook his head. "You'll have to feed him. I need to restrain him. He's close to losing control."

Close to? Judging by the wild look in Blake's eyes, she'd say he'd already lost it. But for whatever reason, she wasn't afraid. Blake wouldn't hurt her. Somehow she knew that.

Lilo slid on the couch next to him and brought the bottle to his lips. His nostrils flared and his head rocked forward. Some of the blood spilled, but she managed to tilt the bottle so the liquid dripped into Blake's open mouth.

He swallowed, and with relief she saw that the blood seemed to calm him. So she brought her hand underneath his chin and continued feeding him, until he'd greedily emptied the bottle. She tossed it on the couch, then twisted the top of the second bottle open.

"There you go, my love," she cooed, and pressed the second bottle to his lips.

Blake didn't seem to register her. He appeared delirious, but he continued drinking, gulping down the red liquid quickly and thoroughly, until the second bottle too was empty.

She exchanged a look with Ryder. "And now?"

Ryder lifted his head in Blake's direction and eased off him slowly. Blake didn't move, instead, his head rested against the cushion and his eyes slowly drifted shut.

"He can only heal during his restorative sleep."

"How long?"

"I don't know. We'll have to let him sleep until he wakes up by himself."

She trembled now. Her eyes fell on the blood that had soaked not only Blake's clothes, but also Ryder's and her own. Everywhere she looked, there was blood.

"Is he gonna make it?" Tears rose to her eyes, and she knew she couldn't hold them back any longer. At least Blake wouldn't have to see her like this.

"He'll make it. Thanks to you." Ryder looked at her, the admiration in his eyes evident. "I'm glad that you're not afraid of us."

Tears were streaming down her cheeks now, but she tried to smile through them. "How can I be afraid of any of you, when I see how you love and protect each other? Like a real family."

Ryder smiled. "We *are* a family." He cast a glance at Blake. "Blake is like an older brother to me and to all the hybrids." He rose. "I'll get him upstairs and put him to bed. You should get cleaned up, too."

But before Ryder could lift Blake from the sofa, they heard the sound of the front door ripping open and then slamming shut again. A second later, identical twins appeared in the living room.

"We lost him. Sorry," one of them said.

"How is he?" the other asked.

"He'll make it. We got the bullet out. Well… actually, Lilo got the bullet out," Ryder said.

The twins looked at her in surprise. "Wow. She's totally like Mom, don't you think, Damian?" one of them said.

His brother jabbed him with his elbow. "Just as courageous. I'm telling you, it's not true what they say about blondes." He grinned, nodding at her. "Our mother is blond, too. And very smart."

"Hey, guys," Ryder interrupted. "Can you give me a hand with Blake? We need to get him upstairs so he can rest."

"Sure," Damian said. "Benjamin can take his legs, I'll take his head. You should follow protocol, notify HQ, and then get the boys out of here."

Ryder nodded.

"Protocol?" Lilo echoed.

While Damian and Benjamin lifted the unconscious Blake and carried him out of the room, Ryder turned to her. "When an attack like this happens, there's a strict protocol we have to follow: we followed the first step, saving the life of the injured vampire. Now we need to put everything else in motion. I need to remove the minors from his house. I'll take them to my parents' house. They'll be safe there. Since it's daytime now, headquarters will send two human guards to watch the house so Blake can recover. And we'll execute a dragnet to capture the assailant."

"It was Ronny," she told him. "Hannah's boyfriend. Blake saw him. He's the one who—"

Ryder interrupted her. "I'm up-to-date on the case. I'll let HQ know. They'll hunt him down. He must have had a car or another mode of transportation nearby, or he wouldn't have risked being out so close to sunrise. I'll find out from Benjamin and Damian where they lost him."

She nodded slowly. "And what should I do?"

He let out a breath. "You've done enough for one night. Why don't you get changed, shower, rest?"

"But Blake, I need to look after him."

"There's nothing you can do right now. He'll sleep a very deep sleep. It'll be hours before he wakes. Take that time to rest. I'm sure once he's awake, there won't be time to rest until we've got that son of a bitch."

She looked down at herself. Yes, she needed to shower and wash off the blood. Blake's blood.

"Are you sure I can't do anything?"

Ryder grinned. "You truly are like Nina." He motioned to the ceiling, where she could now hear footsteps as the twins carried Blake to his bedroom. "You're quite a woman. Blake is a lucky guy."

She opened her mouth, but the automatic protest that she wasn't his girlfriend didn't roll over her lips. Instead, she smiled. "Thank you."

29

After Ryder and the twins had left with the younger boys, silence had descended upon the house. Scanguards headquarters had called shortly afterward and confirmed that two human guards were stationed outside the house, one in front, one in the back, ensuring nobody would be able to surprise them. Ryder had left her a direct number to call should she have any concerns.

She'd taken a shower and changed into comfortable clothes, a loose-fitting T-shirt and sweatpants. She'd also eaten and then tidied up the kitchen, all to kill time. But time had a way of creeping along at a snail's pace when one was waiting for something. In the end she'd started dozing off, and at some point she'd fallen asleep, her body and mind exhausted.

It was still light, when she opened her eyes again.

Lilo shot up from her reclined position on the couch. After cleaning off the blood as best she could, she'd tossed a blanket over the stains. Now she listened to the sounds that had woken her. Above her, a floorboard creaked. Her heart beating like a drum she rose and rushed to the hallway. Everything was quiet there. Nobody had come in.

She walked upstairs. The last time she'd checked on Blake had been three hours ago, and he'd been deep asleep.

At the bedroom door, she paused, then turned the knob gently. If he was still asleep, she didn't want to wake him prematurely. She pushed the door open and stepped into the room, then took two steps so she could peek at the bed. It was empty.

The sound of another floorboard creaking made her whirl around.

Blake stood in the doorway to the ensuite bathroom, only a short towel wrapped around his lower body, his hair and upper body damp. He'd never looked more virile in her eyes.

"You're awake."

Without thinking she walked to him, her eyes zooming in on his shoulder. Where only hours ago a gashing wound had marred his body, almost perfect skin had grown, though she could tell that it hadn't completely healed yet.

She stretched her arm out and ran her hand over his injury. Beneath her touch, he shuddered. "Shouldn't it have healed completely?" She raised her eyes to his face.

His azure-blue eyes pinned her, the smoldering look he gave her making her weak in the knees. When he'd first made love to her, he'd looked like that. And that memory made her insides erupt in flames and liquid pool at the juncture of her thighs.

"It takes longer with bottled blood. It's not as potent."

His voice was strong again. But his words made her curious.

"I thought the bottles contained human blood."

"They did. But when it's bottled it loses some of its potency. Blood coming directly from a human is preferable in a case of severe injury." Blake shrugged. "But as you see, I've recovered. And all thanks to you."

Lilo shook her head. "Why didn't you say something? I could have given you—"

His finger over her lips stopped her. "That's exactly why I didn't. I want your blood, but not as an act of charity. And I didn't want you to feel obligated to give me your blood."

She grabbed his wrist. "But you saved my life. You took a bullet for me!"

He blew out a breath. "The bullet was silver, Lilo. It was meant for me, not for you."

"You can't know that. And when Ronny shot at you, you couldn't know it was silver. Yet you threw yourself on me to shield me. In my book, that's still saving my life." She tipped her chin up in challenge. Did this man have to rile her up like this? Couldn't he just accept the cold hard truth, the fact that he was a hero?

"Woman, do you always have to be so stubborn?"

"I'm not stubborn. I'm—"

"—brave." He smiled at her. "My brave Lilo." He sighed. "I could feel the bullet in my bone. I knew it was lodged in there. I had a one-in-a-million chance of survival. But you did it." He chuckled, shaking his head. "With a spoon."

He snaked one arm around her waist and pulled her to him.

"You gave me strength when I needed it. You said what I was yearning to hear." His eyes started to shimmer golden as he looked at her. "Or did I hallucinate when I heard you say you didn't regret it?"

She ran her hand up his bicep and over his shoulder. "No, you didn't. It's the truth. I don't regret that we had sex."

"That we made love," he corrected softly.

"That we made love," she repeated, feeling heat rise into her cheeks. "I wanted you to know it, because I didn't know if you'd make it, and I would have never forgiven myself if I hadn't told you."

"Ah, my beautiful, brave Lilo. And now? You saw me at my worst. An out-of-control beast. Few have ever seen me like that. It couldn't have been a pretty sight. Yet you're still here. You didn't run away."

"Why would I run away? With you I'm the safest I've ever been in my entire life. And now that I know what the world is really like, and what hides in the dark, I need to know there's somebody who can keep me safe." She smiled. "Besides, I still have to thank you for saving my life."

He rolled his eyes in mock-frustration. "I thought we'd cleared this up. I didn't save your life. You saved mine."

"Fine," she conceded, realizing that she wouldn't win this argument with him. "Then maybe I should get a little thank you from you."

He arched an eyebrow. "What did you have in mind?"

"Promise me first that you'll give me whatever I ask for."

He tilted his head to the side, pondering her request. "Given that I wouldn't be standing here if it weren't for your ingenuity, I can't really refuse you anything. You can have whatever you want. My car? My house?"

She stepped out of his embrace and pointed to his midsection. "I'd like that towel, please."

He looked down at himself. "*This* towel?"

She nodded, suppressing a grin. She'd managed to surprise him. "Yes, *that* towel. And I'd like it right now. You can't possibly deny me such an inexpensive gift."

"No, I can't." He reached for the side where the towel was tucked in and undid it, pulling it away from his body and handing it to her.

She took it and tossed it behind her with barely a glance. "Thank you."

"Already tired of your gift, I see," he commented, pointing to the discarded towel on the floor.

"I've never been very fond of wrappings," she said, and went down on her knees. She reached for his already semi-hard cock and wrapped her hand around it, feeling it grow with every second. "I've always liked what was inside." She looked up at him and reveled in his heated gaze.

"Lilo, I hope you know what you're doing," he warned.

"Don't worry," she murmured. "I believe I'm very good at this."

She brought her face closer and guided his erection to her mouth, licking over the bulbous head with her tongue.

"Fuck, Lilo!"

"Shhh." She blew against his heated flesh. "Let me do this." She lifted her eyes to look at Blake, then wrapped her lips around his tip and slid down on him until she could go no farther.

~ ~ ~

If he didn't know any better, he'd say he'd died from the gunshot wound and gone to heaven, because Lilo on her knees in front of him, his cock in her mouth, was more than he'd hoped for in his wildest dreams. Particularly not this quickly. After having confessed to being a vampire less than twenty-four hours earlier, he'd expected that she would need time to accept him for what he was—and not immediately want to go down on him and worship him with her divine mouth.

But the intense pleasure she was unleashing on him with her soft lips and her wicked tongue was too real to be a figment of his imagination. No, he was truly awake, and Lilo was making love to him with her mouth. Her eyes were closed now and she sighed softly, her breath teasing his engorged flesh, sending a tingling sensation down his shaft and into his balls. They tightened in response.

"Lilo, baby," he groaned and shoved his hands into her hair, not to force himself deeper into her, but to pull back a bit. "Easy, or you're gonna make me come too quickly."

She opened her eyes then and lifted her gaze while she continued taking him into her mouth, then sucking on him as she slowly withdrew.

He'd never seen anything more erotic than the scene that was unfolding in front of him. Her lips were plump and red, wrapping tightly around his hard-on. The warmth and wetness of her mouth felt as if he was diving into paradise. She was all feminine softness as she licked him with such devotion.

"So beautiful," he murmured.

As if to thank him for the compliment, she brought one hand to his balls and cradled them.

A spear of white-hot heat charged through him, nearly robbing him of any control he still had—which wasn't much to start with—and forced a moan over his lips. If she continued like this, he'd spill in her mouth in thirty seconds flat. And he wasn't going to let that happen.

But he couldn't resist the urge to thrust his hips on her next descent, asking for more friction. Lilo wrapped her hand more tightly around his root while she caressed his balls with the other and licked her tongue along the underside of his cock, teasing the sensitive flesh.

"Fuck!"

He wrenched himself free of her and pulled her up to stand.

"Strip. Now! And get on the bed!"

"But I wasn't done," she said coquettishly.

"Oh, no, you were done," he insisted. No way could he have taken another second of her sensual torture. "Now strip!" Because if he had to do it, he'd shred her clothes to rags.

Smiling, Lilo pulled her T-shirt over her head and tossed it to the floor. She wore no bra, and automatically, he reached for her breasts, cupping the perfect globes, loving the weight in his palms. But she stepped back and walked toward the bed, turning her back to him, stopping a foot away from it. He watched her as she hooked her thumbs into the waistband of her jogging pants and pushed them down her legs, letting them pool at her bare feet, before she stepped out of them completely.

She wore a skimpy lace thong today, hiding nothing from his hungry view. Like a tiger, he stalked toward her. And as if she knew what he wanted, she slid onto the bed on her hands and knees, her enticing ass pointed at him. His mouth went dry, and he lost the ability to speak. He couldn't even tell her how sexy she looked, because his brain wasn't working anymore. All blood had rushed to his cock, bringing him to bursting point.

He stepped behind her, reached for her thong and wordlessly ripped it from her. She didn't even flinch, showed no sign that she was objecting to his rough treatment. Even when he gripped her hips with both hands and brought one knee to rest on the mattress while remaining standing behind her, she didn't try to get away. She was offering herself to him despite everything she'd seen: his sharp fangs, his glaring eyes, and his deadly claws.

"Don't make me wait," she murmured now, looking over her shoulder.

The way she gazed at him, with passion and desire in her eyes, nearly undid him. He thrust forward and plunged into her moist heat, seating himself in her pussy. She was everything he remembered and more. And this time everything was different. This time he knew he didn't have to hide his desires, didn't need to hold back, because Lilo understood him now.

Savoring every second, he withdrew in slow motion, pulling himself entirely from her sheath. He took a breath to collect his strength, before he drove back into her, this time gentler, trying to take his time. He didn't want this to end too quickly. Because being inside of Lilo, feeling her interior muscles clamp around him as if she didn't want to let him go, chased away the horror he'd been through earlier when the silver had started eating him alive.

"I need you, Lilo."

Never before had he needed anybody like he needed her. That he gave her power over him by admitting this, he didn't care.

He slowed his thrusts and moved back and forth with more tenderness now. He let go of one hip and ran his hand along her shapely ass, caressing her, reveling in the softness of her skin. Her blond locks fell over her back and shoulders, whipping back and forth, side to side, with every thrust he delivered.

But taking her like this wasn't enough anymore. He needed a deeper connection with her, to look into her eyes when they both came. To know that she saw him, the vampire.

Blake eased himself from her tight channel and turned her onto her back. She gazed up at him with passion-clouded eyes. Her chest was heaving, her heart hammering so loud his vampire senses had no trouble picking up the sound. A thin sheen of perspiration covered her entire body, making her even more beautiful. A long lock curled around her hard nipple as if caressing it. He reached for it and freed the little rosebud, letting his finger slide over it.

A strangled moan broke from her throat, and she arched off the mattress. "Please," she begged, putting her hands on his hips and pulling him down to her, until he was hovering over her center. She reached for his cock then and stroked the hard length.

He clenched his jaw. "Lilo, oh God, you're killing me."

She smiled up at him, mischief in her eyes now. "I didn't realize a vampire would be so sensitive."

He nudged his cockhead at her moist entrance. "Everything we feel is amplified." He plunged back into her, watching with satisfaction how all the air rushed from her lungs, sending moans bouncing off the bedroom walls.

He kept his tempo slow, wanting to prolong their lovemaking, because this time he wanted to show Lilo how perfect things could be between them. Their bodies moved in sync as if they'd done this a hundred times, perfectly attuned to each other. Lilo's pelvis tilted toward him whenever he dove deeper, inviting him into her delicious pussy. Her ankles crossed over his butt to hold him close to her, and he loved the feeling of her heels digging into him, just like her fingernails dug into his back.

"I want you to see me," he said, locking eyes with her.

There was understanding in them. She knew what he wanted to do.

"Yes, Blake, my love."

The word sank deep into him and filled him with an unknown sense of pride. He wanted to howl, instead he opened his mouth and peeled his lips back from his gums, while he willed his fangs to lengthen until they were fully extended.

She stared at them, while he continued to move in and out of her, slow and steady, to show her that he was in control.

Lilo lifted her hand, her face a mask of fascination.

When he realized what she was about to do, he pulled his head back a few inches. "Are you sure you want to touch them?"

"Yes, please." She brought her hand closer, and he ceased his movements.

"You should know something first."

She cast him a curious look.

"Fangs are a vampire's most erogenous zone. By touching me there, you're going to make me come very quickly."

She smiled. "Then we'll just have to have seconds later."

"I like the way you think."

Lilo moved her finger closer, and he remained entirely motionless. The pad of her finger brushed his lower lip, before she ran it over his teeth, sliding back until she reached his fang. At the contact, a jolt went through him, and he thrust his cock deep into her, moaning out loud.

Her finger slipped off his fang, but got caught at his tip. He felt it pierce her skin.

"Oh!" she let out on a stunned exhale.

The scent of blood rose into his nostrils, and made his entire body stiffen. "Fuck, Lilo!" He knew it had been a bad idea to let her touch him there. Because now he couldn't resist anymore. His tongue lapped out and licked the drop of blood off the pad of her finger, closing the tiny incision instantly.

As the blood moved past his taste buds on the back of his tongue and then down his throat, he growled. Automatically, his hips began to move in a tempo he had no control over. Hard and fast, he began to fuck her, to drive his relentless cock in and out of her, while he tried to hold on to the last vestiges of his control.

Beneath him, Lilo moaned despite the rough treatment he was dealing her. She slid her hand onto his nape and pulled him to her, pressing her lips to his, even though his fangs were fully extended. Was she not afraid that he'd hurt her?

He tried to pull back, but already, she'd dipped her tongue between his lips and was running it along his teeth. When the smooth surface of her warm tongue connected with one of his fangs, he gave himself over to the pleasure Lilo was granting him and didn't fight it any longer.

His balls tightened, and hot semen shot through the length of his cock, exploding from the tip. But it didn't slow his thrusts. He continued to plunge into her until, finally, he felt her shudder beneath him, her interior muscles gripping him like a tight fist and squeezing him.

He retracted his fangs and took over the kiss, pouring his soul into it, until they were both breathless.

30

Blake rolled onto his back and immediately pulled Lilo halfway onto his body, loving the feeling of her weight on him, one leg draped over his groin, one hand on his chest, while her head rested on his shoulder. For a few moments, all he could do was catch his breath. Lilo, too, was breathing hard.

He pressed a kiss on the top of her head. "I can't even tell you what it means to me to have you in my bed."

She lifted her head and looked at him.

"To know you've accepted me for what I am." He locked eyes with her. "To feel you lick my fangs. I never dared hope for so much."

Lilo gently ran her finger over his lips. "I've never seen anything more erotic than when you showed me your fangs and let me touch them."

His heart thundered at the revelation. "You weren't afraid."

"You said you wouldn't hurt me."

"You trust me despite everything that happened." He could hardly believe it. But he saw it in her eyes. Lilo had faith in him.

He took hold of her finger and kissed it. "I'm sorry about pricking you with my fang."

"It wasn't your fault." Lilo looked away. "Did you like it?"

"Your blood?"

She nodded.

"How could I not? Lilo, you have no idea what it's like. My sense of smell is so hypersensitive that even now I can smell your blood. And you know what that does to me?"

She lifted her eyes back to meet his gaze. "What does it do?"

He took her hand and guided it to his groin, where he placed it over his hardening cock. "That's what it does."

Her chin dropped. "How can you already be hard again?"

He chuckled. "Because of you. That tiny drop of blood that I licked off your finger is making me want more. That's why the vampire inside me is preparing for it, for you. The vampire inside me wants to seduce you with sex until you allow him to bite you."

He knew he shouldn't tell her this, but he was done hiding things from her. If he had any chance of winning her for good, he had to be honest about every aspect of himself. Winning her for good? The thought suddenly struck him. Did he truly want her in his life? When had he made that decision?

When she didn't respond, he slid his hand under her chin and looked deep into her eyes. "I would never force you. I want you to know that. But you should know that every time we make love, my desire to drink your blood will grow."

Understanding shone back in her eyes. "Is that why you think that Hannah let Ronny bite her?"

He stroked his hand over her head and drew her against his chest. "You said they'd been dating for at least six months. No vampire, no matter how civilized and tame, will stay with a woman for that length of time without biting her. With or without her permission. Though I doubt Hannah would have denied him. She knew what a vampire's bite entailed, before she ever met Ronny."

"Knew, how?"

"Because I bit her."

Lilo shot up to a sitting position. "What?" Her eyes were wide with shock. "You and Hannah? You were lovers?"

At her appalled look, he couldn't help but laugh out loud. "Hannah and I?" He sat up and pulled Lilo to him, but she pushed him back. "Hannah and I were never lovers. We were never attracted to each other. Not for a single second."

She frowned, obviously not believing him. "Then why?"

"You wouldn't by any chance be jealous?"

"Don't be ridiculous!" she shot back.

But he knew he'd hit a nerve, and that fact made his heart beat out of control. Lilo had a fierce streak of possessiveness in her that he hadn't expected. But he had no time to revel in it, because first he needed to calm her down and assure her that the bite had had nothing to do with sex.

"Hannah offered me her blood to save my life."

~ ~ ~

Still skeptical, she searched his eyes. Was he telling the truth? And why should it matter that Blake had bitten her best friend? It was none of her business.

Oh please, just admit that you can't stand the fact that he bit Hannah, but not you, the voice in her head said.

"I had an accident." Blake's words pierced her thoughts.

Slowly she nodded. "What happened?"

He reached for her then and pulled her onto his lap, so she was straddling him, before she could protest. Well, maybe she hadn't wanted to protest because she liked the fact that he sought a physical connection to her.

Blake caressed her back gently. "Baby, there was never anything between me and Hannah, though she did save my life, just like you saved mine last night. And while I was very grateful to Hannah, I never touched her the way I can't stop touching you." He brushed his lips over hers in a feather-light kiss.

Then he leaned back against the headboard.

"I was in pursuit of a suspect one night close to sunrise. The road was wet, and I was driving too fast. There was no time to call for backup. I knew I had to catch him before he was gone for good. It was a winding road in a wooded area. I lost him behind a bend in the road. Or so I'd thought, until I realized he'd managed to pull onto a dirt path to hide. When I saw the headlights in my rearview mirror, I knew he'd outsmarted me."

Her heart beating rapidly, she asked, "What did he do?"

"He shot at me. The rear window shattered, but my seat and backrest were steel-plated. He couldn't know that. But he realized very quickly that he couldn't eliminate me by staying behind me, so he pulled to my side. His truck was bigger and heavier than my BMW. He rammed me. I did everything I could to keep control of the car, but behind the next bend there were road works. The truck managed to get past it. But my car flipped over and rolled down the hill, overturning several times."

She gasped. "Oh my God!"

"I would have been okay even during daylight while I waited for help, because the windows in my car had a special UV-impenetrable coating. Something Thomas, one of our geniuses, invented. But the rear window was shattered. And at the angle the car landed, the rising sun would have fried me. I was at nature's mercy."

Blake ran a hand through his hair, then placed it on her back, and continued to caress her.

"Why didn't you get out of the car and take shelter somewhere?"

"I couldn't move my legs. The front of the car had been crushed and the engine was practically sitting on my lap. I was bleeding. I tried to get free, but I wasn't strong enough. My injuries were draining me of my strength, and while I ordinarily would have been able to push the collapsed engine parts off me and wedge free, in my injured state, I was powerless."

She felt tears brim in her eyes.

"Had Hannah not been out walking her dog, I wouldn't be here today. Frankenfurter found my car and alerted Hannah. When she found me, she tried to call 9-1-1, but she couldn't get reception. My phone had the same problem. We couldn't call anybody, and the sun was about to rise. I had no choice but to tell her the truth. I was as good as dead anyway."

"Don't say that!"

"It's the truth. I had no way of knowing how Hannah would react." He shook his head. And he'd been too weak to exercise any kind of mind control on Hannah to make her help him. "But all she said was *How can I help?* Imagine my surprise. She wasn't afraid. In fact, she seemed excited."

Lilo had to chuckle involuntarily. "That's Hannah. She's game for any adventure. Always has been. She needs that excitement in her life. That constant rush of adrenaline."

Blake smiled back at her. "That was my luck. When I told her that I needed human blood to heal myself so I could gain enough strength to free my legs and escape from the car, she didn't hesitate. I took only as much as I needed. Human blood directly from a living human's vein is much more powerful than any bottled blood. But of course, I had no time to warn Hannah about the side effects. The sexual arousal. The fact that my bite was erotic, even though sex was the last thing on my mind." He sighed. "With her blood, I was able to garner enough strength to free myself. But the sun was already rising, so Hannah took a blanket she found in my trunk and we were able to make it to an old shed she'd seen on her walk with Frankenfurter. We took shelter there."

"And Hannah, how did she take the bite?"

"She was stunned, as was to be expected. And hooked, but that was something I didn't realize for a while."

"Hooked? You mean she fell in love with you?"

Blake stroked his knuckles over her cheek, a gesture that comforted her. "No. She was hooked on the bite. On the feeling it gave her. We talked while we were waiting for nightfall. I told her about Scanguards, about what I do. Who I am. And I told her I'd give her anything she wanted for saving my life."

"What did she want?"

"Very little. She really is too good for this world. All she wanted was a job. See, she'd been fired the previous day. That's why she'd been out all the way in the woods with Frankenfurter. To think about what she wanted to do with her life. It was fate that she was there."

"So you gave her a job."

Blake nodded. "I could have arranged pretty much any job she wanted in this town. Scanguards has lots of connections. But she didn't want to work for any human company. She wanted to work for vampires. I don't think Ronny was her first vampire boyfriend. I think she dated several of the vampires she met as part of her job. I suspect that she was always chasing that high that she felt when I bit her."

He combed his fingers through her hair. "That's why I feel responsible for her and will do anything to save her. Not only because she saved my life, but because I'm the one who thrust her into the world of vampires. Everything that happened to her happened because I introduced her to this life instead of wiping her memory of the accident and how she saved me."

"Why didn't you wipe her memory?"

"She begged me not to. She wanted to remember everything." Blake caressed her face gently, and warmth spread inside her. "And you? Do you want to remember, now that you know what danger you could be in just by knowing?"

The decision was an easy one. "I want to remember everything. Every little detail." She shifted on his lap, lifting herself onto her knees and readjusting her core to align with his cock. "I want to make more memories. Will you help me with that?"

He brushed his lips to hers, smiling. "I thought you'd never ask."

31

Lilo lowered herself onto his cock and took him inside her. He didn't think he would ever get enough of that. Like a cocoon, her warmth and wetness engulfed him, instantly making everything else disappear in the background.

Nibbling on her upper lip, Blake thrust his hips up, seating himself even deeper in her. She gasped in delight and threw her head back, thus exposing her vulnerable throat. Temptation charged through him. But he wouldn't act on it. Lilo hadn't made the decision yet whether to grant him the pleasure of biting her. And he wouldn't rush her into it, because if he did, she would only resent him for it.

Instead, he lowered his face to her breasts and captured one hard nipple in his mouth, sucking on it, making Lilo shiver under his touch. Yes, that was how he would help her decide: by showering her with passion and pleasure, with tenderness and care. And with love. He froze. Love? Was the feeling that was controlling his body and mind, love? Could it be? Could it even happen after so short a time? How would he know for sure?

Her voice made him snap his attention back to her.

"Oh, yes, Blake, please, just like that," she said, riding him faster now.

He helped her by gripping her hips and lifting her up whenever she rose onto her knees, then drawing her down when she sank back onto him. Despite the plentiful lubrication from his semen and her juices, the friction was increasing, and he felt his next orgasm approach.

He continued sucking her breasts, alternating between her nipples, while he plunged his cock deep into her.

"Yeah, ride me hard," he mumbled against her firm flesh.

He lifted his head to look at her face, a face that glistened with passion. Their gazes met, melting into each other.

Lilo suddenly lifted her hand and brushed her hair away from one side of her neck, tilting her head to the side. He stared at the delicate skin and could see the vein beneath its surface pulse in the rhythm of their lovemaking. How many more temptations would he have to resist?

Lilo bent closer, then let one hand trail down the exposed side of her neck, as if to show him the way.

He groaned. "Damn it, Lilo. This is hard enough."

She didn't break eye contact. "I know. I can feel it." As if to emphasize her statement, she drove down fast, practically impaling herself on his rock-hard cock.

He moved his head back, touching the headboard. "If you don't stop teasing me—"

She cut him off by crushing her mouth to his. Her tongue licked the seam of his lips, and he parted them, unable to resist her. When she licked along his teeth to entice his fangs to descend, he knew he'd lost.

A ringing sound drifted to his ears. Was he already delirious from the knowledge that in a few seconds, he'd be piercing Lilo's skin and driving his fangs into her? Was he that far gone already?

The ringing didn't stop. Finally, he realized what it was: his cell phone. It lay on his nightstand. And the ringtone was one he couldn't ignore.

He ripped his mouth from Lilo's. "Sorry, Lilo, but I need to get this."

A disappointed mewl came over her lips, but she stopped moving up and down on him. He reached for the phone, but before he answered it, he said, "Trust me, I'm more disappointed by this interruption than you."

Her eyes sparkled at his words, and he squeezed her hip in reassurance while he connected the call.

"John?"

"Glad to hear you're awake," his colleague answered. "Are you fully recovered?"

Despite the fact that his shoulder still felt a little sore, he answered, "I'm a hundred percent."

"Good, because we have a solid lead."

Lilo who was leaning closer to hear what John was saying, sucked in a breath. "Oh my God!"

"Let me put you on speaker. I'm here with Lilo." He pressed the speaker button.

"Hi, Lilo. So, here's what we've got: we found Hannah's dog at an animal shelter. And listen to this: who do you think dropped off the dog there the night of Hannah's disappearance?"

"Who?" Lilo asked.

"Ronny."

"Why would he—"

Blake cut her off. "Are you sure it was him?"

"Positive. The clerk on duty that night recognized him from the photo we showed him."

"Did he also see how he left? On foot, by car? Was anybody waiting for him outside?"

"No," John said. "But guess what: there's a gas station kitty corner from the animal shelter. And they have surveillance cameras. One of them caught Ronny getting into an old pick-up truck."

"A pick-up? I thought the car we were looking for was a Toyota Corolla."

"Correct, but he wasn't driving that car."

"Please tell me the camera picked up the license plate."

"It did. We already traced it. Looks like it's registered to an address in Napa. We looked it up on Google Maps. Pretty remote area, deep in the woods. Ideal for hiding an illegal operation."

"Let's get a team together, now," Blake ordered.

"Already done. We're just waiting for you."

He checked the digital clock on his nightstand. Not only did it show the current time, it was also programmed to count down to sunset and sunrise. "Sunset is in an hour. I'll be at HQ before that."

"Good. We'll be waiting."

Blake disconnected the call and looked at Lilo. "I wish I didn't have to cut this short, but—"

She put a finger over his lips. "You don't have to explain anything. We've gotta go. Let's get dressed."

"We?" He shook his head. "Oh no, you're not coming with me this time."

"But—"

"No but! We don't know what's waiting for us there. You must be crazy if you think I'd let you put yourself in harm's way."

She braced her hands on her hips, scoffing. "You're calling me crazy?"

"Only in the best possible way."

"There is no fucking best possible way."

He gripped her hips. "While it does turn me on when you swear like that, I'm afraid you're not going to win this argument. You're staying put. And to make sure you do, I'm going to ask my family to keep you company."

"You can't do that!"

"I can and I will!" Furious that she wasn't obeying, he thrust his hips upward, ramming his cock deep into her.

Her eyelids fluttered and he could hear her pulse race. Well, maybe he'd secure her submission by other means. He wasn't above a little manipulation. And nobody would get hurt by it.

Sliding his hand between their bodies, he found her clit well lubricated by their combined juices and rubbed his finger over it.

"That's not fair," she ground out and dropped her head back.

"Life isn't fair. Now be a good girl and come for your big bad vampire."

While he plunged in and out of her, he steadily rubbed his finger over her clit, increasing the pressure and tempo with each second, until he finally felt Lilo stiffen in his arms. A second later, a shudder wrecked her body and she collapsed against him, while her interior muscles squeezed his erection. But he didn't allow himself to come. Instead he lifted Lilo off his lap and laid her on the bed.

He pressed a kiss to her navel. "That's a good girl."

"You're a bad vampire," she murmured, but there was no heat behind her accusation. He'd managed to wear her out, at least long enough so he could get ready to leave.

He rose and smiled down at her. "Exactly how you like it, baby."

32

Blake had left his Aston Martin in Scanguards' parking garage and was riding in one of the blackout vans with Samson and John. Amaury and Wesley were following with Oliver in a second van, while Haven and Yvette followed in their car. It was unusual for Samson to take part in a mission these days, but given the serious implications of a drug that could control humans, he'd decided to get intimately involved in all aspects of the case. He'd been briefed on every detail and now knew as much about the case as Wesley and Blake.

It was busy on the bridge as they crossed the bay, and while John concentrated on the rush hour traffic, Samson turned to Blake. He'd insisted on both of them sitting in the back.

"How's Miss Schroeder holding up?"

"I think you might want to start calling her Lilo."

Samson raised an eyebrow. "So I wasn't wrong then."

"She saw me at my worst when I got shot. I couldn't control the beast inside me. She didn't flinch. Didn't run." Blake smiled at the recollection of how she'd tended to his injury, even though he'd been behaving like a wild animal. "She's brave." And that was the thing he admired most about her.

Samson chuckled. "Reminds me of somebody I know." He paused. "Actually, reminds me of a few women I know. Very special women."

"Me, too."

"You trust her?"

He didn't even have to think about his answer. "With my life. Did Ryder tell you how she got the silver bullet out?"

Samson smiled. "Quite ingenious. I'm glad you're alright." Then he turned serious. "A few things about this case don't make sense for me yet."

"Just a few?" In Blake's mind, there were a lot of things that didn't make sense.

"There's something about this Ronny that doesn't ring true. We believe him to be behind the disappearance of his girlfriend and the manufacture and distribution of the drug. But what's not consistent with that picture is this: why go through the trouble of dropping Hannah's terrier off at an animal shelter?"

"I've been wondering about that, too." Blake shrugged. "Maybe he's an animal lover."

"It's possible. I just don't see him being the caring type. Especially considering he shot you—which by the way is another thing that doesn't make sense. Why attack you?"

Involuntarily Blake rubbed his shoulder where the bullet had entered. "I was wondering the same thing. First I thought maybe he was after Lilo, but considering the bullet was silver, I believe it was meant for me. Maybe he followed us after we left Hannah's flat. Maybe he was watching it?"

"To what end? His associate, Norwood, had already been there earlier."

"True, but he left empty-handed. Well, he got Lilo's cell phone. But from what I could tell, he didn't find what he was looking for. Why else would he ask Lilo where *it* was? I can only assume that he wanted the USB stick. Maybe to cover his tracks."

"That would mean he knew it existed. How would he have found out?" Samson rubbed his nape.

"Assuming that Ronny didn't know about the camera in Hannah's flat, the only person who could have told Norwood or Ronny about it is Hannah."

Which could actually be good news. Samson seemed to think so, too.

"They didn't kill her. Maybe they have no intention of killing her," his boss said.

"You think they're using her? Like they use the other humans for their crimes?" The thought sent a shudder down his spine, and chilled him to the bone. "That means they're using the drug on her."

"To make her compliant, yes, it's possible, though they could do that with mind control, too. No need to waste the drug on her," Samson said.

Blake nodded and fell silent again. He hoped that in the woods in Napa they'd find not only Ronny, but also Hannah. Ronny hadn't returned to his house in the Excelsior since he, Wes, and Lilo had searched it, so he had to be holed up somewhere else. And what better place to keep a kidnapping victim than in a remote cabin where nobody would hear Hannah's screams for help?

"How much longer, John?" Blake asked.

"According to my GPS, we're almost there."

Blake glanced out the window. Dense vegetation lined the narrow road on both sides. "Where are we?"

"On the border between Napa county and Sonoma county. It's only thinly populated. Lots of off-the-grid people out here from what I've heard," John informed him. "Probably why Ronny chose this area."

Samson nodded. "Twenty, thirty years ago, there were a lot of marijuana growers up here. The feds conducted a ton of raids here. But they weren't always very successful. The growers chose pretty secluded spots. That was before they legalized cannabis, of course. Now there's no need for those secret farms anymore. It made space for other illegal operations to move in."

Blake grunted. "Well, let's evict the bastard."

~ ~ ~

The GPS only got them as far as a dirt road that culminated in a dead end a hundred yards off the paved road they'd been on. There was no sign of a house or any kind of habitable structure, though according to the latest map, this was supposed to be a legitimate address. Not that any mailman would ever find it: there was no number posted anywhere, and no mailbox either.

Blake got out of the car and looked around. His colleagues joined him until all eight were assembled. Maybe this many trained bodyguards was overkill, but without knowing how many accomplices Ronny had apart from the one they'd identified as Norwood, Samson had insisted on the best and toughest men (and women) in his employ. It was a shame that Zane was still in New Orleans. Gabriel was running HQ in Samson's absence, while Quinn had agreed to look after Lilo. He and Rose had arrived at Blake's house just as Blake had left. Call him overly cautious, but he wasn't going to take any chances when it came to Lilo's safety.

"Fan out," Samson ordered. "If you see a structure, notify the team by text. Everybody's cell phone set to silent. Now."

Blake checked his phone, then his weapons. A small-caliber handgun was holstered on his hip, a silver knife hidden in his boot, and a stake tucked away in the inside pocket of his jacket, though he hoped he didn't have to use it. Nevertheless, he wouldn't mind inflicting a little pain with his silver knife, to explain how it felt in a language that Ronny understood.

All his senses on alert, Blake stalked into the darkness, aware of his colleagues around him, though everybody was careful where they stepped, trying to remain as quiet as possible.

About a mile away from the main road, Blake saw a faint light. He carefully approached, his eyes scanning the ground for possible booby-traps that might alert Ronny. About a hundred yards away from the structure, which looked like an old, run-down cabin, he stopped and texted his position to his colleagues.

His superior night vision picked them up a few moments later as they circled the building and closed in. Blake lifted his hand to tell them to remain where they were, then walked closer to the spot where a sliver of light was coming from. It was a window. And though the curtains had been drawn, somebody had been sloppy, leaving an inch uncovered. Blake moved his head closer to the glass and peered inside.

A living room. Empty.

Blake shifted his angle, but all he could see was a door, but not where it led to or whether anybody was there. They'd just have to take their chances. Suddenly a sound came from inside. Blake's heart stopped, and his mind tried to analyze what he'd heard: cutlery clanging against metal. Either somebody was eating, which meant it wasn't Ronny, or somebody was trying to give a signal.

He turned around and made hand signs to alert his colleagues that at least one person was inside the cabin. He waved to Wes, and the witch joined him. They'd already discussed earlier what to do. This time, Wes didn't speak the spell to open the door—since Ronny, if he was inside, might hear them out here in the wilderness where there was no ambient noise. Instead, Wes had brought a potion that opened any lock without making a sound. He now poured it over the doorknob, put the empty bottle back into his small backpack, and stepped back as if to say, *It's all yours.*

Blake motioned to his colleagues to cover the windows in case Ronny made a run for it, then nodded at John, who was now giving him cover.

Blake drew his gun, and without further ado, he kicked the door open and stormed in.

There was a sound coming from one of the rooms, and Blake headed for it, hearing his friend rush into the house behind him. He kicked the door to the room open and aimed his gun at the person inside the large kitchen.

"Shit!"

"Ronny!"

The jerk dropped the utensils he was working with and lunged for the door that led into the next room.

"Don't make me shoot you," Blake warned calmly, knowing his colleagues were cutting Ronny's escape route off. "Silver hurts like a bitch."

But Ronny didn't stop—and ran right into Amaury who grabbed him and slammed him against the nearest wall, holding him there, suspended.

"Let me go! Damn it!" Ronny yelled, struggling, but Amaury was stronger.

"You want first dibs, Blake?" his linebacker-sized friend offered.

"With pleasure," he grunted and swung his fist into Ronny's face, slamming his head so hard into the wall that the lath-n-plaster cracked. "That's for the silver bullet you left in my shoulder." He swung again and this time delivered an uppercut to Ronny's chin. "And this is for Hannah!"

Blood ran from Ronny's nose, and Blake's fangs lengthened automatically. His fingers turned into claws, and he lifted his hand, ready for another punch. But his claws didn't connect with Ronny's face. Instead, somebody was holding him back.

Blake whipped his head to the side.

"That's enough. We need him alive," Samson said, before releasing his wrist.

Blake sucked in a breath and stepped back. Then he looked at the others who'd entered the kitchen. "Have you found Hannah?"

They shook their heads.

"Not a trace," Haven said.

Blake turned back to Ronny, narrowing his eyes. "Where is she?"

"I don't know!"

"The fuck you don't!" Blake shot back. "I'm asking again: where is Hannah? Where are you keeping her?"

"I don't have her," Ronny wailed. "They've got her. I don't know where she is."

"You sack of shit! Liar!"

"I'm not lying. Please, let me go. If they know that you found me, they'll kill her."

"Who's they?"

He motioned to the large table in the kitchen, where he'd been working with several bowls and herbs. "The vampires behind all this."

Blake scoffed. "Are you trying to tell me you're just a pawn? How stupid do you think I am?"

"It's the truth! They're using her to make me do what they want. But if they find out that I'm no use to them anymore, they'll have no reason to keep her alive."

Blake moved closer, flashing his fangs. "You'd better be telling the truth." He turned to Samson. "We'll take him to HQ to interrogate him."

"No!" Ronny protested. "I have to finish this batch. If it's not done when they need it—"

"Let's go, buddy," Amaury interrupted and hoisted him out of the room.

"I'm gonna stay," Wes announced all of a sudden. "Hav, can you leave me your car?"

"What are you gonna do?" Blake asked.

Wes pointed to the table. "I'm gonna check on what he's been doing. It might help me understand how the drug works."

"You're gonna be okay on your own?" Haven asked, concern etched in his face. "Want me to stay with you?"

"I can stay, too," Yvette offered.

Wes shook his head. "It's gonna bore you to death. So, no. Just go home. I'll be fine."

"If you say so," Haven conceded.

"No worries." He motioned to his backpack. "I've got all the protection with me that I need. I'll lock up when I'm done."

Oliver raised an eyebrow. "Lock up? I'd say, burn the place down."

"Not yet," Wes replied. "We might still need some of this later. Besides, if Ronny told us the truth, then we'd better keep things the way they are until we've got Hannah. I'll put a locking spell on the house when I leave."

"Sounds good," Samson agreed, then he said to the others, "Let's move it."

Blake nodded at Wes, then followed Samson and the others outside. He could only hope that Ronny had told them the truth, and that Hannah was still alive, and would remain alive as long as her captors believed that Ronny was complying with their demands. But so far he didn't believe Ronny. He needed proof.

33

Wesley waited until his colleagues had left and silence had descended on the house. A quick glance told him that it would be a little while before he left this place. There was a lot to investigate. But just in case Ronny's associates were to show up unannounced, he decided to set up protective wards that would alert him to any intruder. Once the magic crystals were in place—one outside the door, and one outside each window—he went to work. Only another witch would sense the wards, a human or vampire wouldn't even notice the crystals until it was too late.

Wes turned to the table, where Ronny had been mixing the various herbs. There were several bags filled with strange dried leaves, measuring spoons, and various metal containers and other utensils. He looked around in the kitchen, sniffing. On the stove sat a large earthen pot with a lid.

He walked to it and lifted the lid, but instantly staggered back. The smell emanating from the disgusting-looking black sludge was vile. And he was no stranger to vile smells. He'd brewed enough awful-smelling potions in his life, but this concoction took the cake.

There was no way to test the brew here. He would have to take samples back to his lab. He opened his backpack and took a vial from it, snatched a clean spoon from one of the kitchen drawers, and scooped some of the black sludge into the vial, then sealed it tightly and put it in a plastic container so it wouldn't get damaged in his bag.

"Well, then," he murmured to himself and started examining each herb on the table individually. The Höllenkraut he recognized immediately. In the last twenty-four hours he'd read everything he could find about the plant. And the more he found, the more he was concerned. Some of the other herbs he could identify visually, others by their smell. He catalogued each of them on his notepad, and bagged samples. But there were several he didn't recognize. Fortunately, thinking ahead, he'd packed his *Herbal Companion* book, and now retrieved it from his backpack.

He leafed through it and was able to identify all of the herbs Ronny had been using. Some seemed rather innocent: chamomile, for example.

He shook his head. What effect would an innocuous herb like chamomile have in this dangerous concoction? Clearly it did something, but he couldn't figure it out just by looking at it. He'd have to find Ronny's recipe book. Somewhere, he must have written down the exact proportions of each herb he used in the manufacture of the drug.

But no matter how many drawers he opened, how many things he turned over, and how many books he flipped through, he couldn't find anything even remotely resembling a recipe. The closest he'd come to a recipe were the online notes Matt had discovered on Ronny's computer. But it had been evident pretty quickly that the recipe on the computer was an early trial of the drug and was incomplete. Useless, other than that it had alerted him to the Höllenkraut.

He was packing his backpack with the various samples he'd taken, when there was a sudden flash outside the kitchen window. It was the ward he'd set up, alerting him to a visitor. Wesley jumped into action immediately, pulled his gun from the bag and barreled outside. But by the time he ran around the house, whoever had triggered the ward was gone.

He froze for a moment and peered into the darkness. He didn't have a vampire's sensitive hearing or eyesight, but as a preternatural creature, he could sense auras. It was how he recognized vampires. And how vampires recognized him as a witch.

And as a witch he could sense the faint impression of the person's aura that still lingered. A preternatural creature, no doubt, though he couldn't tell if it was a vampire. Nevertheless, he started running, hoping the trail would last long enough to let him catch up.

Wes charged through the forest, not caring that he sounded like an entire herd of elephants trampling through the woods. It didn't matter. The aura trail became stronger every minute he was in pursuit of the stranger, which meant his endurance training at Scanguards was finally paying off. Whoever it was, Wes was gaining on him.

However, even though moonlight now shone through the less dense vegetation, he still couldn't see anybody. He could hear him now, though. Dry twigs were breaking under the person's feet. Wes used those sounds and the aura trail to keep close behind his target, sucking more air into his lungs as he continued the chase.

The stranger was running uphill now, and from what Wesley could see and hear, he had just reached the peak. The moonlight shining onto that spot should silhouette him against the background, but Wesley saw nothing. Absolutely nothing.

"Impossible," he murmured to himself, and raced uphill.

When he reached the spot where the person had been only seconds earlier he looked down the other side of the hill. He saw twigs and leaves flying, as if somebody were hurtling down the hill in a hurry, but there was nobody. Nobody *visible* anyway.

Wes barreled down the hill, careful not to fall. If he broke his neck, it wouldn't help anybody.

At the bottom, he finally saw what the person was heading for. A wooden shack. Its door flapped. The stranger must have just entered it. Wes charged toward it, kicking the door in with one foot, while aiming his gun into the middle of the wooden hut.

But this wasn't an ordinary shack, he realized immediately.

At the far end of it was a stone wall with an opening larger than an ordinary door. Past it, he finally saw the person he'd chased. The stranger whirled around, their gazes meeting for a moment.

"Destroy it," the stranger said.

Stunned, yet still pointing the weapon at the man dressed in dark clothes and a long black coat, Wes asked automatically, "Destroy what?"

"The drug. It'll only play into the demons' hands."

Wes hesitated. "Who are you? Identify yourself!" Because this man was no vampire.

"We're on the same side, witch!" Then he lifted his hands as if in surrender, and suddenly a stone wall appeared in front of him.

"Shit!"

Wes ran to it, pressed his hand against it, but it was solid rock. How the fuck had the guy done this? It couldn't have been witchcraft, because for certain, the stranger was no witch. Yet he'd recognized Wesley as a witch. He was preternatural. That much was certain.

But what was he?

Wes dropped his head, when something caught his attention. He stared at the stone in front of him and concentrated on the grooves in its surface. Then he saw it: somebody had carved a dagger into the boulder. A perfect, beautiful ancient dagger. Wes traced the outline with his fingers and felt the stone heat under his touch. Simultaneously, it started to shimmer.

"Fuck!"

He pressed against it, but the heat subsided, as did the glow. The stone was cold again. But the dagger was still there. And he knew he'd seen this dagger somewhere before. Somewhere in a book.

34

Lilo listened anxiously while Quinn spoke to somebody on his cell phone.

Several hours ago, Blake had left, leaving her behind at his house, even though she'd wanted to go with him. But he'd used his sexual prowess to make her submit to his wishes. And she was still fuming about that. This was exactly what she didn't like about men: their dominance—and her own weakness of giving in so quickly.

And to top it all off, Blake had asked Quinn and Rose to babysit her. Not that she didn't like the couple—in fact she liked them very much—but she didn't like being manhandled like that. Without her wishes being taken into account. And she'd tell Blake exactly that—just as soon as he was back.

Quinn disconnected the call, slipped his phone into his pocket and walked back into the living room. "That was Oliver."

Impatient, Lilo asked, "And? What happened?"

"They've got Ronny."

Her heartbeat accelerated. "And Hannah? Is she alright?"

She suddenly felt Rose's hand on her forearm. Lilo shot her a look, then stared back at Quinn.

A regretful expression crossed his face. "I'm sorry. They didn't find her. She wasn't there."

A sob tore from her chest. "Oh no! He killed her, didn't he?" It was too late.

"Oh, no, luvvie," Rose cooed and stroked her arm.

"She's alive," Quinn said, approaching.

Lilo met his gaze. But she couldn't utter a single word.

"But we don't know where she's being kept. Not yet anyway."

"But then how do they know that she's alive?" Lilo choked out.

Quinn sighed. "She's alive because they need her." He exchanged a look with his wife. "I think we should go to headquarters. They're bringing Ronny in for interrogation. We'll get more details then."

Lilo nodded. She couldn't wait to be face-to-face with Ronny, and tell him what she thought of him.

By the time they reached Scanguards' office building in the Mission district, a bustling working class neighborhood with predominantly Latino influences, Quinn had already gotten word that Blake and his team had arrived with their captive in tow.

"They're just starting the interrogation," Quinn said, and led her and Rose down a long corridor, before opening a door with his ID card. "We can watch everything from up here."

He motioned for her to enter, and Lilo walked into the room. It looked like a control booth from which a sound engineer monitored a recording studio. Only, the recording studio was a two-story room with nothing but a chair and a table in it. A large window allowed the occupants of the control booth to watch the goings-on in the room below, where several men were milling about. Microphones and loudspeakers ensured that the sound was transmitted into the booth.

Lilo heard the door close behind her.

Quinn now addressed the man sitting at the controls. "Thomas, you know Lilo, don't you?"

The blond man in leather pants and a black T-shirt nodded and smiled at her. She remembered him now as Eddie's blood-bonded mate. "I saw you at the meeting last night. Take a seat. They're just starting." He turned up the volume.

Lilo took the seat next to Thomas, while Quinn and Rose remained standing behind her.

She looked down into the room. Ronny was sitting in the only chair, while John hovered over him together with another man she'd seen at the meeting, but hadn't been introduced to.

"Who's that?"

Rose bent to her. "That's Oliver. Our son."

Quinn squeezed Rose's hand, giving her a ravishing smile. "Well, he's actually my protégé. I turned him, which makes me his sire, his father, whatever you want to call it. And Rose has graciously accepted him as her son. He and Ursula, his wife, and their son live with us."

"Oh, I've met Ursula and Sebastian."

"Aren't they wonderful? You know, they were talking about getting their own house. Oliver sure can afford it, but I would miss Sebastian so much if they moved out. He's such a sweet kid. And our house is too big for just the two of us anyway," Rose said.

Lilo suppressed a laugh. A sweet kid who got into trouble the moment he was hanging out with his pals. "He is."

The door to the interrogation room suddenly opened and Blake, followed by Samson, marched in, joining their colleagues. She couldn't help but let her eyes roam over Blake. He was all male, all power, all confidence. He appeared almost unapproachable the way he now strode into the room and approached Ronny. Superior was the word that came to mind.

John and Oliver stepped aside to make space for Blake. He now faced Ronny, turning his back to the window from which Lilo was watching with the others.

"Let's talk, Ronny, man to man."

Ronny glared at him. "If she dies because you're holding me here, I'll rip your heart out!"

"Then you'd better answer all our questions truthfully, and maybe—"

Ronny scoffed. "Maybe what? We've already wasted too much time. If I don't have the next batch ready by the time they call me, Hannah is as good as dead."

"Then why don't you start talking? From the beginning." Blake leaned in. "I want to know every fucking detail, do you hear me? Or I'll be the one ripping your heart out." As if to underscore his threat, Blake lifted his hand.

Lilo sucked in a breath. His fingers had turned into claws, and she had no doubt that, should he really want to rip the guy's heart out, it would be an easy task with those razor-sharp instruments.

"It wasn't my fault," Ronny grunted, his eyes wild when he glared at Blake.

Blake moved back and crossed his arms over his chest. "Wasn't it?"

"No! I wanted to get out."

"Get out of what?"

"Making the stuff. I'm into chemistry. At the beginning, I was just experimenting. You know, making the stuff to get high."

Lilo turned to Rose. "Why didn't he just do coke?"

"Conventional human drugs don't work on a vampire. Alcohol, nicotine, and any other prescription or non-prescription drugs have no effect on us."

Surprised, she focused her attention back on the interrogation.

"What happened then?"

"Well, it didn't work," Ronny barked. "None of the stuff I brewed was getting me high. I wanted to toss it all out, because there was no way I could sell this to a vampire when it didn't work."

"So you wanted to make a drug that worked on vampires and sell it on the street to make money?"

Ronny shrugged. "A guy's gotta live. It's not like I have a lot of job opportunities."

Lilo rolled her eyes. There it was again: Ronny was full of excuses.

"But you didn't destroy the drug," Blake prompted.

"I ran into an old friend. He'd just gotten out of prison."

"Steven Norwood," Blake supplied.

There was a flash of surprise in his eyes. "So you're onto him already."

But Blake didn't offer any more information. "What did Norwood want?"

"He needed money, too, just like I did. And he knew a few guys who weren't opposed to doing anything it took to get ahead. When I told him about the drug I'd tried to manufacture for vampires, he had an idea. He thought that maybe it would work on humans, and instead of selling it to vampires, we could sell the drug to humans."

Blake scoffed. "You're trying to tell me you sold those drugs to the humans and then they committed those break-ins all by themselves? How stupid do you think I am?"

Ronny lifted his hands. "No, that's not what I'm saying. That was the plan at first, but it didn't work out like that. The drug didn't give the humans a high. But it put them into an almost catatonic state where they did practically anything they're told." He swallowed. "Steven saw the potential in that. And once I tested how to control the human over a long distance, we put the plan in motion."

"Hold it," Blake interrupted. "How did you make sure the vampires could control the human over a long distance?"

"Every batch of the drug is the same, but before it gets administered, the vampire who's in charge of that human mixes it with his own blood. It creates a short-lived bond via which the vampire can control the human's mind. It assures that the human will only listen to his master, the vampire whose blood is in him. Nobody else can give him any orders. And mind control by any other vampire won't work."

"And without the blood?"

"Without it, the human goes into the catatonic state, and can be controlled by anybody. Even a human. We had to eliminate that possibility, otherwise we would have lost control over the humans we used."

Ronny shoved a shaky hand through his hair.

"Continue," Blake prompted. "What happened when you realized you could control humans with the drug?"

"Steven figured we could order them to rob stores for us, and homes. We wouldn't have to get our hands dirty. And we could do it during daylight. Nobody would ever suspect us. It went well for quite some time. But I hadn't really had any occasion to test the drug's long-term effects, and I started seeing something..." He visibly choked back something akin to a sob. "We kept using the same humans, and I started to see what the drug did in the end."

"Side effects?" Blake asked.

"You could say that. The long-term effect on a human is devastating. The longer the exposure, the more of the human's mind dies. Like with an Alzheimer's patient. It's gradual at first, but it's inevitable." Ronny looked straight at Blake, his gaze open. "That's not what I'd signed up for. I didn't want to do this anymore. I wanted out. But—"

"Norwood wouldn't let you," Blake guessed.

A slow nod. "I was the only one who could manufacture the stuff. The others are nitwits. But Norwood, he knew how to keep the pressure on me. He knew about Hannah."

Lilo's heart contracted painfully.

"He confronted me, said he would hurt Hannah, if I didn't do what he wanted."

The video, Lilo recalled. The two had argued.

Ronny continued, "I tried to convince Hannah that we needed to leave, but she was stubborn and wanted to know why."

"She didn't know what you were doing?"

He dropped his head and shook it. "No. I had no choice, but to tell her then. I've never seen a person so disappointed. She threw me out. Oh

God, she was so angry. I think she hates me now for what I've done. For what I've allowed to happen." He sniffled. "I left, hoping she would cool down, but when I got back a few hours later, she wasn't there anymore. Her dog was wandering around outside the building."

"You brought him to an animal shelter."

Ronny nodded. "She loves that dog, and I couldn't take care of him, because I needed to find Hannah. I didn't have to search for long. Steven called me. He put her on the phone so I would believe that he'd captured her."

"So you know where they're holed up then," Blake said.

Ronny lifted his lids, his eyes brimming with tears. Red tears. "Steven and the others had already moved their hideout somewhere else right after our argument. They figured they couldn't trust me anymore. I checked out their old place. They were gone. I don't know where they went or where they're keeping Hannah."

Lilo felt tears well up in her eyes. If Ronny didn't know where Hannah was, how would they find her now?

"But they won't kill her," Ronny added. "Not as long as I keep delivering the drugs."

35

Blake rubbed his neck and paced in front of Ronny. Was he telling the truth? His demeanor was sincere enough. Even his tears looked real. But he had to be sure.

He turned to Samson. "I want Gabriel to delve into Ronny's memories to find out whether he's telling us the truth."

Samson nodded up to the mirrored window. "Thomas, get Gabriel down here."

"Okay," Thomas replied via the loudspeaker.

"I'm telling the truth," Ronny yelled.

"Yeah? Well, I hope you don't mind if I check that out, do you? Because if you're such a choirboy, then why the fuck did you shoot me? That doesn't fit with your pretty little story." And Blake was still feeling a little pissed off about almost having died from a silver bullet.

"I didn't want to do it, but I had to," Ronny snapped.

"Let me guess: Norwood made you do it."

"He said that somebody was onto us, and that if I didn't take you and that woman who was with you out, they'd hurt Hannah."

Blake growled low and dark. "You were planning to kill Lilo, too, not just me?" He practically jumped at the guy, flashing his fangs at him, his hands already curling around the scumbag's neck, lifting him out of his chair. "I should rip your throat out just for that thought alone. If you or your cronies ever lay a hand on her, you'll wish you were dead, because what I'll do to you will be so painful that you'll beg me to stake you. Do you get that? She's mine! Nobody touches my woman!"

"Blake, drop him!" Samson ordered. "Gabriel is here."

Blake whirled his head to the door Gabriel was just closing behind him. He hadn't even heard Scanguards' second-in-command enter, so furious had he been at the knowledge that one of Ronny's bullets had been meant for Lilo. At least she wouldn't have to find out. This was one thing he'd have to keep from her in order not to upset her again.

He let go of Ronny's throat and dropped him unceremoniously back into the chair. Ronny immediately rubbed his throat and coughed.

Blake stepped aside. "Do your thing, Gabriel, before I lose my composure."

Gabriel drew one side of his mouth up. "Gee, and there I thought you already had." He remained standing at Samson's side. "Samson is filling me in quickly."

Blake waited impatiently while Samson relayed all pertinent information to Gabriel. Then he said, "I suggest you go as far as two weeks back to verify what he's been up to."

With a swagger in his step, Gabriel approached and stopped in front of the prisoner, addressing him directly, "It's not gonna hurt."

"Unfortunately," Blake grunted under his breath.

But his superiors had heard it. Both Samson and Gabriel shot him dirty looks, but he wasn't going to back down.

"As long as *he* doesn't touch me again…" Ronny mumbled.

"Relax now," Gabriel demanded. "I'll be delving into your memories to verify that what you've told us is true."

Gabriel remained entirely still and closed his eyes. Blake had seen him exercise his gift before. He didn't do it often, believing that it was an invasion of privacy, but on occasion, when a person's life hung in the balance, he used his special skill.

There was no outward sign that he was doing anything at all, which made this gift so dangerous. And there was no defense for it. It worked on any human or preternatural creature. Nobody was safe.

Several minutes passed, then Gabriel suddenly turned around, facing his colleagues. "He's telling the truth. He tried to get out of Norwood's gang—there are five others with him—and he also tried to warn Hannah. He didn't take her. He searched everywhere for her, until Norwood called him and let him talk to her. And he also checked Norwood's old place. It's deserted." Gabriel shook his head. "He doesn't know where they're hiding now."

"And what about him shooting at me and Lilo?" Blake asked.

"He's told us the truth, Blake. Shooting you wasn't his idea. He was desperate to keep Hannah alive." Gabriel sighed. "I have a feeling he'll do anything for her."

For the first time, Blake looked past the crimes Ronny had committed and just saw a man. A man who loved a woman so much, he'd kill for her. And damn it to hell, he understood Ronny now.

"Damn it, Ronny, why didn't you come to us right away? You knew Hannah was working for Scanguards; you knew what kind of work we do. We could have helped you!" Blake growled.

"I was afraid that they were watching me. I couldn't risk it. I love Hannah."

Blake could understand that, too. His heartbeat slowed by a fraction. "What now? When are you supposed to deliver the drugs?"

"They'll call me on my burner to give me the time and the place."

Blake nodded and turned to the mirrored window of the observation booth. "Thomas, can you clone Ronny's phone and monitor it?"

"Sure thing."

He looked over his shoulder back at Ronny. "Do you know when?"

Ronny's eyes darted to the clock on the wall. "In about two hours."

"Okay." He looked at his colleagues. "Let's get IT on this. We'll prepare for any eventuality." They had plenty of protocols in place for this. "And when they call Ronny, our friend here will request that they bring Hannah to the meeting place."

"It's gonna make them suspicious," Ronny cautioned.

"She needs to be there, so we can get to her. You want her back, don't you?"

Ronny nodded.

"Then you'll do as I say." Blake took a breath and rubbed a hand over his face. "Let's get ready."

John put a hand on his shoulder, squeezing it. "We've got it covered. Why don't you take a breather?"

"Good idea," Samson said, before Blake could protest. "That's an order."

"Oh, uh, Blake," Thomas said through the speakers.

Blake lifted his gaze to the window, though he couldn't see Thomas behind it.

"Lilo is here."

"Where?"

"Up here in the observation booth."

Oh shit! How long had she been up there? Had she heard what Ronny had said, that one of the bullets he'd fired that night had had her name on it? He could only imagine how she must feel.

"I'll be there in a second."

~ ~ ~

Lilo followed Blake silently as he led her to his office and shut the door behind them. Too many thoughts were swarming in her mind, producing too many conflicting emotions. Residual annoyance about Blake having left her behind was still coursing through her veins, but now something else was keeping it company. But first things first.

"How are we gonna save Hannah?" she asked. "I heard everything Ronny said. But I didn't hear what Scanguards' plan is now that we know Ronny doesn't have her. What are we gonna do?"

Blake reached for her, but she pressed her hand against his chest, pushing him back. A guarded expression spread on his face. "Let us do our job. Trust me on this. Everybody is working on this already. By the time Norwood calls Ronny, we will have prepared for anything he can throw at us. We've done this many times before. We're good at this."

She breathed to calm herself. Yes, she'd seen Scanguards in action. But she wished she could do something. "I know you and your colleagues are good at what you're doing. But I need to do something, too. I need to help, too."

He shook his head and smiled. "There's nothing for you to do. I know you hate waiting, but maybe I can occupy you until we get the call?" He smiled and leaned in.

She pushed him back. "Not so fast!"

He pulled back, his forehead furrowing. "I get the sneaky feeling that I've said or done something you don't approve of."

She huffed. "Where do I even start?" She planted her hands on her hips. "First of all, you can't just use sex to make me compliant so you can leave without me! I wanted to come with you."

"I told you it was too dangerous."

"Bullshit! Quinn told me there were eight of you and one of him. It wouldn't have hurt if you had taken me. But no, because I'm a woman, you think you can steamroll me."

"Well, apparently I'm paying for it now..." he remarked dryly.

"You think that's all? I haven't even started yet!"

He crossed his arms over his chest. "What else have I done?"

"You're dominant and full of yourself!"

He lifted an eyebrow. "That's harsh. I didn't think you had any objections to my dominance earlier. If I recall correctly, you enjoyed it tremendously when I—"

"I'm not talking about the sex!" She scoffed. "I'm talking about you! How you behaved in that interrogation room."

"How I interrogate prisoners is up to me." He narrowed his eyes, clearly annoyed now.

Well, so was she! "You told Ronny to keep his hands off *your* woman. Damn it, Blake, you have no right to talk about me like that! You told him I was yours. As if I were your property!"

Blake's mouth suddenly twisted into a smile and he dropped his arms. "So that's your problem? That I told Ronny that I would kill him if he hurt you? That's what you take offense to?" He laughed.

How dare he laugh? "This is serious! I won't be treated like one of your possessions! Just because you're a vampire and stronger than I, you think you can order me around! I won't have it."

"Ah, how I love feisty women." He reached past her and flipped the lock shut.

She shot him a stunned look. "What are you doing?"

"I'm ensuring that we have privacy while we discuss our relationship."

She swallowed, her throat parched. "Relationship?"

He moved closer, forcing her to step back until she hit the wall. "Yeah, our relationship. So you think I'm stronger than you because I'm a vampire? I guess you must have forgotten that I was at your mercy not twenty-four hours ago. I put my life in your hands, trusting you to keep me safe. Don't you remember that side of me? And what about when we made love? Don't you remember the power you had over me then?"

"Power? Me?"

"Yes, you, my brave Lilo. You have power over me." He took her hand and pressed it to the spot where his heart was beating rapidly. "I wasn't planning this. But from the moment I first kissed you, I knew I couldn't stay away from you. You have more power than you think, because you hold my heart in your hand."

She shook her head. When Blake had held Ronny by the throat, she'd seen something she didn't like. "You're possessive."

"I know."

"It scares me."

"Why?"

"Because I don't want to be told what to do. I don't want to be suppressed or dominated. I don't want to be controlled."

"Oh, Lilo, baby. You think just because I'm possessive I would do all that?" He shook his head, smiling softly. "A vampire is possessive by nature. But it's solely to protect and take care of those he loves." He brushed a lock of her hair behind her ear and tipped her chin up with his index finger. "The only place I might occasionally show my dominance or control will be in bed—and only to give you more pleasure."

He dipped his mouth to the crook of her neck and pressed a warm kiss to her skin.

"Do you want me to demonstrate?" he murmured and pulled her into his arms.

"Blake…"

How could she be mad at him when he sounded so reasonable? After all, he was right: she had seen more than one side of him. Not just the dominant one, but also the vulnerable one. And the soft one. And it was that knowledge that made her shiver now. Because she had to admit to herself that she liked all sides of him, not just the soft one. She liked his rough edge and his dominance. Even if it spelled trouble.

"Lilo, I'm in love with you." He lifted his face to meet her gaze. "I don't know how it happened, but it happened. All I want to do is keep you safe and make you happy. Is that so wrong?"

In love? Her heart stopped. This big bad vampire who managed to rile her up like nobody ever had before, was in love with her?

"Blake," she murmured, and pressed her lips onto his.

He responded to her kiss, drawing her closer and robbing her of her breath, until he released her lips a few moments later. Panting, he said, "Now about that demonstration…"

He lifted her up and carried her to the other side of the office, where he pressed a switch on the wall. At first she only heard a loud grating sound, then she saw something from the corner of her eye. She snapped her gaze to it. The paneled white wall was lowering.

"You have a Murphy bed in your office?" She gaped at him in disbelief.

"A necessity in my job. Looking after thirteen hybrids isn't exactly a nine-to-five job. Sometimes I have to get shuteye whenever I can. So Samson approved having it installed." He grinned mischievously. "But I've never used it for sex before. We could baptize it together. How about it?"

"You can't be serious! This is your office."

"I know it's my office. Samson told me to take a breather. I'm just following orders."

She pointed to the bed, which had now lowered completely. Clean-looking crisp sheets were stretched over the mattress. "I don't think Samson meant this when he told you to rest."

Despite her words, he lowered her onto the mattress and began to undress in front of her. "Trust me, baby, this will give me more energy than many hours of rest."

"We can't have sex now! We have to prepare to rescue Hannah. We need to be ready when Ronny gets the call—"

"—which won't be for at least another hour and a half, maybe two. My team is already taking care of everything. There's nothing else we can do but wait." He winked at her. "Let's kill some time."

"You're incorrigible."

He shrugged. "Another one of my many flaws. I'm sure you'll get used to it. Now strip, baby!"

36

Blake was already naked in front of Lilo, as she started peeling her clothes off.

So she thought him possessive? She'd seen nothing yet. She would be just as possessive of him once she was his. And he couldn't wait for that. Couldn't wait for her to claim him. But all in good time. First he had to woo her, and show her what it was like to be loved by a vampire.

He watched her undress, feasting his eyes on her as she peeled away layer after layer, until all of her creamy skin was exposed and she lay back on the sheets. She angled one leg and coyly looked up at him from under her long lashes, her hair draped over her shoulders, reaching her rosy nipples. She looked like a pinup girl, and he was determined that only he would see her like this in the future. He just had to play his cards right.

He pinned her with his eyes, then slowly lowered his gaze to his cock, making her follow his look. He was fully erect now, his hard length pumped so full with blood, it was curving toward his navel. His balls had drawn up tight, too.

"Look at what you're doing to me," he urged her and wrapped his hand around his hard-on, giving it a quick tug. Pre-cum was already seeping from the tip.

Lilo shifted, propping herself up on her elbows, her breasts jiggling from the sudden motion. "Is that the demonstration of your dominance you were talking about?"

One side of his mouth curled up involuntarily. "Are you trying to mock me?"

"What if I were?"

He crooked his finger. "Sit up. I think you need a little lesson in how to treat your man."

She pulled her lower lip between her teeth, but sat up and scooted to the edge of the bed. Blake bridged the distance between them with one step, bringing his groin level with her head.

"Now be a good girl and suck me until I tell you to stop." He nudged his cock at her lips.

Her tongue emerged and she flattened it over the head of his erection. She lifted her eyes to meet his gaze. "Like this?"

"So you're gonna play innocent now, are you? When we both know what a hot-blooded woman you are."

Again he nudged against her lips, and they parted on a moan, allowing him in. He eased forward slowly, giving her time to adjust.

"That's it, Lilo, all of it." He slid his hands into her hair and massaged her skull gently.

She took him a little deeper, his cock sliding over her tongue.

"Damn, you're good at this," he praised and drew back his hips just as slowly.

Lilo exhaled and her breath blew over his heated cock, making him shiver with pleasure. "Again," she murmured and reached for him, wrapping one hand around his root.

He held her head motionless, while he descended once more, sinking into the wet cavern of her mouth. He wanted slow this time, very slow, so he could savor every second of their lovemaking, and prolong their pleasure.

"Look at me," he ordered.

She lifted her eyes again.

"I've never seen a more erotic sight than you with my cock in your mouth." He couldn't suppress the moan that was rising from his chest.

She held his gaze and started to move up and down on his erection, wrapping her lips tightly around him, sucking harder than he'd allowed her until now. He felt shudder after shudder race through his body, obliterating any sane thought he might have ever had.

Lilo was turning him into a creature driven only by lust and passion. Nothing else counted. With every second his body heated more, and he knew if he wanted to remain in control, he had to make her stop.

"Enough!" Before it was too late, he stepped back and pulled himself from her mouth.

She looked up at him, her lips in a pout. "You always make me stop just when it starts getting good."

He chuckled. "Nice try, baby, but I'm the one who's in charge right now. Maybe some other day I won't stop you. But for now I have other plans."

He gave her shoulders a gentle shove so she landed flat on the mattress. He rolled over her, aligning his cock with her center and plunged inside.

"Yessss!" she cried out, arching her back, thus thrusting her breasts at him.

Unable to resist the delicious offering, he dipped his head and captured one nipple between his lips, sucking and licking his tongue over it.

"More!" she demanded, and undulated her hips.

He thrust into her in a steady rhythm, filling her, then withdrawing, while he continued feasting on her breasts, alternately teasing one, then the other, while she writhed beneath him.

She was panting heavily. Her arousal permeated the room, making his nostrils flare and his cock pulse. But he didn't want to come yet. Taking a deep breath, he slowed his tempo to a more tender rhythm, rocking against her more gently.

"Blake…"

He lifted his head from her breast and gazed at her. Concern jolted through him. "What's wrong? What do you need, Lilo?"

He noticed her swallow, before her lips parted. "I want you to bite me."

His heart stopped, and his body froze in mid-movement. "What?"

He couldn't possibly have heard correctly. He was probably hallucinating.

"Bite me," she whispered. "Anywhere you like." Her cornflower-blue eyes shone back at him with untamed lust. "I want to know what it's like."

He lifted his hand and ran his fingers along her graceful neck. "You mean it?"

She nodded.

"I must be dreaming."

"You're not," she said. "Please, show me what it's like."

Slowly he resumed his movements, thrusting slow and deep into her, then withdrawing just as slowly. Their gazes locked, he willed his fangs to descend, and parted his lips to show her what she would feel pierce her skin in a moment.

"It won't hurt," he promised, but hesitated. "Anywhere I want?"

"Anywhere."

The choice was an easy one. He could always take the vein at her neck some other time, but for their first bite—and he hoped it was only the first of many—he wanted something special.

Still continuing to slide in and out of her warm pussy, he lowered his head back to one breast and rubbed his fangs along either side of her nipple. She trembled beneath him, and instinctively he grabbed both her wrists and pinned her arms to her sides.

"Do it," she encouraged him.

He set the tips of his fangs to her skin and pressed down. Like scalpels, his fangs drove into her flesh, sinking deep and lodging there before he drew the first drop of blood. The rich red liquid ran down the back of his throat filling all his senses with wonder and awe. He'd bitten other humans before, but sinking his fangs into Lilo was different. He'd suddenly found what he'd been looking for all his life. Nothing before had ever tasted so good, and nothing after would ever be better. He couldn't imagine ever drinking bottled blood again, now that he was drinking his fill from Lilo's gorgeous breast.

His vampire body was taking over now, increasing the tempo with which he thrust his cock into her. Ever harder and faster he was taking her, while she moaned and sighed, and her heartbeat raced.

He was still pinning her down by her wrists, but he couldn't make himself release her, because the knowledge that she was at his mercy turned him on even more, made his cock swell even more. Lilo moved with him as if they'd done this a thousand times before, her pelvis slamming against his with every thrust.

More and more blood filled his mouth, and he knew it was time to stop, or he would take too much. He eased his fangs from her and licked over the tiny incisions, closing them instantly. When he lifted his head to look at her, he saw a woman in ecstasy, her face glistening, her lips parted, moans rolling over them, and her eyes gleaming with lust. She was close. And so was he.

Adjusting his angle, he plunged deeper and harder, his pelvic bone slamming against her clit over and over again. Until, finally, she tensed. One more thrust, and he was there with her as they both hurtled over the edge. He captured her moan of release with his mouth and swallowed it down, letting it bounce against his heart.

He couldn't tell how long it took to come down from the high, but at some point he rolled to the side and took her with him, cradling her to his chest, draping one of her legs over his thigh, so he wouldn't slip out of her drenched pussy.

"I can't even begin to tell you what this means to me," he murmured against her lips before he kissed her again.

"I thought I was floating on a cloud. I've never felt anything so… so amazing." She opened her eyes. "Is it always like that?"

He smiled. "Between lovers, it's like this. A vampire's bite arouses, but it only turns truly erotic when it happens during lovemaking. Only then can the vampire's bite fully unfold in all its facets."

"Now I understand why a human would let a vampire bite her."

He rolled onto his back, pulling her with him, readjusting his groin to fully seat himself inside her again.

"Thank you for letting me drink your blood," Blake said, combing his fingers through her hair. "I wish I could tell you what it felt like to take you like this. To feel you give yourself to me so freely. Without reservation." He pressed a kiss to her hair.

"But for you it can't be anything new. You must have done this many times before."

He slid his hand under her chin and lifted her head to make her look at him.

"Lilo, I've never bitten a woman during sex. I've never experienced this before. Sure, I've bitten humans before, but it was never like this. Never while making love. No bite has ever felt like what I just experienced with you. It was out-of-this-world. I'm afraid, Lilo, I'm going to get addicted to this, and to you."

An almost shy smile crossed her lips. "So you might want to do this again?"

He pressed his head back into the pillow, closing his eyes for a moment. "Lilo, just like I could make love to you all day and all night, I would love to sink my fangs into you every single time." He stroked his fingers over her cheek and traced the outline of her lips. "And I'd be the happiest man on this earth if you allowed me to bite you again."

He rolled, bringing her underneath him again. "And now, I'd like to thank you for your generous gift." He began to move inside her, thrusting back and forth.

Lilo gasped. "But you just——"

"——came? Yes, but I have your blood inside me, and guess what it's doing to me." He smirked and motioned to his groin. "It's your own fault for asking me to bite you. I'm afraid naughty women like you need to be taught a lesson."

She chuckled. "How?"

"Let's discuss that after your next orgasm."

37

"Lilo."

Blake's voice was close at her ear. She opened her eyes and shot up to a sitting position, finding Blake sitting at the edge of the Murphy bed, fully dressed. "Did I nod off?"

He brushed his knuckles over her cheek and smiled. "Just for a few minutes. You needed it. I took a lot of blood from you."

At the recollection of what that had felt like, she sensed heat rise into her cheeks. There was nothing on earth that was even comparable to a vampire's bite. Now she understood why Hannah had sought out a vampire as her boyfriend. It practically ensured a satisfied sex life.

"Is that a blush?" he murmured at her ear.

She lifted her chin. "What if it is?"

"Then I'll take it as a compliment. And as an invitation to do it again."

A knock at the door and the rattling of the doorknob made her whirl her head toward it.

"Blake?" It was Wesley's voice coming through the door.

"What do you want?" Blake responded, rising from the bed.

"Why's the fucking door locked? Open up, I've gotta talk to you. It's important!"

"Give me a minute." Blake tossed her an apologetic look. "Sorry, baby." He walked to the wall next to the Murphy bed and pressed against it. A door that had looked like a panel opened up. "It's just a tiny bathroom, but you can get dressed in here while I see what Wes wants."

Stunned, she rose and looked into the small room. "You're full of surprises."

He shrugged. "Rose's idea. She grew up in the Regency period, and they had secret panels that led into hidden rooms all the time. She figured it would be nice to have a place to freshen up when I sleep here on occasion."

"What's taking you so long?" Wes grunted outside the door and banged against it once more.

Blake grimaced. "I'd better talk to him before he flips." He paused. "Oh, and come out when you're done. I have no intention of hiding you in the closet."

She snatched her clothes from the floor and hurried into the bathroom, and pulled the door shut behind her. She only took a few minutes to clean up and get dressed. She'd never been one to spend a long time getting ready. Besides, she was curious about Wesley's important news.

When she opened the door and stepped back into Blake's office, he and Wesley were bending over his desk, a large, old book open before them. Wes looked up and spotted her. He didn't appear to be surprised at seeing her. From the corner of her eye she saw that the Murphy bed was back inside the wall, and that fact made her relax.

"Hey, Lilo."

"Hi, Wesley. Any news?"

"Lots."

"Go on," Blake encouraged him. "You were saying…"

"So when I reached the shack that I'd chased him to, he suddenly materialized. I knew he wasn't a vampire, but he was preternatural. I just couldn't tell what he was. He told me to destroy the drugs because they'd only play into the demons' hands. You can imagine how stunned I was. But I had no time to question him. Suddenly that boulder just moved in front of him and he disappeared."

"What boulder?"

"Some massive stone. And this—" He pointed to something in the book. "—was carved in it. I'm telling you it was a portal. Some sort of transportation system. Here, Francine writes about it, too."

Curious, Lilo joined them at the desk, moving next to Blake. He made space so she could look at the book, simultaneously snaking one arm around her waist.

The book looked like it had been published in Gutenberg's time. Printed on a page headed *Stealth Guardians*, was a drawing of a dagger.

"Stealth Guardians? What are those?" she asked.

Wes glanced at her. "That's what we're trying to figure out. We've never encountered them before."

"Do you think they have something to do with Ronny and his friends?"

"No," Blake answered firmly. "If they were in league with Norwood and his guys, they wouldn't have asked Wesley to destroy the drug." He looked at Wes. "You're sure you heard right?"

"I might not have a vampire's sensitive hearing, but I'm not deaf, man."

Lilo looked up at him, surprised and confused. "But why don't you have a vampire's sensitive hearing? Don't all vampires have that?"

Wes chuckled. "Oh they do. But I'm not a vampire."

"You're not? But I thought—"

Wes looked at Blake. "You didn't tell her? I thought you had no secrets from her."

Blake pulled her closer to him. "I don't. But there was a lot to fill Lilo in on. And I'm afraid you weren't that high on my priority list."

"I guess I'll have to remember that the next time you want a favor."

"So what are you then?" Lilo interrupted, too curious to wait another second.

"I'm a witch, of course." There was pride in his voice. "One of the best."

She had no words. But was it really so far fetched? If vampires existed, why not witches, werewolves, and gargoyles? Why not demons and angels?

"A witch," she murmured to herself, then shrugged. "What else is new?"

"Well, a little more awe would have been nice," Wes said dryly. "But maybe I'm asking too much."

"I didn't mean to—"

Blake squeezed her to him. "Don't pander to him, Lilo. He's just fishing for compliments." Then he tipped his chin in Wesley's direction. "I'm not sure what you want to do with this information, Wes, but I don't think it's gonna help us rescue Hannah."

"I realize that. But these guys, these Stealth Guardians, they have powers we don't. They can make themselves invisible and walk through walls."

At Wesley's revelation, her chin dropped.

"I figured," Wes continued, "considering they seemed to be on our side concerning the drugs, we could make them our allies. With their powers—"

"How would you even find them?" Blake shook his head. "We don't have the time or resources to spend on this right now."

"But it might help us."

"It might, but what if it doesn't? We don't know who these guardians are. We don't know their agenda, or whether they're friendly to vampires. You were the only one they met. And you're a witch. What if they're not that peaceful when it comes to vampires?" Blake shook his head again. "With Hannah still in Norwood's hands, I'm not going to risk a distraction or accidently start a war with a species we know nothing about."

"I don't need any backup. I can do this on my own. Nobody from Scanguards would be pulled off his duty to search for Stealth Guardians."

"Wrong!" Blake poked his index finger into Wesley's chest. "*You* would be. And we need you. You're the only one who knows how to cast a spell or brew a potion. What if we can't defeat Norwood with conventional weapons? We need you, Wes. *I* need you."

For a few seconds Wes seemed to war with himself, but Blake's plea—laced with compliments Wes clearly appreciated—won him over. "Fine. I'll stay here. But once Hannah is safe, I'm going to search for them."

Slowly Blake nodded. "And I'll support you when you bring it up with Samson. Ultimately he'll have to approve."

"He will."

Without a knock, the door flew open and John appeared. "Showtime," he announced. "Ronny just got the call. We don't have much time. They want him to bring the drugs to Fort Mason. In thirty minutes."

"Did he get assurances from them that they're bringing Hannah to the meeting?"

Blake released her, hurrying to a cupboard and ripping open the door. Inside were several guns, knives, and stakes.

John nodded. "Ronny played the suffering boyfriend pretty convincingly. He begged them to let him see her. They agreed."

Blake grabbed several weapons and turned back to his colleague. "Then let's go." Then his gaze drifted to her. "Stay here."

"Please take me with you."

"No, Lilo. We've barely got enough time to get there. There's no time to implement any safety measures for you. Stay by the phone." He motioned to his desk. "I'll call you as soon as we know anything. Promise."

He was right, of course. She knew that. "Okay. I'll wait."

A quick smile and Blake was gone, his colleagues with him. Now all she could do was wait.

38

They'd parked the cars and vans at the end of a cul-de-sac surrounded by greenery. On the other side of it, an embankment covered in trees and shrubs led down to three broad piers, which held old warehouses that had long ago been converted to a center for art and culture with regular exhibitions, artists' work spaces, and large private events.

Blake and his colleagues walked down the embankment, using the trees and shrubs for cover to get an overview of the warehouses and surrounding area. Besides the three large warehouses on the piers, a small firehouse sat just below the embankment. Five more structures, each almost as large as the warehouses, sat on solid ground near the water.

Blake gave his colleagues the sign to spread out. He'd brought a large contingent of men with him: for every guy that Norwood had, Scanguards had brought three, many of them crack shots, who could take out a target from a long distance. However, everybody had to remain hidden until the enemy showed himself.

John remained next to him, watching a red dot on his cell phone move around a map. "Ronny's just entering the first gate."

Blake peered into the distance. "What's he driving?"

"His own truck. We figured Norwood would be less suspicious if everything looks normal. We put a tracker in Ronny's shoe to make sure we can keep an eye on him if he has to leave the car somewhere and continue on foot."

"And the drugs?"

"He told us they came in liquid form, so we filled plastic bottles with colored water."

"As long as they don't smell it, I guess we'll be fine."

"And by the time they do," John added, "we'll already have them by the balls."

Blake heard a crackling sound over his earpiece. "Positions?"

"This is Wes. My team is at the south end, opposite buildings B and C."

"Oliver here. We should be at the northern end of building A in about sixty seconds."

There was a pause.

"Amaury?"

"Yeah. Sorry, had to adjust the volume. My guys and I are stationed behind some crates at the entrance of the walkway between buildings D and E. We have a good view of the parking lot. Ronny's just pulling up."

"Good. John and I are overlooking the Festival Pavilion, and we can see the entrance to the Herbst Pavilion, too." Several shadows approached from the back of the firehouse and slowly crept past the shrubbery there. "Shit, I can see somebody approaching from the east. Anybody got eyes on them from below?"

He exchanged a look with John, indicating that if nobody was closer, he and John would try to take them from behind.

The three figures froze. "It's us," Samson suddenly said through the earpiece. "I've got Haven and Yvette with me. I texted you that we were coming."

Just then, Blake felt his cell phone vibrate and looked at it. Samson's text message appeared on the screen. "Just got it now. Glad you're here."

For a few minutes, everybody remained silent. Blake glanced at the dot that represented Ronny. "Amaury?" he asked through his mic. "What's Ronny doing?"

"Waiting around next to the car."

"They're late," Blake said.

"Yeah, or something," John said next to him, frowning. "I don't like it."

"Yeah, you and me both." Thirty minutes hadn't given them any time to prepare for this. They were winging it, and Blake could only hope that everybody would think on their feet and make the right decisions when it came to it.

"I hear something," Oliver suddenly said. "I think it's a boat."

"Samson? You see anything from where you are?" Blake asked.

"Definitely a boat approaching. A small motorboat," Samson confirmed.

"How many people on it?"

"Not sure. One driving it. But there could be more hiding in the hull."

"Okay. Sharpshooters, get ready!" Blake started issuing his orders. "All teams: move in." He motioned to John and they descended all the way down to the embankment until they reached the paved area. Communicating by signs now, so as not to be overheard by the approaching vampires, they moved closer, using the buildings and parked cars to give them cover.

Blake could hear the engine of the motorboat being throttled down, and knew the boat was coming to a stop now, somewhere between buildings A and B.

A loud bang suddenly jolted him.

"What's that?" he hissed into his mic.

"Fuck if I know," Amaury cursed.

"I'm going in," Blake growled.

"Wait!" Samson cautioned, but Blake was already running.

"Cover me!"

~ ~ ~

Lilo paced back and forth in Blake's office. There wasn't even a window to help her wile away the time, something she hadn't noticed until Blake had left. Every few minutes she looked at the clock on his wall. There were actually three clocks. One showed the current time, the second counted down to sunrise, the third to sunset. And the less time there was left until sunrise, the more nervous she became.

She wished somebody would tell her what was happening. Had Ronny's associates brought Hannah with them? What was happening right now? Were they all safe?

The ringing of Blake's phone made her jump. She raced toward it and grabbed the receiver, afraid that the ringing would stop before she could get to it.

"Blake?"

"Lilo? Oh thank God, it's you."

The female voice couldn't possibly belong to the person she thought. "Hannah?"

"Yes, Lilo, it's me. Oh God! It's terrible. I'm free, but Lilo, he's hurt so bad. Blake is hurt so bad, and some of the others, they're dead. I don't know what to do."

An iron fist clamped around her heart and squeezed. "Blake? Oh no! Please no!" She couldn't go through this again. She'd almost lost him once, she wouldn't survive a second time.

"Listen, Lilo. I'm in Blake's car. He's with me. We'll be at HQ in a minute. But I don't have the strength to get him into the building. He's too badly hurt, he can't move on his own. Help me!"

"I'll be down there. Please, Hannah, hurry. I can't lose him."

She slammed the receiver down and charged to the door, ripped it open and ran for the elevator, pressing the button several times before the doors opened. She jumped in. The ride down to the first floor couldn't have taken more than fifteen seconds, but it felt like an eternity. All she could think of was Blake. He was hurt. He needed her.

Oh God, what had happened at Fort Mason? What had these monsters done to the men of Scanguards? How many of them had died? A sob worked itself up from the pit of her stomach to her throat. She tried to force it down. Blake needed her. She had to remain strong.

When she reached the first floor she practically flew through the lobby, ignoring the questioning look of the woman behind the reception desk.

A guard stood at the glass exit door. He glanced at her visitor badge and nodded as she breezed past him and barreled outside onto the sidewalk.

She searched for Blake's Aston Martin, but couldn't see it. Had Hannah not gotten here yet?

Please, please!

She prayed silently. Don't let him die.

"Lilo! Here!"

She whirled her head to the side and saw Hannah wave to her from the corner. "He's here."

Lilo ran toward her friend. "Hannah!" She'd never been more relieved to see her friend. Hannah looked exhausted and worn out, dark circles under her eyes, her red hair an unruly mess, her clothes rumpled.

When Lilo reached her, Hannah was already running toward the car, which was parked halfway down the block.

"You should have double-parked right in front!" Lilo called out, tears brimming at her eyes. How were they gonna carry Blake inside?

"Help me, Lilo!" Hannah waved to her as she opened the passenger door of Blake's car. "Quickly. He hasn't got much time left."

She raced to the car, and Hannah stepped aside, so she could tend to Blake. Lilo reached out and bent toward the interior—but nobody was sitting in the passenger seat.

"Where is he?" She spun her head to Hannah, but it was too late.

Her friend pressed a cloth to her face. Lilo gasped in surprise and sucked in the vapors emanating from the cloth: chloroform.

"No! Help!" But nobody heard her muffled cries.

She tried to fight it, but every ounce of strength seeped from her body and she collapsed, darkness descending on her.

39

Blake stared at the human who'd arrived with a small motorboat and then calmly walked into the arms of the vampires waiting for him. With a permanent marker somebody had written *For Scanguards* on his white T-shirt.

"They sent a fucking pawn!" Blake ground out, while the man continued to stare blankly into the distance.

"Drugged out, just like the other guy," Wesley confirmed. "They must have known we were coming."

Blake kicked against a trashcan. "Fuck!" No matter how careful they'd been, he'd always known that there was a chance that Norwood and his guys had been watching Ronny, though there hadn't been any indication of it. "How're we gonna find Hannah now?"

Several of his colleagues grunted in displeasure, and in the midst of it all, his cell phone vibrated. He pulled it from his pocket and looked at the display.

Pressing the answer key, he said, "Thomas?"

"Can you talk?"

"Yeah, they didn't show. They sent a drugged human instead. No sign of Hannah."

"I wish I could say I was surprised, but I just got alerted that Hannah's access card was swiped to enter the garage."

"You mean somebody took her access card and managed to get inside Scanguards? How is that even possible?" There were more levels of security than just the access card. "They would have had to have her fingerprint, too."

"I know. That's why I pulled the video feeds from the levels accessed with Hannah's card. Hold on." He paused for a second. "Thanks, Eddie. Blake, you're not gonna believe this: Hannah entered the garage. It's her, without a doubt. She went to the main parking level and accessed the emergency key hold."

This made no sense. "If she escaped somehow, then why wouldn't she just go upstairs to the staff office and report back?"

"Blake, I don't think she escaped. There's something about her... Eddie, zoom in on her face again... There! Blake, I think she's drugged."

"Oh shit! Where did she go?"

"That's just it, she took one of the keys, then went to parking level B2. Eddie, go to the recording for level B2... There, she comes out of the elevator, heads for the cars. Oh no."

"What?" Blake barked into the phone.

"She took your car. Let's see..."

What was she planning to do with his car?

"She left with it. I don't know where to, but she drove out of the garage about twenty minutes ago."

"It makes no sense. Why would Norwood make her steal my car? They must realize that we can trace it with its built-in locator chip. Something isn't right."

"I'll go through all the footage again to see if we're missing anything, or if she let anybody else in, but so far I see nothing."

"Blake!" Ronny suddenly called out, holding his cell phone in the air. "It's Norwood. He wants to talk to you."

"Stay on the line, Thomas," Blake ordered and took Ronny's phone with his other hand, already barking into it. "Norwood, you little shit! What're you up to?"

"Is that a way to greet the man who's in possession of the one thing most precious to you?" Norwood drawled.

"I know you drugged Hannah," he started, but Norwood cut him off.

"But I'm not talking about Hannah. I'm talking about Lilo."

Blake's heart stopped.

"Such a beautiful woman. A little limp right now, but," Norwood continued, "she'll wake up eventually."

"You really think I'm gonna believe you have her?" He pressed the mute button, then switched to his own cell phone. "Thomas, run to my office and check on Lilo. Now!"

"On my way."

He pressed unmute on Ronny's phone and concentrated on Norwood's words, continuing to listen with one ear to his own cell phone.

"I'd like to trade her and Hannah for Ronny and the drugs. And this time, no games," Norwood warned.

Meanwhile, Thomas's voice came through the other phone. "She's gone, Blake. Disappeared."

Blake's fangs descended and his hands turned into claws. "I'm going to rip your throat out when I find you!"

"Such idle threats," Norwood said coolly. "Guess you believe me now. So let's see how much she's worth to you."

~ ~ ~

Blake slammed his fist into the wall of his office, leaving a dent in the drywall. "How could this happen?" He'd failed Lilo. He hadn't kept her safe. She was in the hands of a madman. "Why didn't I see this coming?"

John stood in silence next to Ronny, who appeared to be crushed by this setback.

Wes put a hand on his shoulder, but Blake shrugged it off. "Nobody saw this coming. They must have drugged Hannah to somehow get her to trick Lilo into meeting her. The guard said Lilo went rushing out the door, but he didn't see where she was heading."

Blake nodded to himself. "Lilo is smart. She wouldn't have fallen for it if Hannah hadn't been convincing."

"Maybe that's why Hannah stole your car," Wes mused. "What if she needed it to convince Lilo that *you* sent her?"

For a moment, he contemplated the question. "However they convinced her, we need to find where they've taken her. Quickly."

"We've already located your car. I've sent a team there, but I'm pretty sure they just dumped it. Hannah knows the car is equipped with a GPS tracker. She would have ditched it as soon as she didn't need it anymore," John said.

Blake turned to Wes. "Can you scry for Lilo?"

"With what? It was hard enough finding something with Hannah's DNA in her flat. And the little I found didn't get me a reading on her. It's even harder with Lilo. So unless you have a vial of her blood, I'm afraid, we're out of luck. A couple of hairs won't be powerful enough to make the crystal work." Wes gave an apologetic shrug.

Ronny suddenly lifted his head. "You said with blood you could locate somebody?"

"Yeah, I can."

"Maybe you can find Norwood or one of his associates. The drug they put into that human with the motorboat has blood from one of them in it."

Wes approached him. "What do you mean?"

"But you can't scry for vampires, it doesn't work," Blake interrupted. "You weren't at Ronny's interrogation. He already told us about the other vampires' blood."

Wes lifted his hand. "Let me hear him out. How is it done?"

"Well, I give them the raw drug, but if we don't individualize it, it won't work over long distances. We might as well use mind control. So if the vampire wants to control the human over long distances and make sure nobody else can control him, he has to mix some of his own blood with the drug. Like a bond, so to speak. So the human will respond to his master, and only to him." Ronny looked at Wes, as if to verify that he understood.

"I get it." Wes paused and started pacing. "Hmm. Like a homing pigeon. Clever." A spark appeared in his eyes. "I think I have an idea."

Blake's heart beat excitedly. "What kind of idea? Please tell me you know how to find them."

Wes nodded. "I might. But I'll need Ronny's help in the lab. Where's your recipe book? I didn't find it in the cabin."

"Recipe book?"

"The formula for the drug."

Ronny tipped his finger to his temple. "That's the only place it's safe from Norwood. That's why I'm still alive."

Wes nodded. "Good. Blake, keep that drugged human we picked up tonight ready for me. I think there might be a way of using the bond to his master as a way to turn him into a homing device. If I can isolate the vampire's blood from the drug and alter the composition a little, I think I can do it."

Blake's chest swelled with hope. "Wes, if you can do this and find them, you know I'll owe you big."

"And this time I might just cash in on all the favors you owe me."

Blake met Wesley's look and nodded. To get Lilo back, he'd do whatever was necessary.

40

Lilo felt groggy, her limbs were stiff, and her head ached. She was coming out of a daze, and somebody was shaking her with both hands on her shoulders. With difficulty she managed to open her eyes. At first, she had trouble focusing.

"Lilo! Oh God, Lilo!"

The voice brought her back to reality. In an instant she remembered everything. Her eyes flew open.

It was Hannah shaking her awake. Lilo shot up on the uncomfortable cot.

"Hannah?"

"What did they do to you? How did they get you? What are you even doing in San Francisco?" The questions were fairly spewing from Hannah's mouth. She looked distressed, close to tears. At the same time she looked different from earlier. More lively. More animated. Real.

"You don't know, do you?" Lilo asked, grabbing Hannah's hands and squeezing them.

"Know what?"

"Hannah, you called me at Scanguards and told me to come down because Blake was hurt. You said he was dying, and you needed my help."

She shook her head. "Lilo, I've been in here, locked up for I don't know how many days."

"Honey, they drugged you. The men who took you, they made you set a trap for me, and I marched right into it."

Tears rose to Hannah's eyes. "Oh, no, Lilo! I'm so sorry!"

Lilo threw her arms around her friend and pulled her into an embrace. "No, I'm sorry. If I'd been there for you when you needed me, this might not have happened."

Hannah sobbed. Lilo took her by the shoulders and eased her back to look at her. "Don't cry. Please. I'm here now."

"You shouldn't have come to San Francisco. Now we're both in trouble. And it's my fault. I should have listened to Ronny and left with him."

"Ronny told us everything."

"You saw Ronny?" Her eyes widened. "How?"

"Blake and his men captured him."

Hannah slammed her hand over her mouth. "Oh my God!" Then Hannah cast her a cautious look. "How much do you know?"

Lilo sighed. "Everything. Or almost everything. I know about Scanguards, I know about the vampires, the drug Ronny is producing for Norwood, the danger we're all in."

Hannah shook her head. "I'm so sorry I dragged you into this. I never wanted you to have to deal with this."

"We can't change that now. I don't blame you, you know that, honey, don't you?"

"Oh Lilo, I don't deserve you."

Lilo ran her hand over Hannah's auburn hair. "Blake will come for us."

Hannah forced a smile. "He's a good man." She sniffled. "How did you even find out about Norwood and about Scanguards?"

"I went to your apartment, and Norwood broke in."

"Oh my God! Did he hurt you?"

She shook her head. "Blake showed up just in time. He saved me, and Norwood ran. But he was looking for something. I suppose it was the USB stick you hid."

Hannah sighed in relief. "You found it! I was hoping somebody would. I was afraid that Norwood would kill me, so I told him that I had evidence that showed what he was doing. I told him I had the formula for the drug. I knew he wanted it so he wouldn't need Ronny anymore. And that if he killed me, the authorities would find it."

"But there was nothing on the recording other than Norwood and Ronny turning into vampires. You can't even tell what they're talking about; there's no audio. And we didn't find the formula for the drug either."

Hannah winked. "Because I don't have it. But Norwood didn't know that."

"I still don't understand. You couldn't have known that you would be kidnapped when you hid the memory stick."

"You're right. But after I accidentally recorded Ronny and Norwood arguing, and Ronny told me he wanted out of what Norwood was doing, I had a strange feeling. So I hid the USB stick. I figured if something happened to me, at least somebody would know where to start. Scanguards would know."

"But didn't you realize that Norwood would go to your apartment, trying to find the evidence you told him you had? What if he'd found it before we did?"

Hannah shook her head. "I told him because I wanted him to go to my flat. I was hoping that by that time, Scanguards would realize that I was missing, and set up a watch on my flat. I was counting on Norwood going and hoping that he'd be caught by Scanguards."

"You were right. Except that Norwood was able to escape." She sighed. "Blake's worried about you."

"He's a good friend."

"He told me how you two met."

Hannah dropped her lids. "You probably think that I'm impulsive and irresponsible, but even when he told me that he was a vampire, I couldn't just let him die."

Lilo smiled. She'd been in a similar situation. And she hadn't had the heart either. "Thank you for saving him. If you hadn't, I never would have met him."

Hannah's chin suddenly dropped. "Are you serious?" She shook her head. "You and Blake? How? I mean I don't understand. You're not the impulsive one. That's me. You're so... so reasonable... and you think everything through."

"Sometimes things just happen. And there's nothing I can do about it. And our captors somehow found out about me and Blake, and they used it against me. When you called to tell me that Blake was badly injured, I didn't even stop to think for a split second. I just acted. You had his car. I had no reason to believe you weren't telling the truth. I was so scared to lose him, Hannah." Even now the thought clamped around her heart like a vice and squeezed.

"He'll come for us," Hannah said, her voice stronger now. "But now that you're here, maybe we can figure out how to get out of here."

For the first time, Lilo let her eyes wander around their prison. It was a large room with high ceilings, bare concrete walls, and a couple of windows high up. Both were painted black. Steel reinforcements, possibly an earthquake safety retrofit, criss-crossed two of the walls. It appeared that this was a room in a warehouse.

Lilo tapped her finger to her lips.

"What would Morgan West do in a situation like this?" Hannah asked, putting her arm around her shoulder.

"I'm not sure even Morgan West is clever enough to outsmart a bunch of vampires. We might have to put our money on Blake and Scanguards."

~ ~ ~

"Everybody ready?"

Blake looked at his colleagues. They were all standing in a side street behind a large truck in the Potrero Hill neighborhood. Wedged between two freeways, the northern part of the district housed mainly businesses: predominantly warehouses and wholesalers. Farther up the hill to the south, the area was framed by a residential neighborhood.

Wesley's idea to use the blood inside the human they'd caught at Fort Mason had worked like a charm. The human had led them to a large warehouse in Potrero Hill as if he were a homing pigeon. While a Scanguards employee escorted him back to HQ where he would be debriefed—or rather, where they'd wipe his memory—Blake and his men got ready for their rescue mission.

Thanks to their contacts with the city, Thomas had already sent the blueprint of the warehouse to a computer in one of the vans they'd arrived in. But what had really helped in strategizing their approach was Lilo's blood.

Blake pulled in a fortifying breath. Because he'd bitten Lilo only a few hours ago, her blood was still strong inside him, and as soon as they'd gotten within a block of the warehouse and out of the van, he'd smelled her. He'd been able to identify where in the building she was being kept.

Blake now looked at his colleagues, who were putting on their goggles. They weren't for night vision; the vampires didn't need that. Instead, they functioned as thermal imaging devices. Blake shouldered a rope with a hook at its end, as well as some climbing gear. His backpack held several stakes, small-caliber handguns and enough ammunition to take out half an army. He wasn't leaving anything to chance.

"You know what to do," he said and turned his back to his colleagues.

"You sure you wanna do this alone?" John asked.

Blake looked over his shoulder. "I have to. If we go in guns blazing, they'll have enough time to kill Lilo and Hannah. Wait for my text."

Not waiting for John's response, Blake turned into the next street and walked around the block until he reached the street behind the warehouse Norwood and his cronies were holed up in. He knew he didn't have much time. In less than an hour the sun would rise, and any rescue attempt would have to be delayed.

It was easy to find the building that stood directly behind the warehouse. It was a plumbing supplier, and the building was two stories high, whereas the warehouse had three levels.

Blake assessed the building on both sides. No fire escape. He'd have to do it the hard way. Blake lifted the rope off his shoulder and got ready. Luckily this had been one of the many things he'd been taught during his training at Scanguards many years ago: how to swing a rope onto a roof and hook it on the ledge so he could climb up.

It wasn't quite as easy as it looked in all the cat burglar movies, but on his second attempt, the four-pronged hook found purchase. He pulled on the rope to make sure it held and ascended. His vampire strength made the climb easy. Once on the roof, he unhooked the rope and crossed the flat surface until he reached the edge. There were no windows on this side of the red brick building, but there was a gap of about two yards. Easy to jump, if the buildings were of the same height, but not even he could jump up twelve or fourteen feet to the roof of the warehouse.

He made sure the rope was properly rolled up, before he swung it again, aiming the hook at the ledge of the warehouse's roof as if he were swinging a lasso at a calf. This time he succeeded on the first try. Again, he pulled at the rope to make sure it didn't loosen.

Then he wrapped part of the rope around his right hand, held onto it a little higher with the left and stepped back a few feet. He ran and jumped toward the red brick wall feet first. When the soles of his feet hit the wall, he bent his knees, absorbing the impact, and steadied himself.

He took a breath and listened. Had somebody heard the bang against the wall? He waited another few seconds, but heard nothing in response, so he climbed the rope and reached the roof. Not even taking a second's rest, he rolled up the rope and crossed the roof, being careful not to tread too heavily for fear the occupants would hear him.

When he reached the ledge, he inhaled deeply, letting the scent permeate his body. Lilo was somewhere below him. He laid flat on the ground and edged forward, looking down. There were several windows along this wall, one about six to eight feet below him. He slid back and rose, reaching into his backpack to retrieve his thermal imaging goggles. He put them on. Then he fastened the rope to a chimney a few feet away.

Blake tied the rope around his waist, giving himself enough length to reach the window, then started to lower himself over the edge. He gripped the rope tightly and released more and more of it, until his feet touched the window ledge. He looked through the window, but it was painted black. Luckily, this was no obstacle for his goggles.

Inside the room he perceived two bodies, though he couldn't tell whether they were vampire or human, because the heat signature of either species was the same. However, Lilo's scent was strong here. It was seeping through the single-paned window. Blake made a quick assessment of the window and its mechanism. It was latched in the middle, meant to be opened at the top and tilted inward, rather than opened to the side. A little inconvenient to enter through such a tight space, but not entirely impossible. He'd worry about that after he'd managed to open it.

Blake reached for a knife in one of his many pockets and wedged it in the gap between window frame and lintel, sliding it to the latch in the middle. When he felt the lock, he wiggled the knife until he heard a click. He kept the knife there. Checking that his rope was holding, he let go of it with his other hand and then reached for the window, pushing it inward slowly and silently, until it had tilted to a forty-five-degree angle on its bottom hinges.

He took off his goggles and hooked them onto his belt. It was dark in the room, but even without his night vision he would have known who was inside: Lilo's scent was strongest here.

"Lilo," he whispered.

He heard somebody stir, then he saw her and Hannah appear in his field of vision, looking up at the window.

"Blake!" Lilo said.

"Shhhh," he cautioned, put his finger to his lips and motioned for Lilo and Hannah to approach. He took off his backpack and reached it through the opening, before he let go of it to drop it into Lilo's waiting hands.

Checking out the window's opening once more, he held onto the window frame and balanced himself on the ledge, releasing the rope. Once he was without the safety of the rope he reached inside the room and gripped the metal frame of the window that was anchored to the inside wall. He pulled up his knees and swung his legs through the opening, catapulting his body forward into the middle of the room, where he landed. The impact was hard, but he rolled off instantly.

Immediately, he listened for sounds from within the warehouse, but nobody seemed to have heard him.

Lilo and Hannah rushed to him. Lilo wrapped her arms around him, and he pressed her to him for a brief moment. "You're alive." He pressed a kiss into her hair, then reached for Hannah's shoulder and squeezed it.

"We don't have much time," he murmured.

Lilo raised her eyes to the window. "How're we gonna get up there?"

"We're not," he said. He snatched his backpack and opened it. He pulled two guns from it and handed one to Lilo and one to Hannah. "Have you fired a gun before?"

Lilo nodded. Hannah shook her head, so he quickly showed her how to handle the gun.

Satisfied, Blake reached into the backpack again and pulled out a heavy silver chain. Even through the thick, double-layered leather gloves he could feel the silver, though it didn't burn him. He laid it on the floor and pulled out his cell phone, sent a pre-typed text message to John, and put the phone back.

Then he looked at Lilo and Hannah. "Listen carefully. In a few minutes Norwood and his people will storm in here and try to use you as shields. I want you to go to that corner of the room." He pointed to the corner, which, once the door was thrown open, would be in the entering person's blind spot. "Keep your guns ready. Only shoot if one of them comes at you and I can't take him out. Understand?"

Both nodded. Then he took the chain from the floor and walked toward the door. Next to it, he saw steel beams criss-crossing the wall. Perfect.

He climbed halfway up the wall, chain in his hands, ready to pounce.

Suddenly, his vampire hearing picked up the sounds of a commotion from downstairs. Scanguards had just kicked in the door. Norwood and his men were finally aware that they were being ambushed.

Moments later, he heard approaching footsteps, then a key turned in the lock and the door flew open. A vampire rushed in.

Blake jumped, looping the silver chain around the hostile's neck on his descent. The vampire released a choked cry, loud enough to alert his associates, and tried to pry the chain away from his neck. But Blake was already knotting the chain and wrapping it around the asshole's neck a second time, before kicking him in the back to push him to the ground and hogtie him with the silver chain. The vampire struggled, kicking and screaming. He turned his head to flash his fangs, thus giving Blake a good view. It wasn't Norwood, but one of his associates. Ronny had been able to give Scanguards most of the names of Norwood's men and several of them had been in the database. The vampire currently hogtied on the floor was one of them.

Blake heard the commotion downstairs. Yelling. Grunting. Loud thuds. His colleagues were hard at work. He glanced at Lilo and Hannah. Both had come out of the corner.

"Stay here," he ordered the women and motioned to the vampire on the ground. "He can't get free."

Lilo's eyes suddenly widened and she raised her weapon, pointing it in Blake's direction. "Nooooo!" she screamed and pulled the trigger.

Blake dove away and rolled, jumping up a second later, but Lilo kept shooting—not at the spot where he was now, but where he had been. Blake looked over his shoulder.

"Oh shit!"

Lilo was emptying her clip into a vampire that had tumbled to the floor, a stake rolling out of his hand. Norwood. Blood was oozing from multiple wounds. Finally, one shot hit him in the head, and within seconds, Norwood disintegrated into dust, the silver bullet in his brain eating him alive.

Blake jumped up and rushed to Lilo, taking the empty gun from her shaking hands and pulling her into his embrace. She'd saved his life a second time.

But he had no time to thank her, because another sound coming from the door made him whirl around, push Lilo behind him, and rip the gun from Hannah's hands, aiming at the vampire entering.

"Hold your horses," John said.

Blake blew out a breath and lowered his weapon.

"We got four. You?"

Blake pointed to the hogtied vampire, who was whimpering with pain. "Two. This one and Norwood." He tilted his head to where the dust had settled.

"Then we've got them all."

"Anybody hurt?" Blake asked.

John smiled and shook his head. "Those amateurs were no match for us. Piece of cake."

Blake turned to Lilo and Hannah. "It's over. Let's go home."

Lilo flew into his arms, and he reached out one arm to pull Hannah into the hug.

"I don't know how to thank you," Hannah murmured.

"Don't thank me. Thank Lilo. She did all the hard work."

Lilo lifted her head from his chest. "I was scared."

"But you did it anyway. That's what being brave means."

And he'd never met a braver woman than Lilo.

41

Blake tossed a look over his shoulder to glance at where Lilo was standing talking to Hannah and Delilah. Samson's house was packed to the rafters with Scanguards employees and their families, all celebrating the successful rescue of Lilo and Hannah, and the elimination of Norwood's crew.

"And I got sent on patrol while all this was happening?" Grayson groused when John had finished recounting the rescue mission.

Blake turned to his charge, though considering Grayson's age, he really should relinquish his duties where they concerned Samson's hotheaded second-born. "You wanted your own patrol. You got it."

"Yeah, a patrol where nothing happened. Tell me the truth: my father had you assign me to the safest neighborhood, didn't he?"

Blake lifted his hands. "I had nothing to do with your assignment." And he wasn't going to throw either Samson or Quinn, who handled the patrol schedule, under the bus.

Grayson huffed. "You're a big help." He turned and marched away.

Blake exchanged a look with John, who simply shrugged. "He's still got a lot to learn."

"He's crazy if he thinks I'd let him join a mission to save my w... uh Lilo's life."

John nodded, the smirk on his face suddenly gone. "You were lucky this time. Not everybody has that kind of luck."

Blake dropped his head, nodding. "I know that. I wish you'd had better luck." He didn't have to ask whether John still thought of his blood-bonded mate every day.

"Excuse me. I should have a word with Amaury," John said, in a clear attempt to escape the conversation.

Blake didn't stop him. If he lost the woman he loved, he wouldn't want to talk about it either. The only reason Blake knew about John's loss was because Cain had informed the Scanguards management team about the tragedy at the time of John's transfer four years ago.

Suddenly standing amidst the crowd by himself, Blake turned and searched for Lilo.

But before he found her, Wesley and Samson came toward him. Samson nodded to him, then jerked his thumb at Wes. "Wes said you're supporting him in this cockamamie idea of going after these Stealth Guardians, of whom we really know nothing at all."

Blake nodded. He'd made a deal with Wes and he would keep up his end of the bargain. "If anybody can find them and possibly hammer out an alliance, then it's Wes. I have confidence in him. We need to do this."

Samson looked between him and Wes, and grimaced. "So you guys have decided to pull in the same direction this time. Well, then, I guess I don't have a choice." He addressed Wesley directly, "I want you to take all possible precautions when you attempt this. We don't want to lose you."

Wes grinned triumphantly. "You won't. I can't wait to tell Haven."

"Tell me what?" Haven's deep voice came from the side.

As Wes dragged his brother to another corner of the room, Samson came closer.

"I'm very proud of you," Samson praised. "The threat is contained, and we're safe again."

"For now," Blake conceded. "What are we gonna do with Ronny?"

"A difficult decision. The two surviving members of Norwood's gang are on their way to the facility in Grass Valley, and they won't be out for many years. Luther will make sure of that."

Luther, who was bonded to Katie, Wesley's sister, had once been an inmate of that same facility. After he'd been released, he'd subsequently broken back into the prison to follow a lead on a kidnapping, and the council had decided to hire him to improve prison security. He now divided his time between the penitentiary and Scanguards.

"But Ronny is a different case," Samson continued. "I haven't decided yet what to do about him. He showed remorse and helped us in the end. However, he's also the one who knows the formula of the drug and how to produce it. The same thing could happen again."

"It's a difficult decision. Luckily, I'm not the one who has to make it," Blake replied.

"Yeah, the perks of being the boss."

"Wouldn't want to be in your shoes." Blake paused, motioning in the direction of Hannah, who was currently chatting with Roxanne. "Or in Hannah's. She visited Ronny in lockup last night."

"Is she going to reconcile with him?"

"I didn't ask."

Samson nodded. "Well, even if she is, it won't influence my decision. Whatever it may be in the end. We have to think of the common good. That's our mission."

"Yes, so many people rely on us."

"Let's not disappoint them," Samson said, and smiled, before turning around and leaving.

Finally, he was free to join Lilo again. He'd barely seen her since they'd arrived at the party two hours earlier. When he finally saw her, she was being cornered by Nicholas and Adam, both talking excitedly. Zane and Portia, who'd returned from New Orleans the same day, watched with smiles on their faces.

Blake walked to Lilo and slid his arm around her waist from behind, leaning in to bring his head next to hers.

"Are these hoodlums bothering you?"

She turned her head to him, smiling. "They're just—"

"Look what Lilo gave us!" Adam interrupted, his voice full of awe. He held up a book Blake recognized. It was a Morgan West bounty hunter novel.

"So?" He shrugged, surprised that Adam could get so excited about a book. "I mean, I read it. It's great, but I didn't realize you were into books. Had I known—"

"But Lilo autographed it!" Adam opened the hardcover to the title page and pointed to it. "Look! *To Adam and Nicholas, lots of love, Maxim Holt.*"

Blake stared at the page. Why would Lilo autograph a book by Maxim Holt? He turned her in his arms.

"*You* are Maxim Holt?"

She chuckled, a sparkle in her eyes.

"Why didn't you tell me?"

"We all have our secrets."

"Touché." Blake shook his head. "And I was feeling bad for praising Maxim Holt's writing in front of you. You must have had a good laugh behind my back."

"I'm sure you'll get over it."

From behind them, Nicholas interrupted, "When are you writing the next one?"

She turned to look at the teenager. "Just as soon as I can get back to work."

The words sank deep into him. Lilo had responsibilities, a thriving career, adoring fans. And she wanted to get back to work. Did that mean she wanted to return to Nebraska? Or would he be able to convince her to stay? Nothing had been decided yet. And despite the chemistry between them in and out of bed, Lilo hadn't once said what he needed to hear. He'd confessed his love to her hours before she was taken, but she hadn't done the same.

Was she not ready?

42

Lilo turned the light off in the bathroom and walked into Blake's bedroom, dressed only in a short, thin nightdress. Her eyes fell on the bed where Blake was already waiting for her, sitting halfway up, his head and shoulders resting against the headboard. His chest was bare, and she knew he wasn't wearing anything underneath the sheets either—he hadn't in the few days that they'd spent together after her and Hannah's rescue. Every day with Blake seemed better than the next. But she also knew that neither she nor Blake had raised the subject of what would happen next. As if they were both afraid to talk about it for fear of destroying what they had. It certainly was the case for her.

Slowly, her gaze wandered up to his face. His eyes were like embers, already shimmering golden at the rim, the vampire inside him awakening. She could tell now whenever he was close to showing his preternatural side, because she'd seen him make the change many times. A week ago she'd been frightened by it, but now she welcomed it, no, hungered for it. And just like she craved his kisses, she yearned for his bite. She understood the draw now, because she felt it physically. She felt the power he had over her, a power he could unleash with a mere smoldering glance, a casual touch, or a quiet whisper. This kind of power would have frightened her not too long ago, but it didn't anymore, because she knew she exercised the same power over him.

Her vampire lover fulfilled her every wish before she was even able to utter it. Whenever they made love, she felt his desire for her. But there was one thing he hadn't said since the night she'd been taken. He hadn't said the words he'd so freely uttered before he'd made love to her in his office. Did he regret having confessed to her that he was in love with her? Had it only been a temporary feeling that he realized wasn't love after all, but mere lust?

"Aren't you coming to bed?"

His seductive voice drifted to her, and she approached. He lifted the duvet, revealing one naked leg, and she slipped under the covers next to him. Immediately, he pulled her onto his lap, making her straddle him.

"Is something wrong?" he asked, brushing his fingers along her cheek, before sliding them into her hair.

She forced a smile. "No. It's just, I've been staying at your house for a week now, and maybe it's time…" She hesitated, not really knowing how to bring up the subject.

Blake nodded. "Yeah, I guess it's time." He pressed a kiss to her lips. "Time to talk."

Her heart beat erratically, but she needed to say what was on her mind. "The night I got captured, you said you loved me. But you haven't said it since."

He searched her eyes. "Did you want me to say it again?"

Lilo dropped her lids. She hadn't expected the question.

Blake put his fingers under her chin to make her meet his eyes. "You didn't say it back. So I figured I needed to give you more time to let it all sink in. You're human. You need more time than I do: a vampire's emotions are amplified. When they fall in love, it can happen so quickly that they sometimes frighten the human they care about." He sighed. "When you revealed at the party that you were Maxim Holt, I realized something: you have a whole other life away from all of this. I realized I have no right to take you away from your old life. I didn't want to pressure you, that's why I didn't declare myself again. All I could hope for was that you'd fall in love with me in time."

Her heart leapt. "Does that mean—"

"That I love you?" He smiled. "More than I thought I'd ever be able of loving anybody. It frightened me at first, but then I realized my heart would be safe with you. And when they took you, I knew I wouldn't survive if I lost you. What I feel is real, and it won't vanish."

She sighed in relief. "Oh, Blake!" She threw her arms around him and buried her face in the crook of his neck.

"Maybe now would be a good time for you to tell me that you love me, too," he said into her ear.

Lilo lifted her head and looked at him. "I love you, Blake."

He rubbed his thumb underneath her eye. "No need to cry about that, baby. I'm sure you could have done worse than me. I'm not such a bad catch."

She laughed through the tears.

"Lilo, there's something else."

She jolted a little, shifting back.

"Don't look so frightened. It's something good. Or at least I hope you think it's good."

He turned to the nightstand, opened the drawer, and reached inside. When his hand emerged, he was holding a small black velvet box.

Was this a dream? She gasped.

"Wait," he cautioned, chuckling. "You've gotta let me get to it first." He opened the box, revealing a solitaire with a beautiful round stone in its middle. "I called every jeweler in California to find a diamond the color of your eyes. I finally found one, but not even this blue diamond is as brilliant as your cornflower-blue eyes when you look at me. I want you to always look at me like that."

She shifted her gaze away from the ring and met his eyes. "Blake, I don't know what to say."

"Say *yes* to becoming my wife."

"Yes," she choked out, while tears streamed down her cheeks.

Blake removed the ring from the box and slipped it on her finger, tossing the box aside. Then he pulled her to him and captured her lips for a tender, but altogether too brief, kiss. Resting his forehead against hers, he said, "I'm not done yet. There's another question I need to ask you."

Her mind immediately went back to her conversation with Delilah and Nina. She knew what was on Blake's mind.

"The answer to that question is yes."

He moved his head back, looking at her. "How could you know what I wanted to ask you?"

She smiled, and ran her fingers through his hair. "Every time you sink your fangs into me, I sense it. Besides, your friends told me enough to know what a vampire who asks a woman to marry him, truly craves."

"And that doesn't frighten you?"

"I love your bite."

"But the bond is more than just a bite. You'll drink my blood, too. And then there's the telepathic bond."

"Telepathic bond?" Neither Delilah nor Nina had mentioned anything about that.

"Yes, a way for the bonded couple to communicate without speaking."

She smiled. "Doesn't every couple in love communicate without speaking?"

He chuckled. "Oh, I'm sure some of them do. But this is different. It's like hearing the other person's thoughts. You wouldn't be able to hide much from me at all. Nor I from you. We wouldn't have any secrets from each other."

Lilo leaned into him. "I'd like that."

"A bond is forever. Only death will sever it."

She kissed a path along his jaw to his ear, then down his neck. "Forever sounds good."

"I wouldn't be able to tolerate bottled blood any longer. You'd have to let me feed from you every day."

She moved to the other side of his neck, planting kisses along his pulsing vein. "Only if you make love to me every day."

A moan rolled over his lips. "I have no problem with that. But we should make sure you get on the pill for a while."

She lifted her head and looked at him. "Why?"

"I won't be sterile anymore once you complete your first menstrual cycle after the bonding. And as much as I'd like to feel your belly grow with my child, I want you to myself for a while first."

His words made her heart expand even more. "You'll make a wonderful father."

He laughed, and she suddenly found herself on her back with Blake hovering over her. "I'll make an even better husband and lover. How about I start right now?"

"I'm up for that." She reached down between his legs. "And apparently so are you."

He tugged at her nightgown, shoving it higher. "Now: I can either rip this flimsy thing to shreds and buy you a new one, or you could lift your arms and take it off. What's it gonna be, baby?"

She shivered at the thought of his first suggestion and met his eyes, her lips parting.

~ ~ ~

Blake shuddered when he looked into Lilo's face, realizing what she'd chosen. Heat spread in his body and shot into his fully erect cock.

"You're one naughty girl, but who am I to deny you anything?" He willed the fingers of his right hand to turn into claws. "So you want it wild?"

Her chest heaved, and her hard nipples pressed against the thin fabric. She licked her lips, making him moan in response.

"I want you, the man and the vampire," she said, arching toward him.

In response, he sliced through her nightgown, cutting it off her body, while letting the back of his claws slide against her smooth skin. When she shivered, satisfaction filled him. Lilo would make the perfect mate.

"I love you, Lilo," he murmured against her lips, and drove his cock into her welcoming pussy, before he took her lips and kissed her.

Just as in the previous days and nights he'd spent with her, he found his rhythm and the perfect angle to give Lilo the pleasure she craved. With every thrust of his erection, his pelvic bone rubbed against her clit, teasing moans and sighs from Lilo's lips. Moans he now captured with his mouth.

To see what he could give her filled him with pride, and that feeling made his cock swell even more and his balls begin to burn with the need for release. But today would be different from the other times they'd made love. Today they would truly join and become one.

Breathing hard, he released her lips and looked at her. He would never get enough of what he saw: a woman on the verge of ecstasy. When her eyes met his, he smiled at her and slowed his strokes.

"It's time," he murmured, and she nodded.

Again he let his fingers turn into claws. With one of them he sliced into his shoulder. Blood dripped from it.

"Drink from me, Lilo," he demanded and lowered himself to bring his shoulder to her lips.

When her lips touched his skin and her tongue licked up the blood, he shuddered. His hips began to pump, driving his cock hard into her.

"More!" he cried out.

She laid her mouth over the incision and sucked.

"Oh God, yes!" This was what he'd been craving ever since he'd met her: that she'd drink his blood and take him into her, accepting him fully.

Thrusting in a steady rhythm now, he lowered his face to her neck. His fangs were already extended, and when he rubbed them against her skin, a jolt went through him. He pierced her skin a second later and drove his sharp canines into Lilo's flesh.

Blake pulled on the plump vein and let the rich blood run down his throat.

Everything would be different from now on. She was his, and he was hers.

He felt what she felt now. Sensed the approach of her orgasm like a wave about to crest. He let go of his control and gave himself over to her, climaxing with her. As he pumped his seed into her and rocked inside her, he continued to drink from her.

He sent his thoughts to her. *I'm yours, Lilo, forever yours.*

She would hear him in her head now. As if he was there with her, because he was. Just like he could feel her now, she could sense him.

Blake!

He heard his name echo in his head.

What's happening to me?

Don't be afraid, baby.

She clung to him, her lips still on his shoulder, drinking from him.

I'm not afraid anymore. I'm with you now.

I'll keep you safe, forever, he promised.

EPILOGUE

Wesley hiked into the woods until he reached the old cabin that Scanguards had raided only a week earlier. When he saw it appear in the darkness, he could sense that his locking spell was still in place. Nobody had entered the house, not even an animal.

He set his backpack on the ground, removing the accelerant he'd brought together with a box of matches. It wouldn't take much to destroy the house and every sign of the illegal drug manufacturing that had gone on there.

Wesley opened the door and stepped inside. A stale smell greeted him. It got stronger when he reached the kitchen. This was where he'd start the fire. He glanced around and gathered a few old newspapers, a wooden cutting board, and a few books, and piled them up on the kitchen table. Slowly, he poured the accelerant over the pile and tossed the empty canister to the floor. He pulled a match from the box and struck it. A small flame lit up.

"Good riddance," he murmured to himself and tossed the match on the pile.

The flame shot up instantly, but he didn't wait to watch it burn. He turned on his heel and left the cabin. Outside, he grabbed his backpack, collected the crystals he'd left on his previous visit, and hoisted the backpack over his shoulder.

He waited for a few more minutes until the flames grew and engulfed the house, breaking the windows and pushing through the old tiles on the roof. Only now did he exercise control over the blaze and command it to remain contained to the house.

He chanted the spell and waited for the fire to react. And just as he'd commanded it, the fire consumed only the house and didn't jump to the surrounding trees. There would be no wildfire.

He exhaled, satisfied. The Höllenkraut drug was destroyed. He could only hope that nobody else would ever try to mess with the dangerous herb again.

Turning his back on the smoldering embers that remained of the old cabin, he headed in the direction he'd followed the stranger a week earlier. Thanks to the notes he'd found in one of Francine's books, he was almost one hundred percent certain, that he'd chased a Stealth Guardian, a preternatural creature who could not only render himself invisible—which would explain why he hadn't been able to see him during the chase—but also pass through solid objects like walls and doors. If Francine's research was to be believed, the Stealth Guardians were a benevolent race who'd made it their mission to protect humans. Just like Scanguards had. Which was reason enough to establish contact with them and see if they could help each other.

Who would have thought that one day he'd be grateful to Francine, the witch who'd very nearly killed him and his siblings over two decades ago? After Francine's well-deserved death, he'd had the foresight to appropriate any of her possessions related to witchcraft. Francine's books and tools had become the foundation for his quest to regain his powers. A quest he'd won. Though he could never truly forgive Francine, he could appreciate her research and her dedication to her craft.

It didn't take long until he'd reached the shack in which the stranger had disappeared. Everything was quiet. Still, he entered with caution. The interior was empty. Wes pulled a flashlight from his pocket and pointed it at the stone boulder. At first, he couldn't see the dagger that was carved into the stone, but when he shifted the light, he recognized it. He hadn't imagined it.

According to Francine's book, the portal, which worked as some sort of transporter, opened only to the touch of a Stealth Guardian. However, Wesley had experimented with a variety of spells that could unlock all kinds of locks, and he knew just what this particular lock wanted.

He himself had to become the key. It was the only way in. But he was prepared.

Chanting softly, Wes started putting himself into a trance, while focusing on the face of the stranger he'd burned into his mind. He felt his facial muscles move, his skin shift and stretch, his hands curl and uncurl, his breathing change.

"I am you," he continued his mantra. "I am you. I am you."

Gently, he placed his palm over the carving. Beneath it, he felt warmth. It turned hotter with every second, but he didn't dare open his eyes, didn't dare distract himself. He only thought of the stranger and that he was like him.

Something suddenly shifted under his hand, and a second later, he felt nothing. He opened his eyes. The boulder was gone.

Not losing a moment, he stepped into the portal that had opened before him and looked around for any buttons or signs, anything that would tell him how to operate the portal and close the opening.

But there was nothing. The walls on the inside of the portal were smooth, free of indentations.

How the hell was he going to get anywhere now? It was like that time he'd been traveling with some of his college buddies, and had run out of money and gotten stranded. Where had that been? Yeah, somewhere on the East Coast.

Suddenly the boulder moved and closed the opening. He was hurled into the air, floating, losing his balance.

"Oh shit!"

But it was too late now. The portal was in operation.

He could only hope that he wasn't going to end up in hell.

~ ~ ~

If you want to find out about Wesley's adventure, please read Master Unchained (Stealth Guardians #2), where Wesley enters the world of the Stealth Guardians. In Warrior Unraveled (Stealth Guardians #3) Wesley will find love.

Reading Order Scanguards Vampires & Stealth Guardians

Scanguards Vampires

Prequel Novella: Mortal Wish
Book 1: Samson's Lovely Mortal
Book 2: Amaury's Hellion
Book 3: Gabriel's Mate
Book 4: Yvette's Haven
Book 5: Zane's Redemption
Book 6: Quinn's Undying Rose
Book 7: Oliver's Hunger
Book 8: Thomas's Choice
Novella 8 ½: Silent Bite
Book 9: Cain's Identity

20 years pass

Book 10: Luther's Return
Book 11: Blake's Pursuit
Novella 11 ½: Fateful Reunion

Same time period

Stealth Guardians

Book 1: Lover Uncloaked

Next

Book 2: Master Unchained
Book 3: Warrior Unraveled

Next

Book 12: John's Yearning

Next

Book 4: Guardian Undone
Book 5: Immortal Unveiled
Book 6: Protector Unmatched
Book 7: Demon Unleashed

8 years pass

Scanguards Hybrids

The Scanguards Hybrids will also be numbered within the Scanguards
Vampires series (SV 13 = SH 1) to preserve continuity.

Book 1 (SV 13): Ryder's Storm
Book 2 (SV 14): Damian's Conquest

More to come...

ABOUT THE AUTHOR

Tina Folsom was born in Germany and has been living in English speaking countries for over 25 years, since 2001 in California, where she married an American.

Tina has always been a bit of a globe trotter. She lived in Munich (Germany), Lausanne (Switzerland), London (England), New York City, Los Angeles, San Francisco, and Sacramento. She has now made a beach town in Southern California her permanent home with her husband and her dog.

She's written 46 romance novels in English most of which are translated into German, French, and Spanish. Under her pen name T.R. Folsom, she also writes thrillers.

For more about Tina Folsom:
http://www.tinawritesromance.com
http://trfolsom.com
http://www.instagram.com/authortinafolsom
http://www.facebook.com/TinaFolsomFans
https://www.youtube.com/c/TinaFolsomAuthor
tina@tinawritesromance.com

Printed in Great Britain
by Amazon

23560618R00138